The Widow Spy

The Widow Spy

A NOVEL

MEGAN CAMPISI

ATRIA BOOKS

New York | London | Toronto | Sydney | New Delhi

ATRIA
BOOKS

An Imprint of Simon & Schuster, LLC
1230 Avenue of the Americas
New York, NY 10020

First Atria Books hardcover edition April 2024

ATRIA BOOKS and colophon are trademarks of Simon & Schuster, LLC

Simon & Schuster: Celebrating 100 Years of Publishing in 2024

For information about special discounts for bulk purchases, please contact
Simon & Schuster Special Sales at 1-866-506-1949 or business@simonandschuster.com.

The Simon & Schuster Speakers Bureau can bring authors to your live event. For more
information or to book an event, contact the Simon & Schuster Speakers Bureau at
1-866-248-3049 or visit our website at www.simonspeakers.com.

Interior design by Joy O'Meara

Manufactured in the United States of America

1 3 5 7 9 10 8 6 4 2

Library of Congress Cataloging-in-Publication Data
Names: Campisi, Megan, author.
Title: The widow spy : a novel / Megan Campisi.
Description: First Atria Books hardcover edition. | New York : Atria Books, 2024.
Identifiers: LCCN 2023045763 (print) | LCCN 2023045764 (ebook)
| ISBN 9781668024850 (hardcover) | ISBN 9781668024874 (paperback)
| ISBN 9781668024881 (e-book)
Subjects: LCSH: Warne, Kate, -1868--Fiction. | Greenhow, Rose O'Neal,
1814-1864--Fiction. | LCGFT: Biographical fiction. | Spy fiction. | Novels.
Classification: LCC PS3603.A4885 W53 2024 (print) | LCC PS3603.A4885 (ebook)
| DDC 813/.6--dc23/eng/20231023
LC record available at https://lccn.loc.gov/2023045763
LC ebook record available at https://lccn.loc.gov/2023045764

ISBN 978-1-6680-2485-0
ISBN 978-1-6680-2488-1 (ebook)

To my mother and father
And to the original Mary Alice Heaney

Part One

— One —

I'm standing on the front step beside Detective Allan Pinkerton, head of Abraham Lincoln's secret service, when our suspect answers the door.

She's a handsome woman, somewhere on the far side of forty. Tall, like me, but with an olive complexion, dark hair, and slim build. Dressed in black mourning silk.

Does she know who we are? She knows enough to take a paper from her pocket and shove it into her mouth. Right there in front of us, she tries to swallow the damn thing. I lunge over to fish it out. When a suspected spy starts eating messages, you know you've found something.

Pinkerton pushes me toward her. I'm scrabbling at her lips, trying to get my fingers on the evidence. He pushes us both deeper into her house and shuts the front door behind us, so no curious neighbors get to talking. The suspect, the widow Mrs. Rose O'Neal Greenhow, is still trying her damnedest to chew up the paper.

I can't get to it. She'll bite off a finger, if she catches one. Pinkerton is hissing directions from the side. He's not a patient man, my employer. Finally, he shoves me aside and gets in there himself. He cradles the woman's head in his hands just like a baby and jams a sausage-sized finger in through the space of a pulled back tooth.

And he does it: He pries the woman's jaws open and fishes out the message. Well, half the message.

"You must be iron-willed." He waves the soggy mess of chewed paper in my face. The widow is a bent heap of fury beside him. There's enough of the letter left to see it's enciphered. And there's hardly a doubt it's a Confederate cipher. We found our spy.

———

About two minutes later, Pinkerton puts the widow under house arrest in her own parlor. It's an incredible piece of luck finding our evidence so quickly. But that's just the beginning of the work. Our job now is to get the woman's cipher key. Most people cannot commit an entire cipher to memory, so they keep a key written down. We find that, we can intercept Confederate intelligence regarding their next moves.

But the moment we put Widow Greenhow under arrest, the clock starts ticking. We've got a narrow window of time before anyone discerns she's been compromised and the cipher gets changed. Now, we've exercised extraordinary care in the widow's capture. And Pinkerton has given orders to sequester any persons who come knocking at her door, be it the milk boy or some big bug, so as to keep word of the woman's arrest within these walls. As long as the widow doesn't start sending smoke signals, we've got ourselves a window. How long? Pinkerton estimates it at about two days.

We could end the whole war right here from this house. That's our aim.

— *Two* —

It was hate that opened my heart. Cracked it right open. The Confederate spy, Rose Greenhow, she was the one to finally do it. Wasn't her intention. Wasn't mine either. But there it is.

This is the story of how my heart got the way it was. How it got sealed up as a Pinkerton detective and Union spy and how, at the story's end, I was changed. Changed for good by what I hated most. Finally able to find my way to love.

There's other versions of this story. But none tells the truth of what I've lived. I'm hardly the only person whose story hasn't been told in full. Hardly the first whose entire existence is memorialized in but one or two slips of paper—baptismal records, ship manifests, certificates of death—or not even that. I acknowledge it fully. But I'm taking my chance, here and now, to make an account. My own memorial to what I've lived. That's what this book is. My version, looking back on what all happened. Thought you should know.

———

Allan Pinkerton founded his National Detective Agency in 1850 to prevent and detect crime and bring criminals to justice. He took me on in 1856; the first woman detective, Kate Warne.

Like most of his agents (and Pinkerton himself) I wasn't born to

this country. And I wasn't born Kate Warne, but Mary Kate Heaney.
You'll know all Irish girls are named Mary:

Mary Kate	Mary Rose	Mary Susan
Mary Ellen	Mary Louise	Mary Claire
Mary Jane	Mary Ursula	Mary Eliza
Mary Anne	Mary Alice	Mary Margaret
Mary Beth	Mary Belle	Mary Elizabeth

The second name is the true name, the one the parents choose for
the girl. The Mary is almost parenthetical—like a title that means "girl
child" in Irish. All of us Marys: virgin, mother, or the other one. I was
born with three names and sacrificed two in America—tithes paid to
my new home for my place in it.

Being a Pinkerton detective is like always being in on a secret. Inside
the inner circle. It's a thrill that quickens the blood like nothing else.
On the trail of a criminal, we operate in disguise, sometimes under
cover of an entirely new persona. We seem to be as much a part of
the humdrum, everyday world as any other body, but in truth we are
above it, soaring like falcons. A secret society to which only a select
few belong. It is a powerfully strong feeling.

By the late 1850s the whole country had become all-consumed
with the question of slavery. In response, Pinkerton began to direct
more and more of the agency's detective work toward the abolitionist
cause. Pinkerton was raised in a Glasgow slum that makes Chicago
look like the Sultan's Garden. And he was a proponent of "moral
force" in support of the labor movement in Scotland as a young man.
His abolitionist ardor was of a piece with his labor politics. He let it
be known any operatives who weren't prepared to devote themselves
to abolitionism best leave his employ. None of us did.

It was Abraham Lincoln who asked Pinkerton to direct the United
States Secret Service in 1860. Our main job? Spying on the Secessionists.

You'll likely know this next bit of history: In April 1861, Fort Sumter fell to the rebels and the Civil War began. But what you may not know is this: It didn't feel like a war yet. From where we sat in the North, it was just a rebellion—the one the South had been threatening since the formation of the United States. The way we figured it, the rebels would be beaten in a matter of months, if not weeks. On a high horse, we were.

In July 1861, it happened. I was sitting in Pinkerton's provisional offices in Washington when we got word of the Union defeat at Manassas. The Battle of Bull Run was lost.

As I said, we hadn't believed it was a real war. We thought it would all be over at Manassas. The whole thing. Finished. Done. Washingtonians came out to watch the battle with picnics, for Christ's sake. The news wasn't just news of one defeat. It was the news that we were wrong: It was a true war we were in. One that might go on longer than months. And the blood that ran would be ours too.

The day we lost at Manassas, Pinkerton burst through the office door holding a telegraph, his whole body shaking with fervor. "We have orders!"

It turns out the battle of Manassas at Bull Run was won with arms, yes, but also with espionage. The Confederate forces were alerted to the date of the Union's attack and its plan to intercept rebel reinforcements. Our job was to track down the spy ring that managed to move such intelligence to the rebels. That was Pinkerton's telegraph. An order from Major General McClellan himself.

It was not long after that Hattie Lawton, an agent working undercover in Richmond, first sent word of a wealthy Washington widow whispered about by the Confederate wives, a Mrs. Rose O'Neal Greenhow. Greenhow was high society, vocal about her Southern sympathies, and well connected to a wide range of political big bugs. Senators and the like. Word was she was up to more than social calls and knitting socks for soldiers. Pinkerton sent a few of us to surveil this widow at her Washington home and report if there was anything of note.

Well, there was note. Enough note—significant note—that the

war department approved Pinkerton's request for a surprise raid on the widow's residence to search and seize proof of espionage. This is how I found myself looking at a half-eaten Confederate message in the widow's foyer on the morning of August 23, 1861.

———

I signal the rest of the team who've been waiting around the corner, and we set to work. The house is a stately red-brick affair, with three floors on an enviable parcel of Sixteenth Street. There's a small garden and carriage house beside it with a loft for a groom to sleep. The front door of the house opens into a fine foyer as big as a tenement apartment with floors of wood polished so smooth you could walk on them in your bare feet without a splinter.

Now, to get the widow's cipher key, we must:

1. convince the woman to hand it over, or
2. discover its hiding place

The first option is typically the quickest, but, of course, it all depends on the nature of the person you've got to convince.

Pinkerton brought six of us, plus him, for the job. One agent posts up outside in the garden to keep watch. Another gets the three servants—a cook, a lady's maid, and a groom—sequestered in their rooms in the basement and carriage house.

Two other agents, John Scobell and John Tully, join me in searching room by room.

The last agent, Pryce Lewis, one of Pinkerton's finest, attends Pinkerton in the parlor where he's holding the widow and her eight-year-old daughter (the only other family who was at home). Their task is persuading the widow to give up the key and save us poor sods from searching for the damn thing.

It's a la-di-da sort of place, the house, just a'choke with fashionable pretensions. The main floor is outfitted for entertaining with not one, but two parlors, a dining room, and a large indoor kitchen. Adjoining the kitchen is a small room expressly made for laundry. Upper floor is family bedrooms. A house this size in the Massachusetts mill town where I grew up would've fit three families on the first floor alone, another three wedged in the upper-floor rooms, and a dozen goms just off the boat down there at the basement level.

Scobell, Tully, and I begin in the front parlor. Top to tail, searching goes, ceiling to floorboards, looking for hiding spots. Oil basin of a lamp. False leg of a chair. A few years back, there was a bank employee we were investigating for embezzling paper currency. Hadn't turned up a thing searching his house until someone pulled down a portrait of the Virgin Mary and found two thousand dollars pasted right there inside her frame.

The three of us search together as neatly as the teeth of a gearworks sliding into place. Tully unscrews the several porcelain lamps and hands Scobell the sections to check. Scobell passes them on to me to fit back together. Scobell and Tully lift the two floral-upholstered couches so I can pat down the undersides. Tully gets a boost from Scobell to check the top molding above the pink papered walls, while I do the wainscotting below.

Tully turns to a great standing clock. He stops the pendulum, and I hold out a choice of tools. He selects a screwdriver and opens the clockworks. John Tully's English. He's the sort of operative Pinkerton typically uses only for search and muscle. He was born looking like an old, drunk man (aren't we all), but never outgrew it. I doubt Tully's more than thirty, but he could be taken for sixty. He's as bitter and gnarled as an old walnut, but he's good with his hands. He closes up the clock, pushes the minute hand forward one, and lets the pendulum go.

Scobell's already lifting pictures off the wall. I step right over. He turns each so I can inspect the backings. Scobell and I have worked a few jobs together. I know he's married, though I haven't ever met his wife, and that he was born enslaved and bought his freedom. He's wiry-built. Medium height. Medium brown skin. Close-cropped black hair. He has almond eyes, fringed by thick lashes, that gleam like a lamp when he's angry or joking or making an observation. And he's steady even in a tight fix. He's a little older than me, somewhere past grown but before middle-aged. His accent says South, but whether it's Birmingham or Baltimore isn't clear. He's had some education, but converses in a way you can't quite tell. It's purposeful, the ambiguity in the way he talks and carries himself. A gentle blurring of his past, so no one can quite pin him down. Still, something about him has always put me at ease, like it's half our lives we've known each other and not just the better part of a year. It happens that way in this work; you learn quickly who you trust.

Scobell rehangs the pictures on the wall. They're portraits mostly. The widow in her salad days standing beside her late husband, Robert Greenhow, a onetime doctor, then government paper pusher of some garden variety. According to our background research, the couple was living in San Francisco when one day, walking down the middle of one of the city's raised sidewalks, Robert Greenhow fell through a hole and died. (May I opine that the Far West sounds like a terrible place? At least the East avoids the trouble of sidewalks altogether, and you know what you're in for: mud, more mud, and some mud on the side.)

The other portraits are the widow's older daughters at the occasions of their coming-of-age, all trussed up like Christmas geese at the butcher counter. Florence is the eldest, now married and living in Utah territory. The other grown daughter, Leila, is journeying to her sister's place right now. In truth, most ladies left the city for safer locales weeks ago. Washington these days looks like one big camp for the U.S. Army armed against Southerners like the Greenhows.

There's no portrait yet of the youngest girl, Little Rose, the one presently sitting with her mother in the back parlor. Hers will no doubt wait until she's ready to be apportioned out for marriage to the highest bidder.

Scobell straightens the last portrait, then pauses a moment at the wall, looking at something. There's one more hook, but this one's sitting empty where a last portrait must have recently hung.

"Gertrude?" Scobell suggests quietly, throwing me a glance.

I nod back. "Must be." There was a third grown daughter, Gertrude. Twenty-two years old, same as me. Passed from typhoid fever just this past spring. She's why the widow is wearing black. The family must have taken the portrait down.

I move on to the window casings. As I check them, I catch a glimpse of myself mirrored in the glass. Freckled cheeks. A mess of mouse-colored hair already weaseling out of my bun. Blue eyes that people say have an "intelligent cast" to them. That's what people say when they can't call you pretty. "Your face has an intelligent cast to it." I tuck a few stray hairs back into their pins.

Tully and Scobell start pulling up the heavy, foreign rug. I step over and tap-tap-tap the floor under it, checking for loose boards. We work so fluidly we hardly need to speak. But we're also staying quiet because there's only a red gauze curtain separating the front parlor, where we're searching, from the back parlor, where Pinkerton and Lewis have the widow and her daughter. We're hoping to listen in on the proceedings.

She's a special case, the widow. Our targets are usually criminals, sometimes able, sometimes not, but they never know who we are. As detectives, we pose as friends, neighbors, acquaintances, all the while laying traps, drawing in the target, gaining their confidence, and finally stealing their secrets. But the widow is something new. Not only is she an (allegedly) adept spy, but she knows who we are for a fact.

And then there's her sex. Every primary suspect we've ever targeted has been a man. Sure, we've worked on wives who're abetting their criminal husbands or girls who know the details of their fathers' crimes, but this is our first female perpetrator all on her own.

She's well connected too. I did most all of her background work: She was born Maria Rosetta O'Neal. Her older sister was named Mary Ellen. That's already a lot of Mary for one family, and there were three more sisters besides. You might guess we're dealing with the Irish-Catholic persuasion. The widow and her older sister were sent from the family plantation in Maryland (another Mary, for those counting) to the capital at Washington as young women. Lived with an aunt, Maria Ann (we're at four), in her boarding house, a domicile known as the Old Capitol. Congressmen and justices boarded there. The sister Mary Ellen married Dolley Madison's son, and *their* daughter married Stephen A. Douglas, a known abolitionist.

If you're lost, appreciate this digest: The widow's connected at the highest level of American politics, both Democrat and Republican. She is noted to have been particularly friendly with John C. Calhoun and former president James Buchanan. She's also a common sight in Congress's galleries (read: big-game hunting for the widowed sort of lady).

In short, the widow is a true adversary. I wish it were me in there persuading her to give up the cipher key. Me, who Pinkerton brought in especially, instead of Pryce Lewis.

A few years back, I was working a case, and I lost my nerve. Since then, Pinkerton hasn't put me in the fire, so to speak. He keeps me in reserve—doing background research, interviewing witnesses, searching houses like this one. Sticking my hand in the widow's mouth with Pinkerton a foot away as backup is the riskiest encounter I've had in months. The toughest jobs—working undercover, infiltrating enemy ranks—go to others. I won't pretend it's not a source of shame. I won't pretend I'm content to be passed over. Searching isn't the winningest work. Certainly not why you become the first female detective.

As I tap the floorboards, I try to get a peek through the gauze curtain. Pinkerton's on his feet, and I wager he's been on his feet the whole time. Everything in the widow's house is upholstered in such deep plush that sitting would be like dropping into a floral bog from which any retreat would prove at the least awkward, and at the most requiring a hand up. Pinkerton's avoiding that indignity. He's also a stander, plain and simple. Your man can stand all day surveilling a target, then walk to another job, and stand again all the night long. He's the type. Doesn't eat much either. Steam engine, Pinkerton is. Fueled by cooled tea, sipped from the saucer. Thus, the scene: The widow on a sofa, her eight-year-old daughter at her side; Lewis on a straight-backed chair across from them, legs crossed; and Pinkerton, standing over them all, blue eyes flashing like a Pentecostal.

Pinkerton's a fearsome interrogator, to be sure. His face is one large scowl. His body is all lines, hard and squarish, like a crate built to carry every past worry and grief with him. His agency is an extension of that body. His offices in Chicago (and now here in Washington) are multiple rooms of floor-to-ceiling shelves weighted by ledgers, account books, operative reports, and case logs. File upon file of notes on suspects' daily habits, their vices, their known associates and past occupations. Pinkerton stands before those shelves like another man would before a personal arsenal, assured and emboldened by its power. The Pinkerton National Detective Agency has been in operation for eleven years catching counterfeiters, train robbers, murderers, and thieves. And this obsessively detailed stockpile of observations is the secret behind its uncanny success in detecting crime. *We Never Sleep!* is the agency's motto, but a truer slogan would be *Thorough and Complete!*

I listen hard but can't hear but a snip and a snap of their conversation, even if it's only that red gauze curtain and half a dozen sinkhole sofas between us. There's Pinkerton's raised voice here and there, barking commands. There's the widow's low voice singing out words like *habeus* and *corpus*. There's Lewis's soft lilt coming in now and again.

Lewis is an Englishman, like Tully, but loose in his body and affable in nature. He's got thick mutton chops and bright blue eyes. A great charmer, Lewis. (And talker—the kind who will say with twenty words what the rest of us get out with three.) He's the carrot to Pinkerton's stick.

I finish the floor and smooth the rug back down, while Tully and Scobell move on to the seams of the drapes. A seam is easy to slice, slip in a note, and sew up because it's naturally stiffer than the rest of the fabric, and most fingers won't notice the added thickness. They run their fingers all up and down those drapes, while I check a carved end table for hidden drawers.

We all perk up a moment at a loud exclamation from the widow. We wait, but there's nothing more. Tully sucks his teeth and whispers, "Why's Pinkerton wasting time talking to her? Can't he beat the cipher out of her?"

"Damn, Tully!" Scobell hisses.

"What?" Tully hisses back. "Don't the ends justify the means, if the ends be justice?" He's more or less quoting from the forest-green handbook we all received upon being hired: *General Principles of Pinkerton's National Detective Agency.*

Scobell throws me a glance, assuming I'll side with him. But while Tully's suggestion also makes me balk, women aren't generally believed to be tough enough for detective work. I'm still trying to convince Pinkerton I am. I shrug noncommittally. "Pinkerton can't beat her. The widow is too well known and too 'high' society. When the arrest gets out, Pinkerton aims to look a hero, not a lout."

"That's a cold summation." Scobell snorts, but there's the hint of a smile behind it.

"You think it's Pinkerton's lamblike disposition keeps him from violence?" I chaff him back.

"Keep your voices down," snips Tully.

All at once, Pinkerton himself stalks into the room, the red gauze curtain getting caught in his bristled beard. He swats it away, then stands a moment, glowering at our progress. "Haste!" Pinkerton says, just the one word spoken like a sneeze. Then, he stomps off.

It appears spontaneous, Pinkerton coming through, leaving Pryce Lewis with the widow and her daughter in that back parlor all alone. But don't be fooled. Right about now, Lewis will be pouring a drink of something sweet and cool to allay the widow's thirst, all the while murmuring gentlemanly things in a gentlemanly tone. It's a classic mule race, this job: carrot and stick, hurrying the widow across the finish line however we must.

Lewis will break the widow shortly, I'd wager. Only Timothy Webster and Hattie Lawton—presently in disguise among the rebels in Richmond—are better than him. How could she not break? Before noon, it'll happen. Or sunset. Let's say sunset. Lewis will convince the widow to give up the cipher key and maybe even hand over the names of the rest of the spy ring. We'll celebrate with a glass of whiskey and a good night's sleep.

We finally finish searching the front parlor. Tully and Scobell head over to the kitchen. I do a final sweep, then follow. I'm halfway down the narrow corridor between the parlors and the kitchen when I hear the widow's voice coming clear as a bell through the back parlor's side door. I stop a moment to listen.

"It is a most remarkable fact," the widow is saying, "that in their native Africa, the Black race has made no progress. In Jamaica, the emancipated slaves have retrograded to barbarism, while even in our own North, the free Black race is generally found in the jails or poor houses. I ask you, what does the good of society require—the freedom or servitude of such people?"

All at once I hear a creak, and look up to see someone standing a pace away in the kitchen doorway. It's Scobell, listening like me, eyes bright and hard. How long has he been there? My heart tightens, knowing what he's hearing her say about people with skin dark like his.

The widow's voice continues, "It's only right for the barbarous among us to serve."

Scobell nods as if considering her point, then steps to me and whispers with a grim smile, "Tell her I could find someone to take her on as a house girl." He leans over and spits on the floor by the parlor door, then retreats back into the kitchen. My eyes follow him, wishing I could say something to erase the widow's words. But her words are in him, and nothing can take them back.

Through the parlor door, Lewis's reply to the widow is all velvet, soft and rich. "I admire your passion, madam, but surely it's better for you to leave the city. We could convey you to safe haven." Pure strategy, Lewis, maneuvering right around her hatefulness.

"Haven? This home was my haven!" the widow's voice gets lower, not shriller. "My refuge and shelter that you have so uncivilly invaded! Why, I would need no safe haven, but for your coarse accomplices and their egregious acts of trespass! 'Convey me to safe haven,'" she mocks. "I'd never trust the promises of such savages."

I hear footsteps again and quickly look up, but it's not Scobell, just Tully. He tiptoes over to where I'm listening, the floor creaking despite his efforts. He bends down and puts his ear next to mine. Tully's nose whistles with his breath. I give him a nudge, and he switches to breathing through his mouth.

"Madam, well informed as you plainly are"—this is Lewis again—"you must be sensible to the reality that Washington now operates under martial law. Such protections, as exist in more civil times, have ceased. Your friends have fled. Indeed, you have few friends left. Let me be a friend to you now."

"You must think me a fool to suggest entrusting the safety of my person or that of my child to you and your German Jew employer!"

Tully stifles a snort. Glasgow accent thick as butter, Pinkerton has, and she calls him a German Jew. There's no end to her hate.

"Abolitionist—is that the title to which you lay claim?" the widow goes on. "Well, you've been sold down the river by that bean-pole president of yours. If you took the opportunity, which I am certain you have not, to learn what transpires in your own Congress, you would know the Northern senators are fighting to preserve the union of states, not for the freedom of slaves. They are bullies, plain and simple. Just like your vile colleagues and that grubby little female."

Tully raps a knuckle against my knee at the widow's mention of me. I give him a swift kick back. But would you believe it, he doesn't wholly cover his groan. We both hold still a moment, wondering if we were heard.

Lewis's voice comes next. "Madam, you cannot leave."

"Oh, I'm not leaving," the widow says. I hear her footsteps near the door and just get clear before she jerks the door open and shut sharply, effectively boxing Tully about the ear. "Just clearing my hallway of rats." Tully clutches his ear in pain, breathing heavily through his mouth. "Beware, my dear," the widow says loudly to her daughter. "There's vermin loose in our house. Their filth is catching."

The standing clock sounds twelve noon.

— Three —

We search the rest of the downstairs but don't turn up a thing. It's already early afternoon when we move on to the second floor. Just as I start for the stairs, I hear a heavy tread behind me. I turn to find Pinkerton, eyes ablaze.

"We need you," he snaps.

My heart jumps. Maybe this is it: him calling me in to help with the widow.

"Female servants need interviewing," he finishes.

My heart goes back to what it was doing before: nothing much. I don't know why I got my hopes up.

I take a set of narrow, dark stairs down to a sort of half-basement where the servants lodge. There's windows, but they're all up by the ceiling, letting in a poor light even in the middle of the day.

You'll notice it's "servants" Pinkerton said and not "slaves." Don't be thinking the widow innocent of the sordid traffic in humankind in which this country is perhaps fatally embroiled. Or believe that she's somehow morally elevated because she no longer owns human souls. The family sold the two people they kept enslaved. One to himself (I believe he was a man called Clarence). The other person was most likely sold after the widow's husband passed, but before she received her settlement from the state of California for its murderous sidewalks.

I start with Minnie Ann Lyons, the widow's cook. She's Black and in her sixties. Brown hair pinned back neatly. I conduct the interview in her mean closet of a room. The one high window is covered by a drape. Shelves hold her personal effects. Minnie Ann herself sits on a narrow cot made up with pink bedsheets.

I ask her how she came to work for the widow.

"I was a likely domestic, seeing as I done the work all my life. Will Mrs. Greenhow be going to prison?" asks Minnie Ann.

"She's a spy for the rebels," I tell her.

Minnie Ann wipes her brow with a handkerchief. It's August in Washington and warm in her little room, even without direct sun. "Miss, I asked if she'll be going to prison."

"Most likely," I say.

Minnie Ann looks at the handkerchief, then at her lap. Her body speaks of fatigue and concern mixed up together.

"Ma'am, you born a free woman?" I ask.

Minnie Ann's eyes come up, and her expression stays even, but she waits to answer, like she doesn't care to talk with me on the subject. My aim is to sound out who this woman is, if she's likely to help us, or if she's been coerced by the circumstances to believe she should help her employer. Of course, she might prevaricate in talking to me, but what a person chooses to tell is sometimes as helpful as the truth. "I was born a slave," she finally answers.

"Where's that?"

"Kentucky. Later, Virginia."

"Sold?"

"I was sold." Her face doesn't change, but there's plenty going on beneath the surface.

"I don't mean to bring up bad memories, ma'am."

There's a twitch in her hand. "When you sell a mare, the foal goes with it. But that's not how it is with people, is it?"

I nod, because there's nothing else to do in the face of such an awful truth.

"New mistress couldn't watch them parting me and my mama. Said it was too much for her to see."

I feel a rush of sick in my stomach, but continue on. It doesn't help the Cause for spies to get caught up in their hearts. "You see your mama again?"

Minnie Ann looks at me with clear eyes, and I have the answer.

"How'd you come to be here?" I ask.

"My mistress moved to Washington. Her circle had a minister. Good-looking man. Popular, he was. Urging them all, all the ladies, to manumit their slaves. Fashions was changing with the times, as they do. My mistress followed the fashion."

"You were manumitted here?" I ask.

"I'm going to lose my place, aren't I?" she answers.

"Widow Greenhow's been helping the rebels, ma'am."

Minnie Ann reaches into her dress and pulls out a paper sweaty from resting against her heart. "Read this to me?"

I unfold the page. "'To all whom it may concern, be it known that I, Lucille M. Lyons, do hereby release from slavery, liberate, manumit, and set free Minnie Ann Lyons, being of age fifty-two years and able to work and gain a sufficient livelihood. I do declare her discharged from all manner of service or servitude to me, my executors, or administrators forever.'" It's her certificate of freedom. Required to be carried at all times at the risk of being sold back into slavery.

"It promises I'm free no matter what, yes?" Minnie Ann asks.

"I can't promise what the rebels will or will not uphold. But I know President Lincoln will recognize this."

"President Lincoln's been talking again on sending us to Liberia."

"I don't know Liberia, ma'am," I tell her in truth.

"You want to go back where your people came from?" she asks me. "What's in Liberia for me? There a house waiting? A family? A place of work?"

"Mrs. Greenhow going to prison is a good turn." I'm keeping my voice calm, but I'm working at it. If she knows where her employer is hiding her cipher key, she could finish this job.

A hair of a sigh comes from Minnie Ann. "I'm at an age where familiarity is as strong a recommendation for a place as most other qualities." She looks me over. "Do you believe the fighting will come to Washington?" I have the sense her asking is like squeezing the last drops out of a rag, not expecting anything from me but dirty water, but doing it anyway because it's there to be done.

"I believe with people like your employer in prison, the fighting will be finished quicker," I tell her. "My job is to get proof that will put her there."

She looks me right in the eye. "Ma'am, I don't know anything about the affairs of Mrs. Greenhow, excepting serve fish Fridays and don't sugar the tea."

I guess I'll go ahead and admit I thought Minnie Ann might be grateful to us for the work we're doing. To me, in point of fact. I guess that's what I thought. That thing beneath her surface is still there, but so contained I won't reach it. There's an expanse between the two of us, and no question I've asked has started to cross it. Maybe I'm just making it wider. But I'm certain enough she's not hiding anything; there's nothing false about this woman at all.

My next interview is an entirely different affair. Lizzie, the maid, is in her late teens, light-skinned and Irish. I find her perched on the bed in her little room, clutching a pillow to her heart despite the heat. A story-paper sits crumpled at her side. I barely make out the title through the teacup stains:

Diana's Destiny; or Rescued by Love!

No doubt about an insipid, jewel-eyed heroine who needs rescuing by some capable type—frontiersman, Indian brave, Union spy.

Maybe that's what I did with Minnie Ann—tried to cast her as Diana, and me the hero, in my own story-paper. Stands to reason she might resent it.

I said Lizzie's in her late teens, but the girl's younger than that in spirit. She's got thin blond hair, and she's sharp all over except for the hint of a double chin. The girl rewraps her arms around her pillow, revealing two embroidered rabbits on its face. "I'm not saying a word."

There's a stool and tiny dressing table in the corner. I sit myself down.

"Not telling you lot a word, so don't think I will," Lizzie goes on. "Widow Greenhow's a fine employer. Just fine."

I let my own Irish brogue slide right back to where it began, and with it I tell her, "Widow Greenhow's been caught furthering the rebel cause."

Lizzie double-takes my accent before she thinks better of it. She pulls at her dress and petticoats where they're sweat-stuck to her thighs. "And how's that anything to me?"

"Can't make a wage if there's free labor to be had from slaves," I say.

"I was making a wage, weren't I? Until you lot came."

"Slave owners are tyrants. Land tyrants." This last is a term of art from the profession known as being Irish.

"And what is it I should do against the slave owners?" snips Lizzie. "I can't vote. I can't soldier. Shall I quit my place here and go knit socks for the U.S. Army until I starve? Would you leave me in peace then?"

"How long've you worked here?"

"It'll be a year come September. Widow Greenhow don't confide her intimate affairs in me." She squeezes the ludicrous pillow at her heart. "And if she did, I wouldn't tell them to you."

I surely believe the widow doesn't confide in this girl, but I can't help but poke her a little. "You don't confess, you'll be abetting a traitor. Land you in the stir, to be sure."

Lizzie doesn't fully hide her little gasp at the prospect of prison, but all she says is, "Not saying a word, am I?"

I end her interview soon after. I note that Pinkerton has put Agent Dennis Mann on watching the servants. He's a looker, Mann, with curly black hair and a strong jaw. I wager that's why he's down here. When Pinkerton hears Lizzie didn't budge, he'll surely have Mann try to honeyfuggle her, see if he can sweetheart any secrets out of her.

And me? I've nothing to do now but rejoin Scobell and Tully, presently upstairs, still searching for the cipher key.

Tully takes the widow's bedroom. Across the hallway is the library. Scobell says it can use two pairs of hands.

The library's got three walls of floor-to-ceiling books and a ladder on rollers that slides all the length of the longest wall. Under the one window sits the widow's desk stacked high with papers. There's a vase of fresh flowers at its back and a fine wooden chair beside it.

Scobell is sifting through the contents of the desk. On the blotter is an invite list from a supper lately hosted by the widow, including two abolitionist senators and a Union colonel. At this juncture, Southerners in Washington don't generally dine across the political line. In truth, at any juncture, most folks stick to their own political persuasions for supper. This tells us the widow is either entirely obtuse or unusually audacious. Willing to brook social censure. Happy to defy prevailing conventions.

I begin searching the library's books. When Pinkerton mentioned a library, I figured we might be screwed. But that was before I'd seen the place. This is a thorough and complete screw. She must have a thousand books. Or her husband did. One of them reads in three languages, if the books aren't just for show. Of course, you'll guess Pinkerton requires every book paged through leaf by leaf. Looking for hollowed-out books, notes slipped into books, notes on pages. There's a code I've heard of where you prick a pin near certain letters to form a message. I'm like Scheherazade with a thousand stories to get through.

I'm no stranger to tedium. I spent my youth in a cotton mill in Tremont, Massachusetts. Carding, spinning, weaving, and finishing on four floors, all under one vast roof. Spinning Room No. 2 is where I worked, changing bobbins until I was tall enough to tend a spinning frame. It was a cavernous place, flywheel cranks and leather belts running along its high ceiling to power each of the sixty spinning frames below, three to a spinner. It was well lit by double-paned windows, but the air was close—the windows sealed with glue to keep the heat and moisture in and the cotton from drying out. We never dried out either, us mill girls.

And the noise. The roar of machinery crashed against me like a thing of substance. My heart beat to the crashing like a foot tapping out a song, but one whose rhythm shook my very bones. It was the chant of sixty spinning frames rumbling on like a locomotive, rumbling and shaking, but never arriving at any place. And then a thread broke and a girl cut off her machine to piece it back together. When her spinning frame started up again, it was at odds with the rhythm from before. The whole room seemed to stutter-step, trying to fit itself back into the beating thunder of the chant, and I stuttered along with it until my heart found the rhythm again. When the sound finally stopped, at the breakfast or dinner bell, or at day's end—why, the silence was another thing of substance, expanding to fill the space left by the noise. Bread dough rising. A thick cloud of quiet.

How the noise startled me when I first came to the work at age seven. I was hardly able to get my hands to change the bobbins without shaking. But I'll tell you the secret. I'll tell you how to survive it. Days you wanted to push out the noise? You did the opposite; you let it in. You got that crashing riot stuck in you, moved it in your body. Let your very heart take it up. Then the fear had no thrall over you; it became a part of your very being.

The piling minutes of factory work. Piling into an hour. Piling into a day. Then on to a week, a span of weeks, then years. Sometimes the mere thought of a future stuck in the mill was enough to steal the breath from my chest. I think on Lewis down in the parlor with the widow, trying to wheedle the cipher out of her. That's the work that thrills the blood. That's why I got out of mill work when I had the chance.

I climb up on the sliding ladder, right up to the top, and push myself along from one shelf to the next to make the whole thing feel more of an adventure. The ladder knocks against the desk chair down below. I climb down, move the chair out of the way, climb back up.

You can see a person's aspirations in the way they array their library. What does the widow want her guests to see first as they walk in?

Francis Bacon's *Essays*
Thomas Jefferson's *Correspondence Vol 1-7*
Ralph Waldo Emerson's *Self Reliance*

You have to look hard to find the dramas, the whole works of Shakespeare nestled up to some French titles in the bottom corner of the long wall. Some classics (Chapman's translations of Homer). Some domestic romances by that most prolific authoress Mrs. E.D.E.N. Southworth:

The Discarded Daughter
The Deserted Wife
The Wife's Victory

Scobell finishes with the desk and comes over to help with the books. At least there's Scobell to pass the time with. That's something.

He starts in the lower corner with the dramas and classics, pulling out a skinny little book from the end of the shelf and paging through it. "You ever seen it?" he calls to me, showing me its cover. *Romeo and Juliet.*

"I seen it once," I say. The Tremont Cotton Mill had a Betterment Committee for the mill girls. The committee sponsored "improvement circles" like a debate society and a literary appreciation club. One spring, a group of girls performed *Romeo and Juliet* in the community hall.

"Hell of a love story," says Scobell, replacing the book and picking up the next one on the shelf.

"Love story?" I snort. "That's what's called a cautionary tale."

Scobell glances up at me on the ladder. "Cautionary tale?"

"You know, *Little Red Riding Hood, The Little Match Girl, Humpty Dumpty . . .*" I list.

He gives me a look. "I know what a cautionary tale is."

"Fourteen years old and Juliet meets a boy. Marries him in a week's time. Dead the week after that." I raise my hands: point proven.

"She followed her heart," counters Scobell.

"And what did her heart get?" I ask him. "A knife. The lesson is to obey your parents. Had she listened to her mother, she would have married a count and had her happily-ever-after."

Scobell's now working through a collection of Greek myths by

Nathaniel Hawthorne. "Isn't the lesson violence shouldn't answer bad blood?"

"And what should answer it?"

Scobell shrugs.

"You want to know what overcomes hate like what's between the Capulets and the Montagues?" I say, moving on to a shelf of histories. "Young fools and pretty faces. And it's Mr. William Shakespeare who says so."

There's a smile pulling at Scobell's lips. "All right, then." He holds up his book of myths. "How about *Orpheus and Eurydice*? Now, that's a love story."

"It's altogether worse!" I laugh. "How's it go? They meet and get married, and pop! she dies before they even—"

"He's a musician," Scobell cuts me off, plainly not appreciating the direction of my retelling. "He sings about his lost love so prettily, the devil agrees to let her follow him up out of hell. But he's not allowed to look back to see if she's following until he reaches daylight." Scobell pauses to check a loose leaf, then goes on. "But when Orpheus starts up, he can't hear her footsteps. He figures the devil tricked him. He's almost out into daylight—just a step away—and he can't help himself; he takes one peek back. Ooph." Scobell puffs out his lips. "Gets me every time." He sees me already opening my mouth. "Don't say it!"

"Cautionary tale!"

"You're not swayed by the romance of it? Just a little bit?" He's smiling again as he asks.

"Orpheus was a fool to look back."

Scobell sucks his teeth. "You got one hard heart, Mrs. Warne."

"And you, Mr. Scobell, are a romantic."

I expect him to laugh or deny it, but he looks at me soberly, holding my gaze, then nods. "I guess I am, then."

His frank look flusters me a moment, pinking my cheeks. It's like he's opened a little window into himself and let me see in. I cast about for something to say to move us on. "You never told me how you came to work for Pinkerton."

"I started out in Mississippi," Scobell says. He's moving along the bottom shelf, book by book, in a low squat. "Came to Richmond by and by. My wife found work there and I . . ." He pauses, like he's choosing whether to say something. ". . . and I came North, to see what a man might do." He stands a moment to stretch his legs. "This was back in—a few years ago, but Pinkerton was already out interviewing fugitives and free men like me, pumping us for information on the Secessionist activity in whatever places we had come through." He tilts his head to the side and looks over at me. "I thought, this man's clever, asking the right people the right questions. Like he could smell what was coming." Scobell squats again. "And Pinkerton, he sized me up too. Asked how I felt about working in intelligence. I asked back if it was all spying and such, or if I'd need to tussle on occasion. Pinkerton said, 'Oh, there'll be some tussle.' I was relieved to hear it. The Good Book says leave wrath to God, but I had got some saved up." Scobell's got a glint in his eye as he says it.

I wager he's a good fighter. He isn't all that big, but his mind's quick. I can well imagine him two steps ahead of his adversaries. And the glint in his eye is a fierce thing. Like a shard of flint, ready to spark words or movement at any moment.

"I told Pinkerton to put me on the books, and I was on a job the very next morning." He finishes with the dramas and moves on to the shelf above. "And your people?" he asks. "You're a Yankee, right?"

"Not a Yank," I say, sharper than I intend. "Irish born."

Scobell pulls back from the shelf in surprise. "Truly?"

I nod. Scobell's not the only one who can hide his past.

"Ireland . . ." He looks thoughtful. "That's a part of England, right?" He gives me a wink, and I know he's getting my goat. "Your people still there?"

I shake my head. "Fever. Did for them in '46." It gives me a pang of nerves to say it, like all my clothes have dropped off. "I came over to Massachusetts with another family. Mills had plenty of orphans after the Great Hunger in Ireland." I say it quickly, skimming across the memory's surface like a frozen lake, so it can't suck me down into its waters. The truth was the mills preferred Yankee girls to little paddy orphans like me, but with places to fill, the Tremont bosses gave up on their aspirations of homegrown "Yank" labor. Bought my indenture contract along with a boatload of others.

Scobell considers these new details about me with interest. "And Pinkerton?"

"I lost my position at the mill. Heard Chicago had jobs in meat-packing." I don't tell him about the failed protest I took part in back in Tremont. Or taking the train west. The rumbling of the train, the rumbling of everything I'd known, all the familiar constants of *me and mine*, cracking and falling away. I don't tell him, either, about arriving in Chicago and finding the meatpacking factories at the lakefront. Red streams pulsing out the drain pipes at their sides. Ghost-faced packers going in and coming out. The stink of working people and dead animals mixed together.

Instead, I give Scobell a pert smile and say, "Chicago was a city getting a feel for itself, and it felt like it might be worth knowing. The woman I had lodged with in Tremont gave me the name of a boarding house. I didn't have the full week's rent, but when the landlady heard I was a mill girl with experience earning a wage, she set me up in a snug little room. Running water and everything. I opened the spigot the first time, and you know what?"

"Tell me," says Scobell. He's now looking through a shelf of phi-losophy books.

"I opened that spigot and a little fish came out, a little fish the size of my finger, right out into the basin, still wriggling." Scobell and I laugh. "Chicago was so welcoming, it provided water *and* food from the very same tap."

"And Pinkerton?" prompts Scobell.

"You rushing my story?" I say in mock anger.

He's picked up *Plutarch's Lives*. "I just want to hear how a mill girl becomes a hard-boiled detective."

"Pinkerton and some of his agents caught a counterfeiter, right near my boarding house. I watched them haul the man away. It was all written up in the paper the next day, 'the local heroes of Pinkerton's National Detective Agency.' Couldn't believe they were real. Guess you'd say I was inspired."

I had read Pinkerton's detective books in the Tremont Circulating Library as a girl.

The Pinkertons and the Railroad Thief
The Detectives Defeat the Murderer

I adored them: Daring exploits so different from my life of tedium and predictability. A group of chosen detectives, bound by secrecy and craft. A hero who always outwits the forces against him—no matter how unlikely the odds. I used to recast myself in those stories while I worked. I was like a kite tethered in the mill, ranging into my own private heaven. The machines crashed on, but my thoughts wove around their relentless beat. I was a heroine in a forest of spinning frames, a daredevil saving the day on a rumbling locomotive.

But I had taken them for fiction. Fairy tales for a girl in a mind-numbing wage job with no family of her own. I can hardly express my feelings in Chicago when I comprehended that Pinkerton was a true-to-life man and his books true-to-life exploits. Poleaxed is the best word for it. In my mind, a new fantasy sprang to life:

The Detectives Save the Lost Factory Girl
Kate Survives Chicago!

But this wasn't a castle in the sky; it was built on earth at 92-94 Washington Street, the address of Pinkerton's National Detective Agency. Providence, it seemed.

Scobell looks at me, all lost in my memories. "You still didn't tell me how you got hired."

"I went to the offices and knocked on the door."

"And that was that? You just walked in and asked for a job?" Scobell plainly doesn't believe me.

He's right, of course. That wasn't that at all. Pinkerton cut a terrifying figure. He eyed me hard and asked my purpose. I introduced myself, leaning on the first half of my surname Heaney like it was a Yankee name, my accent barely discernible. I lied, adding several years to my age, and claimed I was from Erin, New York. Then I told him he should hire me as an agent.

Pinkerton sized me up for no more than half a minute, then asked when I came to this country, which New England factory gave me the calluses on my hands, and why I claimed to be twenty-three when I couldn't be more than eighteen. I thought I was clever; I was transparent as glass. But one thing a childhood like mine conferred was doggedness.

"I had to convince him a woman could be useful as a detective," I recount to Scobell. "Worm out secrets men have no access to." It was the best argument I could drum up at the time. But it seemed all right; the world gets split into women domains and men domains, and crossing between them is a conspicuous business—having someone across the line could be of use to him. "He offered me a trial to see what I might handle. Then another one. Sometimes I think I'm still on a trial basis." I say it as a joke, hiding the hurt behind it. "But one thing about Pinkerton, he doesn't mind running contrary to public opinion. On women in men's jobs or any other thing."

"That's the truth," acknowledges Scobell.

That day I was hired, Pinkerton asked me to pen my name in the employee roster. "I'm calling you a widow for propriety," he told me. "But you'll choose the name you use."

It took a moment to grasp what he meant. When I did, I understood I wasn't the first person who'd been hired hoping to begin again. I left my old name behind. What was it but a tether to a past I'd prefer to forget? I signed the roster with a Yank name, solid like earth: Kate Warne.

Scobell moves to a new shelf in the widow's library. "It was brave, you asking for the job."

I don't know how to tell him it wasn't brave at all. I was terrified.

No, I was running just ahead of my terror. I was desperate, undone by losing my livelihood at Tremont and finding myself alone in the world. "You know what best compels a person to bravery?" I say to Scobell. "Meatpacking as an alternative."

All at once, a page slips from the book Scobell's holding. It floats down to the floor, light as a feather. Both of us watch it breathlessly, hoping it just might be the key we're searching for. Scobell grabs it and peruses it close, front and back, then once over again. He sighs dejectedly and passes it to me.

I look it over thoroughly. "Nothing," I conclude.

He runs his finger along the binding where the page came out. "Cheap stitching. Fell out on its own, most like."

I feel the paper. "Brittle." All at once, I'm seized with a desire to try something. I take the page and push it into my mouth.

"Whoa!" calls Scobell.

I get the paper partly down, but not quickly. It takes a lot of spit. I extract the page from my mouth. "Wanted to see if I could do it. Swallow a message like the widow tried to."

"Oh," Scobell says. He considers a moment, then takes the following page from the book and gently tears it out. He stuffs it in his mouth and starts to chew.

I put my page back in and try again. It's not easy, I'll tell you that. My throat gets all scratched up by the paper's edge. I feel a half-chewed bit stuck down in my gullet. I fish the paper out. Scobell tries a little longer, then pulls his out too.

I hold up my soggy paper. "I think I got farther than you."

He holds up his. "You certainly did not."

Neither of us speaks with much conviction. Our voices are hoarse, and neither of us did as well as the widow this morning.

"Maybe she used thin paper in anticipation of such recourse," I say to cheer us.

"Maybe she practiced," Scobell tries.

We're both quiet a while, nursing our scratched throats and feeling foolish.

Scobell breaks it. "So, a mill girl from Massachusetts . . ." He seems to weigh the fact. "You know, in Mississippi, we'd talk about the poor Yankees up in their factories. White slaves, we'd call them," Scobell says with some bite. "But it's a machine does the work, isn't that right?" He lets that sit a moment. "Machines are the Northern slaves, seems like." He looks up to see my response.

I don't contradict him. Because the man's right. Whatever hardships I endured in the mill, I was a person in the eyes of Massachusetts law. And while we called the mill bosses tyrants, they never could have separated the families that worked within its walls. And when the working conditions grew intolerable, I had the choice to protest or leave, however few the alternatives. There was never an enslaved person with the comfort of such things. "That sounds about right," I tell Scobell.

He looks at me a moment longer. "Nonetheless, it's no good, factory work, is it?" His voice is gentler, the bite gone. "I read a book on it once: *A History of the American Textile Industry*."

"That's some taste you got in books," I tell him.

"I had work as a porter for a publishing house. Publisher specialized in histories. *The History of Captain Lewis and Lieutenant Clark*, *Lives of the Caesars* . . ." Scobell lists some of the titles. "Best thing about being beneath notice sometimes is being beneath notice. Learned to read from those books after hours. Then I went and read their entire catalogue." He glances over to me. I nod, impressed. He goes on. "Only time I've seen Pinkerton dumbfounded was when I told him I knew the Caesar shift."

"And what is the Caesar shift?"

"Just a two-thousand-year-old cipher," Scobell beams. "Substitute each letter in the alphabet for another a fixed number of positions away. Pinkerton started explaining it to me, and I told him I already knew it *and* when it was invented. Impressed him, I did."

"How could you tell?" I ask.

"A particularly approving grunt," Scobell answers, and we both laugh. "Wager it was the first time anything's surprised that man."

"Underestimation is a dangerous thing," I say.

"That's something you and I got in common, isn't it? No one sees us coming." He gives me such a sweet look, I blush.

"What if it had been only cookery books, your publisher sold, not histories?" I ask him. I'm paging through a shelf of *Godey's Lady's Books*. "Nothing to read nights but how to bake a ham."

He nods to the stack of *Godey's* in my hands. "Could've been only ladies' magazines."

"Or etiquette manuals," I answer.

"Mathematical texts," he counters. His eyes are alight, like it's a game.

"Songbooks," I return, and wait to see what he comes back with.

"Romances," Scobell says.

"Poetry," I reply.

"Sewing patterns."

"Dime novels."

"Atlases."

My well is running dry. ". . . Geologic surveys?"

"Farming manuals," he answers before I've hardly finished.

Damn, the man's quick. "And what was your preferred history?" I ask because I can't think of another type of book.

"Oh, now I can't seem to recall the name," says Scobell. "But it's about a woman who resorts to a detour in conversation to distract from losing to a colleague. Tell me if you know the title." He flashes a wicked smile.

"You won!" I laugh back. "And I admit to trying to divert you from the fact via subterfuge. Here's your prize." I climb down the ladder and pluck a flower from the vase on the desk. "Laurels for the champion." I tuck it into the buttonhole of his coat. As I do, I catch the light scent of laundry soap and the warm smell of his skin behind it. "Wait!" I call out suddenly, remembering *Romeo and Juliet*. "Dramas!"

He sniffs his flower. "Too late, I already won."

"Did you have another, if I'd remembered sooner?"

"I'm not telling you!" he says back playfully.

"I'm going to be wondering all day long."

"And I'm going to be peaceful all day long, knowing I beat you, a Northern white woman, at books," he teases. But he plucks a second flower from the vase and offers it to me.

"What's this for?" I ask.

"You deserve one, too, stuck up in this library searching books instead of out worming out secrets." He says it like he knows I want to be doing more. For a moment I feel exposed, like I should have covered myself up better.

I take the flower. His hand brushes mine as I do. It's a surprising warmth. Soft, despite his calluses.

Scobell turns back to the books. I look at him a moment, his concentrated face going over a new volume. It's a fine-looking face. Trustworthy. Maybe it's all right he saw through me.

As I pick up another book, it comes to me that his hand brushing mine may be the first time we've touched one another, skin to skin. Seems such a natural thing, touching someone. I can hardly believe it's the first time. I tuck the flower into a hairpin behind my ear, still feeling his warmth on my hand.

— Four —

Flower perfume. That's the first sign. I might not have smelled it if I were deeper in the library. It's Lewis's boots on the stairs that come after. And only in the following moment do I put together that Widow Greenhow came up the stairs first, passing by the library door. She was the perfume.

I don't see what next transpires, but I surely smell the smoke. I jump down off the ladder and dash out the library door to the widow's bedroom across the hall. Scobell's right behind me.

Lewis is stopped short in the bedroom doorway, which tells me something's awry more than smoke. I duck behind Lewis's broad back for cover. Through the space under his raised arm, I see the widow and her pistol, three paces away.

"I'll shoot you where you stand," says the widow. The neck of her dress is undone, as if she removed the pistol from her corset. Beyond her in the fireplace, there's a bright little pyramid of papers, consumed in flame.

All at once, Lewis darts to the fireplace, grabbing a cushion from a chair and beating down the flames.

"I'll shoot you!" the widow cries.

"You'll have to cock it first," Lewis calls to her, still working at the fire. The pause she takes to check her weapon is enough for me to step in and wrest it from her.

"Don't you presume to touch me!" she spits.

"I'll presume that and more, you point a weapon at us," I spit right back.

Lewis is gathering up the burned bits of paper, trying to identify what they were. God help us if it was the cipher key.

I hear Pinkerton coming up the stairs. No other person in the house has steps so hard and heavy. I hear the murmur of his voice and Scobell's outside the bedroom door. Then Pinkerton charges in. He's wrathy enough he can't get any words out. Lewis gets one of Pinkerton's sausage fingers pointed right at him. It means: *you*. Then he points to the library.

What could have transpired that the widow got out of Lewis's sight? How did she best the great Pryce Lewis? But suddenly I'm getting the sausage finger too. It's not that he's angry with me. If you haven't got it by now, Pinkerton operates at a low fury as his default demeanor. A thing that drives a man to apoplexy early, but don't even think of telling him that. Even his wife, Joan, doesn't, and she has to live with the man. "Library!" he barks at me. I follow Lewis out of the room. I hear Pinkerton telling Scobell to have Tully watch the widow. That's a little punishment aimed at her, being watched by Tully.

In the library, door shut, Pinkerton bends down and pulls off a shoe. He hurls it so it hits Jefferson's *Correspondence* on the shelf. The man can't abide shoes. Any opportunity, he removes them. Pinkerton was meant to appear at the War Department offices in an hour to deliver the news that this morning we placed the widow Rose O'Neal Greenhow under house arrest on suspicion of spying, but that, no, we haven't yet got the cipher key or a confession or much in the way of useful evidence except the half-swallowed message. And now this: an unsecured captive, a pistol, and more destroyed evidence. We've been hired by Abraham Lincoln himself. Pinkerton doesn't need to reiterate that. Nor that how we do reflects right up to him. Pinkerton gets to where words return. "Well?"

Lewis is still eyeing the burned bits from the widow's fireplace by the library window. "Letter. Enciphered," he confirms.

"Not the cipher key?" Pinkerton hisses.

"Not the cipher key." Lewis sighs with plain relief.

But Pinkerton doesn't look relieved at all. In fact, a wild look is coming into his eye. "How?!"

Lewis turns his charm on Pinkerton. He knows he's in shit creek, and deep. "The lady was experiencing great distress. She asked me, as a favor, to see to a private matter"—he clears his throat—"in her water closet. I showed her gentlemanly courtesy, imagining she would appreciate and return my civility." Pinkerton's still seething. Lewis keeps talking. "Women have private . . . situations." He gestures vaguely to his own privates. "That they must at times . . . attend to . . . privately." Pinkerton slowly shakes his head in disbelief. Lewis finishes weakly, "I am the carrot."

"Change of plans," Pinkerton growls at him.

Lewis looks up sharply like he smells what's coming. "Let me go back to working the widow," he urges Pinkerton. "I will not fall for her subterfuge again."

"Threats and deprivations have had no galvanizing effect." He says nothing of Lewis's failed charms. "Waiting us out, she is. Wagering we don't find enough evidence before her arrest is found out, and she can use her connections to secure her release. She needs an incentive to work with us now." His eyes fall on me. "Alone in a house of male jailers. She'll be desirous of sympathy. Common law of human nature."

My heart starts to beat hard. I can see him considering: two white, Irish-Catholic, female spies. Why not sympathy?

Bam, clump, bam, clump, Pinkerton stomps over to me half-shod. We're of a height, and he comes right up to my face. Beard so thick, you can't see skin through it. It would appear intimate, our proximity, in another man. "Kate." His breath is hot on my nose. "You will get that cipher key."

"I'll do it," I fairly shout. No more searching through books. No more trials. No more other people getting the choice jobs while I do background work and interviews.

Pinkerton's eyes are drilling into mine like he's trying to see down into my heart proper. "But can you, girl?" He's thinking on the Maroney case. The one where I lost my nerve. Hell, I'm thinking on it too.

———

Here's how the Maroney case started: It was 1858. Pinkerton was hired by a Mr. Sanford, a big bug at the Adams Express Company. Transporting cash is a service several operations, like Wells, Fargo & Company, offer along the rail-lines. A locked pouch, a safe, and a trustworthy expressman are the means to ensure the funds' secure arrival. Well, one of Mr. Sanford's locked pouches left the Montgomery, Alabama, station intact, but arrived at its destination in New York $40,000 short. Mr. Sanford suspected Nathan Maroney, manager of the Montgomery station, as the man most likely to have done the job. Sanford had Maroney thrown in jail on suspicion of theft, but he knew the charge wouldn't stick without evidence.

In his letter, Mr. Sanford asked Pinkerton to send a detective composed of equal parts horse and alligator, meaning: prove Mr. Maroney's guilt quick and don't worry nothing about manners and gentility in the process. But Pinkerton doesn't do half horse, half alligator. He does Thorough and Complete. So, this is what he did: He traveled down to Montgomery, Alabama, with me and had me dig down into Mr. Maroney's life.

Criminals always need a confidant, says Pinkerton. No human being can hug a secret to his breast and live—the law of human nature. My job was to provide a confidante to Mrs. Maroney, Mr. Maroney's suffering wife. Because with a jailed husband, no income of her own, and a six-year-old daughter to care for, Mrs. Maroney was suffering indeed.

I'll say straight off it didn't go the way I planned. But I'll get to all that soon enough. It was my first true test of working in disguise— and my first time taking on the persona of a Southern lady. I'd long since lost my Irish accent. I'd learned to switch between my natural speaking style and the pristine grammar and ornate phrasing of more educated types. I'd trained to hold myself like a lady. Pinkerton sent me to a tailor in Chicago and had me study an etiquette primer cover to cover, *Beadle's Dime Book of Practical Etiquette for Ladies and Gentlemen.* I'd practiced a light suggestion of a Southern drawl—loosening my jaw, drawing out my vowels, letting the words sit in the back of my mouth—until Pinkerton nodded with satisfaction.

It was afternoon when I stepped out of the carriage outside the hotel near the jail where Mrs. Maroney and her young daughter were staying, ready to begin my work.

As I approached the hotel, I spied two ladies on the veranda having tea. I marked them looking me up and down. I ventured a glance in their direction, offering a small smile of greeting. One looked away. The other's eyes got glassy, looking right through me. I started to sweat. What if one of these ladies was the very Mrs. Maroney I was meant to befriend? I hadn't even made it through the hotel door, and I'd been snubbed.

It only got worse when I descended for supper in the dining room. Not a lady looked up at my entrance. The only person who met my eye was the girl who served my food, and when I asked a fellow diner to pass the salt cellar, she pretended she didn't hear me.

I didn't yet know "true" ladies can sniff out new money, low origins, and questionable circumstances like no others. It's the most proper and well-bred ones that are the fiercest of scrutinizers, always looking for a weakness or a difference in the others, ready to expel the queer one from the fold. Like a flock of hens. Shut hens in the henhouse with an injured bird at dusk, by dawn that injured bird will be pecked to white bones. That's what ladies are like—North, South, it doesn't matter. All at once, I was back in the mill, a paddy among Yanks, standing at a spinning frame trying to build a castle in the sky—who was I to think I could do this?

As I cut into my supper of pork chop, I wondered how Pinkerton would fire me—with lots of yelling? Only in grunts? I was so absorbed in my own failings, I hardly noticed when a new lady and her six-year-old daughter arrived at the dining room door. But I certainly noted the scuffle.

Mrs. Maroney and her daughter, Flora, were trying to navigate their way to their accustomed table through the other diners' overflowing hoops and cage crinolines. Squeezing through a particularly tight spot, Mrs. Maroney politely asked one lady to pull in her chair. She was answered with the same deafness I encountered with the salt.

Mrs. Maroney uttered loud enough for all of us to hear, "I've surely never met with such incivility!" and shoved right past. There were a few clucks of shock and murmurs of disdain, but mostly the ladies persevered in their disregard. As for me, I looked directly into Mrs. Maroney's eyes and gave her an approving nod. Inside my heart, I was thanking my good fortune. It seemed we were both undesirables.

I started playing "the long game," insinuating myself into her trust. I offered a small smile across the dining room at breakfast. Later, a suitable exchange with Flora when we passed on the stairs. I graduated to the happy accident of taking the air at just the same moment. I paid subtle compliments that bolstered Mrs. Maroney's self-esteem, while bringing attention to our shared interests. It's slow work, worming into someone's trust, but every step quickens my blood. It's the thrill I described before. You know something your suspect doesn't. You're disguising your true self. Binding yourself to someone, opening the door between your hearts, but knowing they can't hurt you because at any moment you can cut loose, shut that door, and go.

While I worked Mrs. Maroney, I studied the other hotel patrons, those "true" Southern ladies. I was like a naturalist, observing Southern belles in their native habitat, learning how the species recognized its own. The gaze that alighted only fleetingly on others. The way they circled around the highest-ranking female. The guarded social mask that appraised everything and admitted nothing. How they paraded in their gowns and ribbons like tom turkeys, eager to show their feathers but always fearing another might out-plume them. I observed these ladies' conduct and took it all inside, like I once did the rhythms of the cotton mill, fitting myself to their behavior.

As for Mrs. Maroney, once she came to see me as an ally, I guided her to a secluded bench on the hotel grounds in the shade of a flowering magnolia tree. "Oh, but you must find me the most deplorable company, preoccupied as I am," I apologized. "If you will not judge me too harshly, I will confess my husband is incarcerated for forgery. You must believe me innocent of his crimes, complicit only in my choice to bind our fates through marriage." Cautiously, she listened, barely thinking to extend comfort, lost as she was in her own, not dissimilar, circumstances.

A detective's job is to steal secrets, and the most efficient means to do so is typically persuading the suspect to give those secrets over. The first step is finding common ground.

The second step is locating a sort of break, like a small rent in the fabric of a person, through which you might tap-tap into their heart. An aperture, Pinkerton calls it. Sometimes it's a doubt that makes the suspect vulnerable. Sometimes it's a weakness you can exploit.

The following morning, Mrs. Maroney approached in great emotion, hurried me to our bench under the magnolia, and confessed that she comprehended my difficulties only too well. Her husband was in jail for theft, and she was at her wit's end—terrified for her future.

Mrs. Maroney's eyes were red as she watched her daughter playing near us in the grass. "My husband sent a letter," she whispered. I leaned in closer. "He desires me to send the stolen money to pay the legal fees needed to free him." Mrs. Maroney was in her late thirties, I'd guess. Not a laugh line on her face but plenty of creases across her forehead. She shook her head. "This isn't the first time he's done this. When he gets out of jail, he'll surely lose the money again. Cards," she spat. "And then it'll start right over. It's like a disease, he's got."

Six-year-old Flora turned to us with a great smile from where she was playing, her dress stained all over with green. Mrs. Maroney smiled back tightly, trying to cover the strain on her face. "I've no family to take us in," she said to me. "What's to become of my beautiful girl?" Her hands pressed together. Soft, white hands with nary a callus. "Should I just take the money? Leave him in jail, and go? We could start over, me and Flora." This was her aperture: fear for her child's future.

I just needed to take the final step: use that fear to make her reveal the location of the money. Pinkerton would seize it and gain the evidence to convict Mr. Maroney for good.

But sitting beside that woman, her grass-greened daughter digging in the lawn, something caught in my heart. When Pinkerton seized that money, Mrs. Maroney would have a daughter to support, an empty bank balance, and a ruined reputation. She was a woman stuck in hell with nothing but bitter choices.

I began to think dangerous thoughts. Who would it harm if she took that money? Mr. Sanford, the railroad baron? Mr. Maroney, her profligate husband? What if she took her daughter and the stolen money and went west, bought a boarding house and made a life for the two of them?

Later in the evening, I met with Pinkerton at a tavern to report on my progress. At our little wooden table in the tavern's dining room, I lied. I told him I couldn't "break" Mrs. Maroney, that I couldn't find a way in.

I swear, there in his seat, Pinkerton looked dead into my heart and saw my lie. "You can't do it or you won't do it?" he asked me.

I didn't know what to say.

Pinkerton's eyes stayed steady on me. "If you don't have the guts to stay the course, walk out of here now and be done with it. But I don't ever want to see your face again."

My breath was tight. I didn't want to fail him. The Pinkerton agency was the brightest thing in my short, tedious life. "How—" I didn't even know what to ask. "How do I—?"

"Our ends are justice," Pinkerton spoke. He raised a finger and pointed at my chest. "Don't be who you are, be whoever you need to be."

I let go of my breath. I ran my fingers over my calluses, remembering Mrs. Maroney's soft, white hands. A flicker of resentment needled into my heart. I grabbed hold of that feeling and reminded myself I wasn't a little girl anymore. I wasn't little Mary Kate Heaney. I was Kate Warne, Pinkerton detective.

Pinkerton marked the change. He gave an approving cough. "It's hard to be on the side of right," he told me. "But we are the side of right. Remember that."

The next morning, I dressed myself in my Southern belle persona and met Mrs. Maroney under our magnolia tree once more. I girded my heart, looked her in the eye, and told her to place her trust in me as a friend. I urged her to stand by her husband—to keep her family together for her girl's sake. I pressed her to collect the stolen money and pay his legal fees.

She agreed. In planning how to retrieve the cash, she revealed its location: the basement of a house in New York. I conveyed the intelligence to Pinkerton. Before Mrs. Maroney could reach it, Pinkerton secured the money—nearly all $40,000. Mr. Maroney was convicted for life.

The newspapers made a big to-do about it, Pinkerton's name on the front page with the headline: "JUSTICE DONE!" I never found out what happened to Mrs. Maroney and her daughter.

When I arrived back in the Chicago offices, Pinkerton congratulated me. "You stayed the course." He even asked me to find a second woman to join the agency. But in the coming months, it was that new hire, Hattie Lawton, who he sent undercover. Pinkerton put me to office tasks—background research, clerical work. He called me head of the new "female bureau," which seemed like a promotion, but the truth was it made me a kind of glorified secretary. All the plum jobs—the daring and exhilarating ones—went to his best agents: Timothy Webster, Pryce Lewis, and soon, Hattie Lawton—like he didn't fully trust me in the field. Until now.

———

In the widow's library, I tell Pinkerton once over that I can handle the job, even though my insides are quailing. It's no easy task. Wholly different from the Maroney case. I'm a known quantity to the widow. I'm the woman's jailer, an abolitionist, and, in her estimation, a "grubby little female." Hell, my hand's been in the woman's mouth; she's made me for an adversary.

Pinkerton looks at me sharply. "Our time frame remains the same.

You've got until day's end tomorrow to become her ally and convince the widow it's in her best interest to collaborate and give up her cipher key. Do not underestimate her. Do not underestimate yourself." He says both like reprimands, which is the tone of most of his encouragement.

He turns to Lewis and says one word: "Bangs." George Bangs, the office manager. Lewis has failed. He is returning to Bangs at the Washington offices for a different assignment.

Lewis's face breaks into indignation. "I'm better than paperwork! Let me go back to the widow," he cajoles. "She'll think I'm a soft touch now. Her guard will be down."

Pinkerton doesn't even look at him. He just shouts once over, "Bangs!"

— *Five* —

I'm alone in the library. Conjuring fantasies of how this long game in a short window of time might work. Let me just take a minute and ask you directly: What would you do? What would you do if you were told you had to win the respect of a bigot like the widow such that she'd listen to you? And recall the constraints: She knows you for a poor, Northern female of abolitionist sympathies. I already hear you laughing. So, once you've had your chuckles, do tell: How would you do it? How would you finger the seams of her heart and find a rent in its fabric? I'm listening.

One thing is certain, the widow doesn't believe me her equal and would never take me as such. I need to fit into the mold of the low females she *does* consort with respectfully. I land on Lizzie, her maid, the one sequestered in the basement. Lizzie hasn't given up any information on her employer, not under threat of imprisonment or Pinkerton's fearsome eyes and flying shoes. That means there's something between them more than salary, some goodwill. That could be my angle. Take a cue from Lizzie and play the Good Servant.

I'll keep my eyes bright, but not too clever. I'll present a cheerful bearing without excess sentimentality. I'll also need to inch myself a couple notches along the scale running from Female to Lady until I'm hovering right at Woman.

A Woman:

1. keeps her feet narrower than her hips, so she takes up less space and her base is a little less stable. This makes her appear less forceful
2. shifts one hip to the side when at rest, demonstrating no firmness of purpose
3. remains poised as if waiting, as if her breath doesn't ever fully drop out. This signals a general anxiety about what people think of her
4. waits when other eyes come to rest on her person, looking down or away to give that person time to peruse her (like a dog allowing another to sniff its behind)
5. narrows her shoulders inward, shielding her heart, her person-hood, of which she is ever unsure. Or, alternatively, pokes her chest up and her bottom out to demonstrate she values beauty and allure over functionality (promising a dotage of backache)

You've seen the other end of the spectrum: the nearly sexless Female, legs wide and steady, shoulders broad as she completes some work on the farm or at the factory. There's a functional alignment to the Female body that allows for its most efficient use. Tweak it—narrower here, off balance there—and you're on the move from Female toward Woman. Once you get to Lady, you've lost nearly all your effective mobility. What Southern belle could accomplish the meanest farm task in a corset? The widow can hardly situate herself on a sofa.

You know all this, even if you think you don't. People are a kind of book. Stories written in our bodies. Some of it's plain, like laugh lines showing a good nature or humped shoulders telling of worry. But there are also deeper stories. I remember the way some of the women in the mill walked through the world. Picking their way through the rooms like deer or rabbits. Like they knew they were nothing but prey in a world of hunters.

Tell me, how is it you recognize a friend crossing the road in the distance, bundled as she is in a shawl? In your own household, how do you know whose footsteps it is clumping down the hall to the water closet, with you all tucked up in your bed? Do you believe it some clairvoyance you possess? It is not. Our habits and experiences are etched onto our bodies like words, revealing our true selves. We think ourselves all hidden and cramped inside hearts and heads, but there's nothing private about a life once you know how to read a body. The only unbiased written record. As a Pinkerton, the first training is to cultivate this talent of close reading.

Tully comes into the library with a stack of enciphered paper bits and a jar of paste. His present job is to reconstruct the widow's damaged (half-swallowed, partly burned) messages and see if he can crack the cipher himself. He's got a gleeful smile after his short watch over the widow. "Scared her good and proper just now."

"Where's Scobell?" I ask him. I could use talking through my options, and Tully isn't much for taking on other personas.

Tully shrugs and takes a bite of an apple from a sack he brought. He chews with his mouth open, like it pains him. "The woman was trembling in her boots when I told her Major General McClellan would soon be taking over for General McDowell and that McClellan is an abolitionist cut from the same cloth as William Lloyd Garrison." (A flat-out lie.)

"Who's with her now?" Into my head comes the image again of the widow, in her bedroom, armed with a pistol.

Tully uses a fingernail to scrape apple peel from between his teeth. "Then I told her we detectives were looking forward to the *nice times* we might have with our captive. Trembling in her boots." Tully grins apple bits. Finally, he gets to it. "Pinkerton's with her." Tully looks at the wall like he can see through into the widow's bedroom. "Captivating, that woman is." Tully goes on. "Seduced Lewis as easy as that Union captain."

Tully's talking about a night a week back. He, Pinkerton, and Scobell were surveilling the widow to see if there was anything to the rumors of her spying for the Confederacy. It was near midnight when a gentleman caller approached the widow's front door. It was drenching rain, but they could see that under the man's cloak, he was wearing a uniform. A U.S. Army uniform for a midnight visit to a known Southern sympathizer. Bold? Foolish? I don't even know what to call it.

"Thought we were just looking for a den of spies. Found a brothel too," says Tully. "That captain gave her some papers from his satchel. And then he gave her something else." Tully looks at me leeringly.

"Scobell said you didn't see them doing nothing," I correct him.

"We didn't *see* it, but it happened." He puffs out his lips with emphasis. I get a whiff of apple with booze under it.

"You smell like brandy."

"Widow has a bottle in her bedroom. Found it searching. Had to tipple to be sure it wasn't poisoned, didn't I?"

"Surprised you didn't take the whole thing."

"Oh, there's a case in the basement." Tully's still looking at the wall, imagining the widow. "An officer in his very uniform," he muses. "A captivating woman with a captivating pussy."

I bang the library desk. Tully looks back at me. "You know Pinkerton wants me to gain the widow's confidence."

Tully giggles. "She's a hard case. A damn hard one."

I prod him. "You've got years working thorny jobs. You could be of some use, you know, in helping me prepare."

"Well, now, you did something right clever once, didn't you? Got into a woman's confidence. What case was it?"

"Can you be more descriptive?" I ask.

"Maroney?"

"You're a revelation, Tully."

"I said it was clever!" Bits of apple fly out of his mouth.

"I'll remind you I had recourse to subterfuge in that job. She thought I was a Southern lady."

"Hattie's a captivating one, like the widow. Oh, but she's a pretty face."

Operative Hattie Lawton, he means. The one presently undercover in Richmond alongside Timothy Webster. When Webster rides around town in his carriage with pretty, blond Hattie on his arm, why, every Southern gentleman sees Elysium and lines up to enter Webster's hallowed circle. "How the hell does Hattie pertain?"

"Jealous of her, are you, Katie? You've your ways. It's not always about being captivating. Don't I know it." He gives me a wink.

"Screw you."

Tully's lips broaden into another leery smile. "I'm just getting your goat!" Scobell comes into the library. Tully waves him over. "Come, I'm helping Kate."

"Sure," says Scobell. He leans against the rolling ladder.

Tully sits down at the widow's desk. "So, now, what does the widow want? We figure this, we can discover some insight into her character."

"It's self-interest, her supporting the rebels," I say. "Self-interest dressed in hate."

"Perhaps," mulls Tully.

"Hell if I can make out any other reason," I tell him.

"A child often wants a toy not for the toy itself, but for motivations entirely different." Tully sticks out a squat thumb. "Because his brother has it." Second finger. "Because it reminds him of his mother." Third finger, curiously shorter than the second. "Because he needs a nap."

"The widow doesn't need a nap," I snap at him.

"I'm working up to my argument." He leans his head in. "You still sore over Hattie being ever so much more attractive than you?"

I look to Scobell, suddenly embarrassed, but Scobell's lost in thought.

"Here it is," says Tully. "The Confederacy sees itself as the younger sibling. Lectured, judged, tyrannized by the older North. What does the younger do? Digs in its heels and hollers to Father for justice. Our oldest passions cut deepest. Could be?"

"I don't see her as being moved by jealousy," Scobell finally speaks.

"Nor Kate, but then look at her ire when I mention Hattie."

Did I tell you the best training for composure is talking with Tully? If you can keep from strangling him for five minutes, you'll manage any interrogation.

Scobell ignores him. "That woman's not falling for threats or she'd be broken already. And she'll see through you, Kate, as easily as you would her, I'd wager." He sighs. "She's intelligent."

"There's some part of me just can't fathom that," I say.

"You've known plenty of intelligent women," Scobell says.

"Not her being female. Her being on the side of this she's on."

"Plenty of clever devils too." Tully smiles coldly. "Wish we had three of her. We'd win the war in a week."

"Clever's different," I tell him. "How can an intelligent person, depth and reason and all, look at the spot we're in and choose the side she chose?"

Scobell snorts. "That's your imagination's limits. That's all that is."

"She's in mourning," Tully considers. Suddenly he sits up straighter. "That's her weakness."

Scobell looks at him sharply. "Use her dead daughter?"

Hearing Scobell say it aloud jellies my guts. But I recall Pinkerton's words to me in the Maroney case: *Don't be who you are, be whoever you need to be.* "If it's my way in, it's my way in."

Scobell turns to me, unconvinced.

"It's all she deserves, isn't it?" I say to him.

"Suppose so," Scobell says.

All at once, Pinkerton barrels through the library door. Would you know it, he's a phantom without his shoes. He surveys Tully at the desk with his apple core, Scobell leaning against the ladder, my resigned figure. "Well?!"

"Kate's skittish," says Tully. The bastard.

"I'm not," I say back quick.

Pinkerton raises one long line of eyebrow. "You're going to need to search her. First thing."

It's not the easiest way to start winning over a target, to be sure. But I understand his thinking. She was already searched once when we got here, but just the outer bits: pockets and sleeves. And Tully already searched her bedroom, so it stands to reason the pistol came from deep on her person. The letter she burned too. If there's a chance the cipher's still on her, we've got to do another search. Thorough and complete.

"Don't you be letting a seam go unfingered, girl," Pinkerton warns. "And don't never let her turn her back on you. She's pissing on the pot; you've got her eye to eye, eh?"

"Got it." I nod. "But I'm going to need your help to start me off right."

"How's that?" Pinkerton grunts.

I tell him the idea starting to form in my mind. The Good Servant. The dead daughter. Pinkerton mulls it over, then gives a sharp nod of agreement. "You ready?"

"Ready," I say.

"Good hunting," Pinkerton says back. Then he starts in at a holler.

— Six —

We're just outside the widow's bedroom now, Pinkerton on a rant. "Why, Kate! I hear report that while I've been elsewhere occupied, you've taken the opportunity to play cat with our mouse. Eavesdropping at her parlor door! Rough handling of her personal effects while searching! It does you no credit. It only proves her suspicions that you're a low type, incapable of better!

"Indeed, you drag the esteem of our entire profession down with you. If you were to pause your rude conduct long enough to look around you, you might discern that you are in the company of a lady of some cultivation. You might even find in her comportment the manners and courtesy you lack.

"I tell you, Kate, if I were not privy to the sordid details of the life you've borne, I would sack you now." Pinkerton takes a heavy pause. "However, in recognition of your hardships not only as a widow, but the other, more tender loss you lately endured, I will allow you to continue in my employ. Seeing a mother so closely joined with a daughter in full health has no doubt rekindled your grief, but you must rise above it. We may be at odds with this woman, but we owe her a measure of decency. Ameliorate your manner and make restitution or, on my word, I will throw you out in the street!"

With that, he sends me into the widow's bedroom, where she's overheard his every word and hopefully believes me both shamed by him and recently bereaved by the loss of a child.

For my part, I can hardly credit it's him, Pinkerton, who spoke all that, considering the number of syllables making up his typical discourse can be counted on his sausage fingers. As if he saved up every word from all his other speeches to make up that one.

The widow herself is sitting at her dressing table with a little smile like the cat that ate the mouse, its tail still wiggling between her lips. In my head, I hear again the words Scobell and I overheard her say, and I want to slap her face so hard her teeth crack. But I tuck that all down and sweep into the room the composed, capable operative.

The room's handsome: a honey-colored bedstead with curtains and a plump, white feather duvet like a swan's back. On the bedside table sits an oil lamp and a stack of books. So, she's a reader. We have that in common, which may prove useful.

I take in the rest of the room. A standing wardrobe matches the bed. There's a clotheshorse draped with more black silk dresses. Miniature portraits of four daughters sit on the mantel. Heavy brass candlesticks too. Would make fine bludgeons, they would. I'll watch for that.

The widow's got an appraising eye on me. "The bitch has been muzzled by her master. How humiliating it must be to be put in your place."

"Suffering for my pride like Ulysses," I say, starting to direct us toward common ground.

"The boss's bitch reads Homer," she says back without a pause. "My goodness, I would not have guessed you had the capacity to read at all."

Fair enough wager. Plenty of poor girls don't get any schooling. But Tremont Cotton Mill required its working children to complete three months of school a year until we were eleven. It wasn't much, but I learned to read.

She goes on. "I would sooner liken our present condition to that of Ithaca during Ulysses's absence."

"Penelope?" I tip my head to the widow.

"Suffering at the hands of rude interlopers in my own home," she finishes. Her eyes rake me over. "As nothing in your demeanor or manner speaks to it, I must gather from your dress that you are female."

This is all expected. What's not is for me to respond with the calm, chip tone of the Good Servant. "I'm afraid I'll be needing to search your person, ma'am. My apologies."

I can see the widow contemplating the best response. Argument? Resistance? She chooses competition. She unbuttons her dress and undrapes herself, like slipping cloth off a sculpture. She looks away and back to see if I've made her smooth skin and snug-fit corset above her hoop and petticoats. Hoping, surely, to see envy and self-doubt in a plain woman like me. There were girls like the widow in the mill. Always playing "Who's Prettiest?" with everyone they met. I shut my face to the widow like I did to those girls.

I sit myself on a puffed footstool and start searching the discarded dress. I feel all along the seams for hidden pockets. While I do, I read the widow's clothing. The dress has got jet tulle trim on a high-necked chemisette—a nod to contemporary French fashion while still acknowledging her matronly years. It says the widow is both worldly and conservative. A knife-pleated ruffle on the skirt's one flounce and hem speaks of simple elegance. And the sleeves: gauzy silk through which might glow her pale arms. They remind anyone looking that underneath the mourning garb is flesh and blood. Soft and smooth flesh, to be sure. Another woman might reveal such a thing via her décolletage, but the widow does it with her arms. There's discretion in that. Sensuality and propriety all bound up together.

I lay the dress across the bed. "Will you take down your hair?"

She unpins it awkwardly, searching for the pins. I finger through it as gently as I can. The stuff falls down to her waist and all of it her own. "Oh, the fine times this must remind you of," the widow says. "At the foot of your mother's knee, her picking at your lice."

"My mother passed when I was young," I say quietly. That shuts her momentarily. "May I help with your petticoats?"

"I can manage," she says back, but her fingers struggle with the clasp. She's plainly accustomed to being undressed by others' hands. As she works at it, she eyes my dress. "Look at you in your shabby little clothes. You display as much feminine allure as your employer."

I don't reply. It must agitate her that she hasn't gotten a rise from me, because she digs in again. "Skin like an India rubber doll and aspect of a bookish menial. But that's what you are, aren't you? No husband. Father couldn't provide. So you had to find a profession. Nothing worse than being born to low people." Her petticoats drop off. She stands in her linen undershift, form slim, not at all bunched from birthing, proud as Helen.

I give her nothing, not a frown, not a pause, not a flicker of hurt. Any feeling gets tucked away inside. "Underclothes and stockings," I ask primly.

"I'd rather the men's gaze on me than yours, you *pseudo-woman*." But she acquiesces, turning her back and handing me her linens to check.

I finish my search. There's nothing on the woman. Not the cipher key or anything else.

I re-dress the widow and escort her down to the parlor to rejoin her daughter. Then I take a moment to gather myself in the corridor. All the words she called me are still jostling up and down in my heart.

I told you some stories appear on us just through living. But other stories? They're written *on* us by others. Fictions scrawled across our bodies after which we are slotted, just as in a library, into categories: degenerate, low, worthy, respectable.

At Tremont, we Irish knew such stories. Ones where we were cast as villains. Some of the people who came over with us from Ireland had made it through the Great Hunger whole. Some had taken on a heaviness, like a sigh that was let go and not taken up again. Some had taken on a bone-deep anger that was never soothed their whole life long. And some had been broken. Coming into the mill yard each day I saw Old Peg Burke. She had come apart during the Great Hunger after she lost her two daughters, and when she was gathered up, her pieces didn't fit into Margaret Burke anymore. All they made was Old Peg.

The Yank bosses let her be the ragpicker of the Tremont Cotton Mill grounds. It was meant to be a sign of their humanity, leaving her to pick up the pieces of others. Maybe find pieces of herself in among them.

One morning, all of us girls were walking across the canal bridge toward the towering brick mill building. A Yank spinner named Nabby Fife was just ahead of me. She was eyeing Old Peg beyond us in the mill yard. All at once, Old Peg stopped, as still as one of the herons in the canal. Then she cried out, cackling like a witch. It startled us all near out of our skins.

Nabby went right ahead and hissed, "Drunken mick!" As if it could be drinking that caused Old Peg to be what she was. As if that could be the cause and not the symptom. Well, Nabby's talk got worse in the mill's spiral staircase. Her voice tumbled down those stairs, saying, "That paddy sold her children for whiskey, a bottle each."

And before I knew it, I was shouting, "She never did!" my voice bounding back up the stairs.

Nabby stopped one turn above me, peering down, the whole stream of girls shuddering to a stop. "Calling me a liar?" she said over the railing.

"She lost her girls on the ship over," I cried furiously.

"She's cracked," Nabby answered.

"Because of her girls," I called again. "She lost them because of the Great Hunger and the passage." The anger was beating across my chest, right up the back of my neck.

"Maybe she should've planted more potatoes," said Nabby. "Dirty paddies breed like rats, then wonder why your babies starve!"

I'll tell you, all I wanted was to scramble up the stairs to have a go at Nabby. If the way hadn't been too thick with girls, this story would've gone differently.

"There's the famous paddy temper," Nabby spit down, knowing I couldn't reach her. She talked to the captive audience between us. "Like children, they can't master themselves."

People call rage blind, but when it comes on me, it's always been the opposite. I see it coming, as if watching from the side: a snapping roar rising up from my guts, me witnessing with a sort of fixed shame, unable to stop its course, and at the same time urging it on, knowing when it comes out in kicks and strikes and shouts, I'll be fully in its thrall—that famous blindness will finally descend, sweeping away all my miserable feeling with its force. Shame will creep back in later—shame that something so feral lives inside me, that it's so easily called out, snapping and cracking—but for the moment of my rage, I am free.

Well, my anger was doing exactly this, rising up to sweep me out of myself, when suddenly a Yank named Consider Pritchett was at my elbow, tugging on my sleeve. She was a Quaker, and one of the only Yanks I'd met with a kind word for a paddy. "Don't give her more cause," she whispered. "She's not worth it." She gave me all the reasons for temperance. "You'll lose your place if you fight."

Consider's words were like a damp fog, pressing down on my anger, choking off its force. The thrall subsided, leaving me with nothing but its sour-shame residue there in the crush of girls on the stairs.

Nabby smiled down. "We must have compassion for the less fortunate: drunken waste pickers, dirty paddy orphans."

The line started climbing the stairs again. Consider disappeared in the throng. I had nowhere to drain the leftover swill of feeling, so what could I do but shove it all away inside. I walked into Spinning Room No. 2 past the overseer. His eyes were going over each girl, knowing something was up but not what or who. I closed my face like it all had nothing to do with me.

The bell rang and the canal gate opened. Water flooded into the massive mill wheel, which turned the teeth in the giant crown wheel on the ground floor. The crown teeth turned the bevel. The bevel turned the big flywheel. That flywheel connected by a belt to multiple shafts running along the ceilings of each room. Smaller wheels and smaller belts ran down to each spinning frame—a great and branching machine, churned along by the canal's force. The spinning frames started up, first, second, and the relentless thump began. Eighth, ninth. The clamor and clatter gained in urgency. Twentieth, thirtieth, fortieth. It was welcome that morning. The sound battered into me. Battered down my rage. Crashing and banging with all the thumps I'd have given Nabby if there were justice.

But Nabby's hatefulness was nothing new. I felt the truth as a girl, that some stories were written on us by others.

I remind myself of this now in the widow's corridor. That's all her words are: hateful graffiti scribbled across my exterior. They don't touch my insides if I don't let them. I take a breath and smooth down my persona of the Good Servant, ready to return to my job of winning over the widow.

But I've only just arrived in the parlor when all at once there's a furious knocking at the front door.

— Seven —

I'm in the foyer by the front door. The knocking continues. Tully's got his hand on the knife he keeps in his belt. Pinkerton's sausage fingers are flexing and cracking in a way that makes my arm hairs stand on end. Both slip to the side of the door, out of sight.

I settle my shoulders into the likely shape of an unharried maid and square my feet, ready for a fight. I pull open the door with an inquiring smile.

And who's revealed? Armed rebels come to free the widow?

Two young ladies. Lily Mackall (twenty years old, thereabouts) and her younger sister, Veruna Mackall (sixteen?).

I usher them politely inside. I can already see them for your typical, well-bred fashion plates of Washington society. The older one asks after the widow. The younger one's noticed Tully and is staring at him with big eyes that wonder, *Whose old, drunk uncle is lurking in the foyer at dear Widow Greenhow's?*

Then they see Pinkerton, a shoeless thug in the corner, and that I'm now blocking the exit, and don't the both of them start squawking.

Tully gets the younger Miss Mackall in hand, but would you believe the elder weasels past all three of us into the back parlor where the widow and her young daughter are?

The Mackalls' surprise and distress suggest this is a regular social call and not an indication that the widow's arrest is publicly known.

But word can't be allowed to spread. Pinkerton immediately places both the Miss Mackalls under house arrest, at which pronouncement you never heard such a hullabaloo out of four females. You'd think he'd announced he'd be torturing them next. Lily, the elder Mackall, is on about rough hands and uncouth men-types, decrying such a heinous attack upon women and children. Veruna is weeping loudly. The widow is likening their predicament to Mary, Queen of Scots, of all people. And then, if you will believe it, eight-year-old Little Rose starts in singing "Dixie." I do not lie.

I see the situation plainly: I've now got three captive Southern women (and one child) to win over. I'm going to need some tea.

I whip into the kitchen and find Tully. "Is there ice in the basement?"

"A small store of it," he says.

"Then make some cold tea, quick-like."

"You make some tea!" he returns.

"I'm working the ladies!" I tell him. "Make the goddamn tea!"

Tully puffs his lips into an angry pout but collects a pitcher. "You'd ruin the tea anyway."

A little while after, I push into the back parlor with a tray of glasses and a pitcher of fresh, cool tea. I address the ladies soberly, "I imagine you are thirsty."

"Look at that, Pinkerton's bitch does parlor tricks," says the widow. Her daughter, Little Rose, and the two Miss Mackalls titter.

The back parlor. The lioness's den. The room's smaller and cozier than the front parlor. There's two sofas, one under the window and the other to its side. The second one is upholstered in yellow and shaped like an S so two people can sit beside one another but face in opposite directions, for what purpose, I cannot fathom. The paper on the walls is brown with a pale green vine motif. As someone who was born into a house made of turf, it belies belief that anyone would make it all the way into a fancy brick mansion, and then *choose* wallpaper that looks like earth.

The widow and her daughter take their places on the S-shaped sofa, while the Mackalls situate themselves on the sofa under the window.

I hold the pitcher. Who to serve first? The widow, regardless of her house arrest, will be desirous for this to be done properly. The elder Miss Mackall is the widow's junior in age and social stature, but a guest. So how to pour? This is a sort of deciphering you won't guess needs much doing in the course of spy work, but it does. Let me end your suspense: I pour the widow's tea first. Then the elder Miss Mackall's. Then the younger's. Then Little Rose's.

The Miss Mackalls take sugar in accordance with their hostess (less than she does, which is none; the younger Mackall is disconsolate). They wait for the widow to drink before they venture the glasses to their lips. Even the girl, Little Rose, knows the ritual and follows along. Excepting the sugar. She gets herself three spoonfuls and a disapproving eyeful from her mother.

While they drink, I read their bodies. The Miss Mackalls are not the widow. They are like the widow's shade versions living across the River Styx, eyes less lively, forms less graceful. They do their hair in fat curls to either side of a smooth center part, but their hair's thin and lusterless. They're corseted and hooped and bustled, but the two of them's figures lack the variegation of the widow's; they're all stalk, thick and straight. A corset needs something to pull in from to do its job. Even with their plumped-up bottoms, it's not the same.

The Miss Mackalls are not the widow, I say again, but this time in regard to their personal character. Being put under house arrest by unknown men and a female (!) detective is not a matter of righteous indignation for the Mackall girls. They are *concerned* by this turn of events. Dearly, deeply concerned.

Veruna, the younger (really, the lesser) Mackall's shoulders fall in toward her heart like a leaf folding around its spine. By age thirty, I can say with certitude, she'll be stuck that way. When she stands, it's with her feet at angles, one in front of the other, all her weight on the back foot, making any step forward a two-part affair: shift, then step. Slow to act and unsure in her own body, this one.

Did I tell you people tend to occupy different parts of their bodies? You've heard it slung around in poetry: men occupy the head, women the heart, and all that. But in my experience, it's not so much sex determines where we live so much as type.

Veruna, the lesser Mackall, lives in her heart, moving in the waters of sentiment, victim to all its ebbs and floods. Suggestible. Susceptible. She's the type that gives ladies the reputation of delicacy—all the weak, insipid qualities of womanhood bundled up in her. I don't doubt that if I ask you to summon up a picture of a "Delicate Lady," it's the very image of Miss Veruna Mackall that comes into your head.

The greater Mackall, I can already see, lives somewhere else. Now, I'll tell you where, but you might not like it. Believe my aim is neither scandal nor vulgarity when I say that Miss Lily Mackall lives in her privates. When she stands, her hips are directly above her feet, holding herself in balance. This tells me she's forthright, ready to move at any moment. Maybe impulsive. (I can hope—impulsiveness in a suspect is a detective's dream.)

Too vulgar? Perhaps. But in truth, you can read commitment in a person's privates. Try it for yourself: Stand and take a step forward without moving your privates even an inch. It'll only ever be the most hesitant of steps, your toes out in front all by their lonesome selves. You can't take a decisive step until your privates move. You want to do something full of violence, your hips and privates must be behind it. You think a boxer punches with his arm? Look at him close; he punches with his hips. His arm just carries through the hips' purpose.

So, the privates is where I read a person's resolution. People who live too much in their privates move first, think after (regret after). People who keep their privates back or shift them to the side, like the lesser Miss Mackall, well, those people aren't making moves in their lives anytime soon. They might be thinking about a move, or feeling one coming, but they aren't making one.

The greater Mackall is the one to watch. I'll put money on her being in the widow's circle of spies. The younger one's just here trying to live up to her big sis, shoulders closing in to soothe her heart's ache at falling short. And where does the widow live? Can you guess? I'll go on and give you a hint: She's a mix.

I take my own seat in the parlor, a straight-backed chair with an upholstered cushion, center in the arc of women. Thirst slaked, the widow asks, "Are we permitted needlework? Or is that too threatening an occupation for three ladies and a child to undertake?" Hazard a guess if it's testily spoken.

"Perhaps the needles could be occasioned as weapons," mocks the greater Miss Mackall.

But me? I nod in acquiescence to the widow's request. And go one further, "Might I join you?"

"We're your hostages," she answers sweetly.

I walk with simple efficiency, not a scurry, not a stride, to collect the widow's embroidery basket from its place by the window. I realize the danger is the scissors, not so much the needles. What do I do? I offer those very scissors open-handed to the widow, saying, "You'll need these to cut the threads clean," while my face says, *I know what these are, and I entrust them to you, knowing you're lady enough not to use them in violence.* Trust begets trust. The widow takes the scissors blithely and places them on her sofa's end table.

"I'm afraid I have few patterns of any interest," apologizes the widow. "Might I devise some new ones?" She looks to me. Again, I nod smartly and set about gathering pen and paper.

The widow draws patterns while the Mackalls hoop their backings. The widow presents her patterns to all but me. The patterns she's done up are Christian phrases bedecked with a ring of hearts and flowers. You can't account for taste.

After the others have selected thread, I go in turn to the basket. The Mackalls are curious, the widow seemingly not. What can the *pseudo-woman* mean by selecting hoop, backing, and thread when she's been deprived of a pattern? It suggests either an excess of talent or ignorance of the art. The widow can't help the smile playing at her mouth; she plainly guesses the latter and relishes the coming opportunity to deprecate my womanly accomplishments.

Of course, for white, Yank girls (who are the Americans I know best) embroidery is a training ground for womanhood because it encompasses all its necessary talents: skill, patience, and obedience. For immigrants, embroidery is a familiar path into a strange and foreign America. An occupation we recognize from back home, but one that for us, arriving in America with few belongings to embellish and precious spare time away from our relentless wage jobs, requires different skills: ingenuity, resourcefulness, and speed.

The *Godey's Lady's Book*—that ubiquitous guide to American womanhood and homemaking—always has a few embroidery patterns in its back pages. But would you believe they aren't ever as complicated as the ones from back home in Ireland, the ones our mams had been about and our grannies before them? We didn't bring these patterns with us when we left the old country, only the memories of what they were. And those memories grew in grandeur, as memories will. Well, when we Irish are driven to remind ourselves of something from home besides hunger and death and turf fires or to demonstrate that we are not just shanty dwellers and dirty types, but people with a culture as fine as any here in America, we pick up our needles and do some damn fine needlework. The Irish in the mill, why, they must have embellished every item of cloth to be found in their cramped tenements. Curtains made from old shirts adorned with butterflies. Towels so thick with flowers they could hardly dry a dish. Even the rags were covered tip to tail.

So, when I pick my colors and settle down to stitch with nimble fingers trained by women who stitched by turf fires, which is to say, in darkness, it isn't long before Little Rose and the Mackalls both are baldly staring.

"I prefer traditional needlework," says the greater Miss Mackall, to excuse her gaping.

We stitch all afternoon long. I get up twice to provide refreshment without being asked. The lesser Miss Mackall thanks me the second time, but I suspect it's just habit. For the widow's part, she keeps a cool distance, gracing me with only the barest of glances.

At intervals, the Mackalls try out subjects of conversation. Someone has begun a collection for boots for the soldiers. Someone else is hosting a bee to knit socks. There are visits to Southern captives to be made. This ground gently trod, they stride into bolder territory. "My niece, Mrs. Adele Cutts, had occasion to visit the receiving room at the White House," begins the widow.

"And what did she find?" Veruna asks.

"That Mary Todd Lincoln makes up for a lack of taste with an excess of lace." There are titters all around.

"I heard tell"—Lily takes up the theme—"that the Ladies of the Diplomatic Corps presented themselves at the White House for reception by Mrs. Lincoln and were left in her receiving room for half an hour with no greeting or excuse. And when Mrs. Lincoln finally arrived, she was so small and poorly attired they took her for a maid."

"I am ashamed that foreign dignitaries must encounter such a woman bearing the title America's First Lady," the widow says with a shudder.

They tread and retread over Mrs. Lincoln's dearth of taste, with only the slightest variations: taste in lace, hats, shoes, dress styles, curtain length, duck breed, muffin type . . . (I admit the last few I invented to offset the topic's tedium.) None of their stories are about meeting the woman themselves, just secondhand gossip they're using to shore up their small-minded views. I doubt the younger Miss Mackall has any true convictions, not like her older sister and the widow, but sitting in such a stew of filth, what choice does she have but to soak it all up? I guess that's how most people come to their views.

Convictions are another matter. There's a world of difference between views and convictions. It's the same sort of difference between friend and lover. Views must grow beyond simple familiarity and affection into something intimate, housed in a deeper room of the heart. For me and abolition, my view changed to conviction the night I met twelve strangers and nearly shook hands with Mr. John Brown.

The widow and the Mackalls are quiet for the moment. As I stitch my embroidery, I allow my thoughts to wander back to that night. It was some months after the Maroney job. Several of us agents were at Pinkerton's home in Chicago. Joan (that's Mrs. Pinkerton) was laying the table for twenty-two, every plate, platter, dish, and bowl put to the purpose. Her daughters were setting out cutlery, one per place, no matter it be fork, spoon, ladle, or teaspoon. John Brown had come for supper, and not alone. Twelve fugitives were with him, planning to escape across Lake Michigan to freedom in Canada.

Pinkerton's young sons were upstairs fitting them with coats and wool socks and other items for the weather. Mr. Brown and Pinkerton were standing in the parlor with Pryce Lewis and John Scobell. Me, I was hesitating in the hallway halfway between the parlor and the dining room, confounded to find myself both a woman and an agent. Should I help lay the table like the other women or stand about nodding and shaking hands like the other agents? Well, the short of it is, I was in the hallway hesitating, not five paces from Pinkerton, when he shook hands with Mr. John Brown and welcomed him and the twelve people into his home. And I heard when Mr. Brown said, "Slavery is a thing . . . It's a thing you can't know and then unknow. Nothing you do is innocent again. If you're not fighting it, you're accepting it. People think they're innocent because they live in New York or Chicago or don't own a slave. No one is innocent." And then Pinkerton was nodding and the other agents, too, and me along with them from my halfway place.

That night changed me. While Lewis and two other agents kept watch outside, I helped these twelve people slip into Pinkerton's house on bone-weary, terror-driven feet. I met eyes. I smelled sweat and travel-dirty bodies. I clasped hands in greeting.

We had supper together (less the guards outside and the younger children who were already asleep). And wasn't it a supper, one scooping potatoes with a teaspoon from a roasting pan and another forking them out of a soup bowl. (Me, I had a butter dish and ladle for the job.) All of us looking up at every noise from the street, knowing Pinkerton had people posted to throw up a warning call if there was trouble, but still unable to settle with the heavy danger of our circumstance.

I was sitting next to Scobell. It was maybe the second time I had met him, but the first time I learned he had once been enslaved himself. It suddenly came to me that he was a better spy than any of us because of this fact, because you could look right at the man and not immediately see such an enormity of his past written all over him. I hadn't lived half of what he had, and I was always fearing people would read my truth on me.

He felt me looking at him and turned, mouth full of potato. "Yes?"

"Pass the salt, would you?" I asked to cover my look.

He passed it over but held my gaze a hair longer than salt warranted. "It's a hanging crime to be caught in the company of fugitives, you know that, Mrs. Warne?"

"I know supper tastes better with company," I said back, matching his gaze.

He considered me with the same concentrated look he had paging through books in the widow's library—full of thought, but unreadable. "It does indeed," he finally said.

That night, abolition became not just an idea or a view, but something deeper for me. It became those twelve fugitives. It became Scobell. All the people behind the word "abolition." Any moment my courage wavered or fear made me hesitate in the years to come, I remembered that night, and my conviction resurged.

My mind comes back to the present. I wonder if Scobell is still stuck up in the library, paging through the books, my flower tucked in his buttonhole—

All at once, my wonderings are interrupted by a gasp. The lesser Miss Mackall has happened to glance at my embroidery's progress, her artlessness allowing the ejection. Everyone's attention—even the widow's—turns to my stitching. In less than an hour's time, I've built up layers of flowers and leaves in such a way that their aspect changes when viewed from either side and front on. "Had I a crochet hook, I'd add berries under the leaves," I say aloud. Little Rose satisfies me with an *ah* of admiration.

"Where did you learn such a technique?" ventures the younger Mackall.

"My mother taught me," I lie.

The widow's head turns sharply. "You said your mother passed when you were young. Have you been dishonest with us, Kate?" She says my name like it's a bit of turned meat.

"I learned before she passed," I reply quickly. But the women are already eyeing me skeptically, all the common ground I just built up coming undone. Hell, why did I go and reveal a personal detail to the widow earlier? Pinkerton agents don't do that.

The afternoon wears on. The standing clock in the front parlor chimes four o'clock. The sun streaks unrelentingly through the parlor's western-facing windows. It's the kind of August sun that'll set you to dozing or to agitation. The lesser Miss Mackall stifles a yawn, but worry creases her brow. The greater Miss Mackall, living as she does in her privates and predisposed to activity, shifts uncomfortably. The excitement of their arrest has passed, and they're starting to wonder just what it means. I didn't consider the sun and its swelter for women strapped up in corsets and bustles. I can use it to my advantage. I offer to bring the ladies something more to drink, and hurry off to the kitchen.

Tully is there in shirtsleeves, eating another apple, flour paste stuck all over his front and up in his scrub beard, bits of enciphered letter now laid out before him on the kitchen table. The door's open to cool things off. "Close that up," I order.

"I'm sweating streams."

"Shut the door. Stoke the stove."

Back in the parlor, I apologize to the ladies as I hold up the pitcher: "Warm tea's all we've got."

"I do believe it's hotter than before." The lesser Mackall fans herself with her pattern, slumping down like a sweaty toad. The minutes pass slower, slackened by the heat. Each one swells the Mackalls' worries: Will they be made to stay the night? What must their mother back at home imagine has befallen them? The Mackalls aren't the ones I need to propel toward cooperation, but they might start things off. The greater might break if the lesser does, and like dominoes . . .

Just as I'm thinking this, the widow stands right up. And what does she do? She offers the Mackalls her place on the shadowed S-shaped sofa next to Little Rose. She takes a chair for herself and places it out of the sun. She's not done. "That flush is quite fetching, Veruna," says the widow to the lesser Miss Mackall. Then she looks from lady to lady and announces: "I've heard tepid is how the Empress of China takes her tea."

The lesser Mackall pulls herself up out of her toad slump and sets herself down on the S sofa. The greater Mackall leans right in for a sip of warm tea. And Little Rose? Well, you can just guess what she starts in humming. The widow's eyes flick over to mine, holding just a second longer than casual. Damn her all to hell.

— Eight —

I'm agitated. Agitated with the widow calming the Mackalls. With the sun already heading toward evening, I'm nearly resigned to losing my wager that the widow will be broken by sunset.

I give Pinkerton a report on my meager progress in the kitchen, while Tully watches the ladies. Mann's in the kitchen too, relating how his honeyfuggle's advancing with the maid.

"Took Lizzie to the garden for some air," says Mann. He sweeps his black hair back from his brow. "Told her I felt sorry for her situation, it's no fault of her own, and such. And that I'm no proponent of the Cause, just a working man earning his living far from home. And that if there was anything I could do to ease her way, I'd be glad of it. And then I gave her a slice of ham from the larder," Mann adds with a sober look, "so she knew I meant business."

Pinkerton grunts in approval.

While Romeo and his ham get back to working the maid, I head out to the garden myself. The kid needs to take some exercise. How do I know? Little Rose has begun to emit powerful, swelling whines every few moments:

"I'm too warm."

"I want a cookie."

"Why can't I stitch a heart with black thread?!"

And Pinkerton figures ingratiating myself to the girl will benefit my work on the mother. I don't disagree.

First eyes I meet in the garden are Sam Bridgeman's. He's the agent keeping watch outside, which translates to standing up against the carriage house, smoking a pipe. Sam Bridgeman is a local hire, new to the agency. I don't know much about him, except he's a hulky sort of man-boy who seems more brawn than brains.

Up above in the carriage house window, a man's face watches. Watches Bridgeman. Watches me. It's the widow's groom, Benjamin Early. He looks to be in his twenties. Dark eyes and deep brown skin. He must be hungering for any view. Pinkerton's had him sequestered in his room above the carriage house all the day long. I wish it were otherwise, but we can't have him going and telling anyone we're here, even to brag about the widow getting what she deserves. Absolute silence. And all he's got for company is the occasional visit from Bridgeman. Can't say he's fortunate in that.

Little Rose startles to see Bridgeman in her mama's garden. She looks to me straight off, as the present grown person. I let my eyes pass over him without note. Bridgeman continues smoking his pipe. The girl takes that in and settles into his presence as a thing of no concern. She puts her attention back on me.

She's a miniature widow, the kid. Eight-year-old Little Rose. (The widow called the girl after her own damn self. Like she ran out of names with the older daughters and was too tired to think on it further. I ask you, how full up on yourself do you have to be to call your daughter by your own name? Can't name her for an aunt or a cousin? That says something, I tell you.) The kid does not look to be enjoying my presence any more than I am enjoying hers. She kicks at a big sort of ball-like flower made of little flowers that's blue moving to violet, shaking off a shower of petals.

"How tiresome it is, this garden," Little Rose whines. She yanks off her bonnet petulantly, letting it hang from its strings across her back. Isn't she just as spoiled as an egg salad in August, the heat making her so fatigued. By her age, I was already a working mill girl.

She kicks the blue ball of flowers again. "Wish it were the head of the president."

I met President Lincoln. That's a story you might not hear since it was all hushed up in the aftermath. But I did. He had just been elected president. In response, seven states seceded from the Union. Pinkerton put Hattie Lawton on assignment with operative Timothy Webster. They were sent to Baltimore to investigate Secessionist plots to disrupt Northern industry.

Not long into their detail, Hattie and Webster heard word of a scheme among the Sons of Liberty, a rebel organization, to murder the president-elect. Plots of the sort were a dime a dozen in Maryland at this time. But Hattie confirmed the plot and alerted Pinkerton. He had a time and a half convincing the president-elect of the peril awaiting him, but Pinkerton eventually persuaded him to it.

The night before Lincoln's scheduled passage through Baltimore, I hired a private car on a train running from Philadelphia to Washington. I claimed the car was for my wealthy, invalid brother, and paid a hefty douceur to ensure we were undisturbed on our journey. People go on about President Lincoln's height, but when he met me on the platform in the middle of the night, he was all folded up under a woolen cloak, cap on his head to shadow that great beak. I sorted the tickets and then slid my arm through his to usher him to our private car.

I settled him into his seat, tucking a blanket all about his long body. Then I took up his hand in mine. I took up the president-elect's very hand and gave it a loving, sisterly squeeze.

Outside the car, the station master walked along the platform swinging a lantern. I leaned over Lincoln, muttering "You'll catch a chill" while pulling his cap down farther. The whistle sounded and the train creaked into motion. We were on our way.

We might have been Ulysses returning to Ithaca, the journey felt so long and imperiled. Had the Secessionists intercepted our plan to reroute Lincoln? Were they waiting along the way to ambush us? I was white-knuckled, each screech of a wheel or bump of a rail a rebel posse descending on us.

We barely spoke. The president-elect seemed content in the quiet, not needing, as some do, to fill space with words for the sound's sake. In truth, he appeared calm. I feigned the same, while inside I was aquiver. When we saw the lights of Washington, my spine softened in relief.

Pinkerton met us on the platform. Mr. Lincoln tipped his cap to me. "Thank you, sister." I was shaky with weariness, and yet almost sorry the adventure was finished. I couldn't sleep a wink that night for the lingering spirit coursing through me.

Later the next day, Lincoln's scheduled train arrived in Baltimore without him, to the disappointment of the waiting crowd. Webster and Hattie remained undercover among the Secessionists.

I tell you, this is a country that loves to hate. Loves its blood. Was founded on it, stewed in it. I read most all the history books in the Tremont Circulating Library—calculated Indigenous slaughter, calling enslavement an economic necessity, enshrining enfranchisement and human rights in founding documents with words wiggly enough to allow fifteen million women and four million enslaved people to slip through.

What is it that drives such hate into us? Drives us to divide ourselves into light skin and dark skin, North and South, Yank and paddy, woman and man, lady and pseudo-woman? Smaller and smaller divisions from which we debate and decide each other's worth. Is it our natural state? Or are we pressed into such divisiveness by education and culture and self-interest and all the other noise beating down into our hearts all the day long? I don't know to tell you.

But here's Little Rose in her mother's garden, kicking her blue-headed flower, giving it the name Lincoln. How'd she come to pack that name so hard with hate? What would it take to shake that hate loose, grow her heart into a different shape?

Little Rose looks at me slyly and kicks the flower once over again. She's doing it for me. It's the widow swallowing the message: a spectacle. Or maybe a test, to see what I'll do. But wrapped up in a trust. Little Rose's trust is that I'll never harm her. The widow's trust was in herself to get it done.

Well, I'm not jumping at her bait. I am the bait. I sit and fan myself a bit on a bench in the shade of the house, knowing full well I'm the most interesting thing in the garden. And to be sure, after decimating her mother's flowers in the name of the rebellion, Little Rose ambles on over to see what else might get my goat.

"I got an arrowhead." She pulls a little piece of napped flint from her apron pocket. "It's a Choctaw chief's. Was his very arrowhead."

People forget there's more than just the one war being fought in this country presently. Sioux, Apache, Paiute, Navajo, Wiyot, Comanche, Five Tribes—the list doesn't end of people fighting this very moment for their lives, their freedom, their land.

Last spring, a delegation of Choctaw Indians came to Washington. People packed into the street to see them. Peddlers crawled all over the crowd hawking arrowheads napped that morning and headdresses made of turkey feathers. It was a festive atmosphere. But I tell you, once you got in close enough to see the faces of the delegation members, the thing changed. In truth, it was a terrible affair up close. Knowing they were in a fight against the unceasing tide of the U.S. Army, settlers, railroad barons, and all the rest. The whole thing unfolding before us like some Greek tragedy, spectators knowing the ending and unable to pull away. Kids, even grown men, paying a penny for a souvenir arrowhead to mark the time they saw an Indian walk through Lafayette Square.

"The Choctaw are a race of warriors come to an unavoidable fate," Little Rose repeats someone else's words. She holds up the arrowhead as if aiming it at me. All of a sudden the thing twists in her fingers and falls. She cries out and clutches her fingers close.

"Are you mortally wounded?"

She looks at me sourly.

I pick up the arrowhead and put the damn thing in my pocket. "Come on, now," I coax, pulling gently at her cuff. "Let me see."

Her hand loosens. I kneel down and take it in mine. She's got a thin slice across her second finger just starting to leak blood. "That'll smart." I nod, and she nods with me. I squeeze the finger tight and raise her hand in the air. "We'll just stop the bleeding."

We rest there, me kneeling, her standing, our hands raised together, faces no more than six inches apart. I can see where her nose is peeling from the sun. Pulls off her bonnet on the regular, I wager. "A chief's arrowhead," I tell her soberly. "Got to handle it properly."

The girl studies my face. "Mama says you're a low sort of woman."

"She's right, your mother."

"You're a degenerate." She's trying out the word, seeing what firepower it's got.

"I'm a degenerate and a villain." I raise my brows. "You ever seen one close up?"

She gives the barest headshake. "Is your name truly Kate?"

"I was born Mary Kate," I whisper.

Her eyes glow with this contraband intelligence. "Do you have sisters or brothers?"

I shake my head back.

"I have sisters," she says. "I'd have brothers, too, if all the babies Mama had lived." I let Little Rose's words stay words and not deepen into feeling. Keeping your heart clear of sentiment in the work means keeping words as words, not souls, never faces. "Mama has sisters too," the girl goes on.

"They come around here?" I ask. "They spend time with your mama?"

Little Rose looks exactly like a child who's been warned not to speak on something. I quiet my breath, waiting. "Since the bean-pole became president," Little Rose begins. "Auntie Ellen's been a damned bit frosty." She glows with the heat of her curse. It's like a sugar lump she's been waiting to suck, these scandalous words. She goes on. "Mama says you all hate us. You and Auntie Ellen and the other tyrants. It's your hate what causes the war."

"Our hate, is it? You sure you want to be talking to me?" I say, low. "I might tell you terrible, hateful things." And if the kid's eyes don't brighten at that. Found an aperture. Might as well worm right in. "You've read stories with villains?"

She doesn't answer, but her tongue peeks out her mouth at the thought of a veritable villain, sitting right in front of her. "Are you wearing a corset?" She peers at my bosom and waist.

"Wouldn't you like to know?"

"You're not," she says.

I lean in close and whisper, "Have you ever seen a labor organizer?" Little Rose gets still with listening. "I knew one once. She didn't wear a corset, did she? You know what she wore? Bloomers."

"Mama said queer females wear bloomers!" Little Rose whispers so the flowers won't hear. She's grinning with mischievous delight.

"Do you believe I've had occasion to wear bloomers?" I tempt.

Her look is equal parts disgust and fascination. She says to me, "Have you seen a man's penis?"

I say to her, "Maybe."

I can't help but try a trick Tully turned me onto. I look into the girl's little rapt face. "You best be sure I don't find where it is your mother's hiding her rebel papers. You best hope they're still properly hidden. What if they aren't?"

Tully's trick is used by pickpockets. They announce in a crowd that a pickpocket is at large, prompting everyone to check their valuables, thereby revealing to the pickpockets where to pick. (Pinkerton maintains he doesn't hire former criminals like the French police are known to, but Tully certainly knows a thing or two more than your average upstanding citizen.)

Little Rose's attention is deep inside her head, just maybe fixing on that hiding place. Her mother likely wouldn't have shown it to her, but children notice more than you think. All at once, Little Rose's eyes get their focus back.

"Are you done taking your exercise?" I ask. "Would you like to go back into the house?"

She nods. Perhaps I can trail her directly to the hiding place when she goes to assure herself her mother's papers remain concealed. "After you, dear." I open the kitchen door for her. I'll give her some rein and then follow. Unlike Pinkerton, I can silence my steps.

— Nine —

Little Rose ascends the stairs, hopefully leading me to wherever her mother has stashed her cipher key.

Like a wildcat catching a whiff of rabbit, Tully steps out of the shadowed passage by the kitchen. I wave the man off. Once Little Rose has reached the second-floor landing and disappeared beyond, I whip up the stairs after her. Her plaited brown head bobs right into the library. The next thing I hear is Scobell's voice greeting her.

Risking the whole plot, I slowly, slowly lean my head into the doorway. The girl is facing Scobell. His eyes are on her, but I feel him mark me. I pull my head back out and wait.

"You'll excuse me, won't you, miss?" That's Scobell understanding that I'm working on something and need him to clear out. His voice is mild and body slack as he addresses the girl, telling a story of calm and deference that speaks to years of practice appearing harmless. "I just need to step out and collect an item from downstairs," he says.

"That'd be fine," comes the girl's voice. Fine, indeed.

Scobell comes out, the flint behind his eyes sharp with disdain at his required performance. We both tuck into the widow's room while Little Rose checks the hallway, then goes back to the library. I ask if he'd prefer I do the next bit rather than him, but he shakes his head. "I want to," he says.

Little Rose is up the ladder, hand rooting around on a high shelf, when Scobell strolls back in, eyes down on a paper in his hand. Nearly topples right off the rung, the girl does, she's so surprised. "I'm selecting a story," she lies, and pulls out the first book to hand from a lower shelf. Scobell nods in mock affability and busies himself at the desk while she descends the ladder. But don't doubt it, he's marked exactly where the girl's hands were digging when he came in.

Out in the hall, Little Rose discovers me. I tell her, "I'm meant to return you to your mother."

"I was selecting a story for my mother to read me," she lies again, holding up the book she grabbed. A geological survey of Utah Territory.

"Well, isn't that fine." I steer her down to the parlor where the ladies are still gathered, now watched by Bridgeman. I run back up to the library to see if Scobell has turned up anything.

Walking in the door I see a bitter satisfaction in his eyes and a bundle of papers in his hands. It's not the cipher key, I'll just go on and tell you that straightaway so you don't get your hopes up. We didn't find that. But here's what we did find:

> *You know I love you and will sacrifice anything on my own account.*
>
> *I repeat to you that spies are just upon me but I will try to elude them tonight. If fate is not against me, I will be with you this night.*
>
> *My love is all.*
>
> *Yours and only yours,*
> *—H*

Thirteen such as this. Thirteen love letters. Written on congressional stationery.

Scobell spreads the love letters across the library desk. We start scanning them for clues to the identity of this mysterious H who has access to congressional stationery and possibly congressional secrets and has maybe been passing them along to a certain captivating lady.

Know nothing would soothe me so much as an hour with you.

Oh, the widow's hypocrisy in calling me a low woman!

My love is all yours and only yours.

To elicit such words. Tell me, how do you get a man to such a point that he says:

I will be with you again tonight and then I will tell you again and again that I love you.

My eyes range to Scobell. He's reading the letters too, his body not two feet from mine.

All at once, our proximity is all I can think on. The small heat coming off his body. His quiet breath.

I love you and will sacrifice anything on my own account.

Scobell's body shifts next to mine, and I begin to feel like maybe he's noticed our nearness too. He shifts an inch closer to me. I smell again the light scent of his skin.

At whatever cost, I will see you.

His hand comes up to his hip. I see the hairs along his forearm where he's pushed up his sleeve. I suddenly want nothing more than to touch that forearm. And then, all at once, I remember he's married. I take a step farther from him and clear my throat. He glances at me. I can't tell what he's thinking. I feel like a fool. "You write your wife in Richmond letters like these?" I ask stupidly.

Scobell seems startled by the question. "Oh," he says awkwardly. "Oh." He says it again like he's searching for the words. "My wife and I." He pauses. "I wasn't for staying in Richmond. She was. She prefers a quiet life, and that wasn't for me." He waits a moment, then says, "I'm not telling her what to do, with what she's lived. And she's not telling me. We're exercising our own choices." He says the next bit with care. "It was both our choices to go our own ways."

"Oh," I say.

We stand a moment awkwardly, then we both turn back to the letters. But it doesn't feel like either of us is reading anymore. After a moment, Scobell turns toward me, his eyes soft. "Your husband—when did he pass?"

It jars me a moment. But then I remember Pinkerton has always called me a widow for propriety. "Never was," I tell Scobell. "Fiction of Pinkerton's to protect the agency's honor. And mine."

Scobell looks at me with narrowed eyes, but then I see a laugh in his shoulders. "Here I was wondering all these months on who this man was."

"What do you mean?" I ask.

"Most men are content to sniff after whoever all the other men are sniffing after—whichever gal's flashing her tail brightest at the moment." He laughs as he says it. "But then there's the plain brown birds. All around, none of us paying any mind to them. But when you finally pause to look close at that sparrow or that thrush, why, there it is: a whole marvel of its own. I wondered who the man was singular enough to see that."

All at once, Scobell gets still, as if only realizing he's been talking aloud and not inside his head. He gives another quick laugh, like at the finish of a joke, but when he glances at me, he looks caught out, like maybe the joke is on him.

For my part, I'm stunned, my breath all stuck up in my chest at the idea of him thinking these thoughts, seeing me and thinking them. I want to say something back, to tell him it's all right what he said and dispel his look of worry, but I'm tongue-tied. No one has ever said anything of the sort to me before. Nothing so observant or so tender. I have twice in my life had relations with men, but they were solitary, physical acts. Moments of need, nothing tying my heart to theirs. "There was never such a man," I finally manage with a feigned lightness.

He seems relieved by my tone.

I go on, "I wasn't even awake to that sort of thing—romance and such. Other affairs on my mind growing up."

"Mmm," he says, taking in my words. "Learning to fit in flush like a peg in a plank?" he asks.

It hits awfully close to home. Growing up, I never belonged among the other Irish because I was an orphan. I didn't belong among the Yanks because I was a paddy. What is a human, but a collection of bonds? Sister, mother, friend, lover. I saw the others in my world joined and propelled by these bonds, like spinning frames driven by the force of the canal—a great community humming in time, shaking along together, moved by the waters of love and companionship. And me, I felt like a human frame abandoned in the corner. But Scobell doesn't know any of that. "Why'd you say that?"

"Just a guess, is all," he says back. "You're sanded so smooth. I can see there's more underneath, but you don't show nothing."

It's the same thing I've observed in him. I'm hardly as skilled. "Pinkerton saw through me," I tell him. "Read me like a book when I asked him for a job. And since. Many times."

"Pinkerton"—Scobell scoffs—"is a rare specimen. I didn't even know you were foreign-born until you said it." He shakes his head. "Smoothing over what you lived makes you feel like you'll survive. But a person gives up a lot to be so smooth." He sighs. "A whole damn lot."

He looks right at me. But the look he gives isn't smooth at all. It's just raw cut. There's a history of loss right there in his eyes. I see it. I look into it.

He looks into me too. And I let him. I let him look deep into the currents of my own, old heartaches.

Then it's like my breath is being pressed out, and I have to look away. Whatever I have to give up to never feel those heartaches, I'll give it up.

Scobell turns back to the love letters. But now I'm certain he's as aware of me as I am of him. It's like the look we shared tied something between us, some kind of tether between our hearts. Not because we're the same, but because he let me see him, and I let him see me.

"There's no name I can see but 'H,'" he says, trying to get back to the work.

"He's certainly devoted," I reply.

"'I will see you at all hazard,'" Scobell reads aloud.

I speak from another page. "'Do not doubt me.'"

Scobell finds another. "'I would be yours.'"

And then me. "'For your sake I am compelled to be cautious.'"

And suddenly, we're not just speaking the words from the letters aloud, we're speaking to one another.

"'I have feared bringing us into trouble.'" He risks a glance in my direction.

"'I have thought on you from afar,'" I say.

"'I long for your company,'" he answers.

"'I would be with you if I could,'" I whisper.

He steps closer to me. His forearm brushes mine. I lean into his touch. My breath stills, and all I feel is the bright warmth of his arm against mine, like my entire being is concentrated in that one spot.

I feel his breath when his face turns to mine. I'm so overcome with nerves I'm afraid to meet his eyes. But then I do.

His look is all question. I lean in in answer. Our lips brush. The softest of touches.

And then all at once there's footsteps on the stairs. Scobell pulls away. I step back abruptly.

Whatever just happened to us can't happen. Not between someone light-skinned and someone dark-skinned. Not between two agents. Not in a suspected spy's house who we're trying to break to end a war. Hell, what were we thinking?

Scobell quickly scoops up the letters from the desk. "Best get these to Pinkerton."

He heads toward the library doorway just as Tully appears in it. "Well, did you find something?"

"Indeed!" I call out a little too brightly.

In the kitchen, Tully opens a bottle of the widow's brandy and pours Scobell and me a drink. Pinkerton's on a quick errand to his offices, but he'll be pleased when he returns. The letters are a find, to be sure. Until we identify H, we don't know the exact significance, but at the very least, it's evidence of a forbidden liaison with a public figure, which is ammunition against the widow. No woman can afford such dirty linen aired.

Tully raises his cup in celebration. Scobell holds his up stiffly. He doesn't meet my eyes. I can still feel the butterfly touch of his lips on mine. Does he regret what happened?

Tully senses something amiss. "What's the matter with you two?"

"Fatigue," Scobell lies.

"Better not be," Tully gripes. "We've got three and a half ladies in the parlor hungry for their supper, and I'm not making it. I made the tea," he grouses.

"Who's with them now?" I ask.

"Bridgeman," Tully says.

Behind Tully, Scobell holds up the love letters. "I'ma leave these for Pinkerton and get back to the library."

I watch him go, my heart a fitful riot in my chest.

"How do you think the widow did it?" Tully asks. "Seduced a Congressman?"

"What do I care?" I say, distracted.

"Crabby, crabby!" Tully says. "The widow put you in such a foul mood?" He finishes his brandy, pours himself another, then returns to his paste and reconstructed letter bits.

I scrounge about the kitchen for supper supplies, landing on some hard crackers and a half wheel of cheese. I set about slicing the cheese and piling it onto a platter.

As I do, my thoughts go right back to Scobell. Half of me is furious for letting us do what we did. The other half wants to run back up the stairs and do it all again.

How could today be the first time we touched? It seems unfathomable. All at once I realize it might also be the last time. Because what possibility is there for us?

The thought hurts. It hurts in a manner altogether foreign to me. It's like I'm suddenly looking at a truth in my own heart, a bald truth I never saw before. Something I never fully put thoughts to, never made into words: feeling for this man I've just begun to know.

Orpheus and Eurydice come into my head. A star-crossed couple. Scobell said he loved the story. I didn't admit it to him, but there was a story like that for me. An impossible love story that picked me right up by the heartstrings. It was a different myth.

Demeter was the goddess of the harvest. She had a daughter,

Persephone, who was stolen down to the underworld by the god Hades in his rumbling chariot. Demeter searched for her daughter, and while she did, winter fell on earth, the fruits of the field shriveling. The people too. Demeter never gave up. She loved her daughter so fiercely, she found the girl and persuaded Hades to release her.

But like Scobell's story, it ended badly. Turned out, the poor, precious girl had eaten Hades's pomegranate seeds, the food of the dead, and so had to remain in the underworld half the year. When Demeter learned this, the world changed forever. While Persephone was on earth with Demeter, it was bright summer. With Persephone's return to the underworld, winter descended. The world broke in two, and they never found their way back together for good.

As a child, I loved the story so dearly, I borrowed it time and again from the Tremont Circulating Library. Sometimes stories are like that, you get sweet on them, just as with a person. The library copy was worn, the spine soft with use but for a strip of binding thread that I'd catch on my thumb when I stroked it. I had shoes and clothes and a pig bristle brush, but to hold that book . . . I pretended it was mine. At times I even slept with it.

One night I took a bit of pencil lead and inscribed old words from a long-ago lullaby onto the story's final page by the window's light. I wove them into the illustration, so they might not be noticed: *grá mo chroí*. Words from a different life. I don't even remember their meaning now.

Even long after I'd grown too old for myths, I still borrowed the book from the library now and again, just to see those words I inscribed, pretending I never wrote them at all, just happened upon them by chance there in the pages. And each time I read the story, I nursed a tiny hope that it might, just once, end differently.

I want to tell Scobell the story. I want to tell him I understand what he feels about Orpheus and Eurydice and Romeo and Juliet. I want to say how I feel about him, too, despite reason and practicality, despite hardly knowing him. But I can't. Demeter and Persephone never worked out. As much as I wished otherwise, the story always ended the same. Just like Scobell's stories. Just like our own story would if we went down that path. Young fools and pretty faces—we aren't either of those. I have to put my feelings aside or we'll end up a cautionary tale.

Out the kitchen window, I see the sun nearing the horizon. Just one day and night left to get the cipher key before our window runs out. My mind's got to stay on that. Nothing else.

In the parlor, I relieve Bridgeman from watching the ladies and announce supper, trying to keep the turmoil about my encounter with Scobell out of my voice. The lesser Miss Mackall casts her eyes about nervously, her concern returning as to the nature and duration of their incarceration. Lily, the greater Miss Mackall, looks to the widow.

The widow flashes an arch smile. "Don't worry, my dears. You needn't dress for supper." Lily laughs. It almost appears practiced when both incline their chins to me at the same moment.

The dining room walls are papered burgundy. A sideboard has crystal decanters along it. The table itself is smooth, dark wood. It's on the lesser Mackall that I read dismay when the three ladies and Little Rose view the cheese and crackers composing their evening meal. Stoically, they spread linen napkins across their laps.

"Veruna?" the widow offers the plate of crackers to the lesser Mackall.

I stand by the kitchen door with the comportment of the Good Servant, never the jailer. I refill their crystal glasses with plain water before they ask. Offer to fetch more cheese. Observe them appreciate their reduced circumstances and slowly become sensible to the deprivations that await them.

A future under house arrest is a heavy thing, sequestered from not just updates of the war, but their habitual lives. These are women accustomed to daily social visits, pleasure outings, shopping excursions in the most lively of cities, abounding as it is in news and gossip, priding itself on its worldliness. Those doors are shut to them now.

The effects of their social isolation are like a storm's first clouds gathering on the horizon. Here, tonight, they discern only the first hints of the coming devastation. Tomorrow they will walk the same overly warm halls. They will eat the same savorless food. Stitch the same embroidery on the same sofas. How many more times might they disparage tasteless Mary Todd until the subject is worn thin? I know the ravages of mindless hours and deadening repetition. These ladies? Just perceiving the first change in the air as they pass the dish of hard crackers.

— Ten —

It falls to me to decide where everyone will retire for the evening (except Pinkerton—he'll sleep at a hotel). Little Rose will stay in her mama's bedroom. Little Rose's room, vacated, will do for the Miss Mack-alls. I push open the door to a third bedroom on the same hall just to see whose it is. The portrait on the dressing table is of a girl about my age. Next to it, a hairbrush sits, long brown hairs stuck in its bristles. A perfume bottle stands open beside two others. A handkerchief rests across the chair, lazily thrown. It's a lady's toilette, left as if the maid hasn't come to straighten it.

I look around the rest of the room. There's a canopied four-poster bed, its blankets turned back. A dress hangs across a clotheshorse, ready for wearing. A book lays on the bedside table, a bookmark midway through it. But the air in the room is close and everything's coated in a layer of dust. Where's this young lady who looks like she went off to the water closet months ago and never came back to finish dressing?

Suddenly Little Rose is at my side, her eyes bright with alarm. "That's my sister Gertie's room!"

Gertrude, the widow's dead daughter. Her room left as she last touched it, like a shrine or memorial.

"She passed in the spring?" I ask Little Rose.

"From typhoid fever," Little Rose says. "Mama—" Little Rose looks to assure herself we're alone. "Mama cries 'most every night."

My heart clenches with an old pain. My own mother humped in a bed, leaving me alone in this world.

Little Rose goes on. "Mama was going to make us all go to Florence's in Utah territory for safety, but after Gertie passed, she only sent Leila. She let me stay behind with her."

I feel a twinge of something bitter. Grief. Or maybe it's envy.

"What is it?" Little Rose asks, feeling the change in me.

"Supper sitting wrong," I say quick. I'm not that little girl anymore. I remind myself that this dead daughter is an advantage to me—I've led the widow to believe I've lost a child too. It's our common ground. My heart stutter-steps at the thought of wielding something so painful against her. I take a breath and do my best to tuck those feelings away.

"Was it the cheese?" Little Rose interrupts my thoughts. "It was ripe."

There's voices coming up the stairs. It's the widow and the Miss Mackalls escorted by Tully. I beat a quick retreat away from the dead girl's room, then point the ladies to their respective sleeping quarters.

Tully gets the Mackalls sequestered in Little Rose's room. I follow the widow into hers. She's got no help but Little Rose for her evening toilette. (Imagine an eight-year-old girl trying to remove her mama's hoopskirt. She'd drown in the thing.) I offer my hands. Unlike earlier, the widow agrees.

I let my fingers be their nimble best as I help her out of her dress. Little Rose sits on the bed watching me. "Little Rose" is all the widow needs say, and the girl starts getting into her own nightclothes.

Once everything's off the widow but her linen underclothes (Did you know she wears dress shields? In the armpit between skin and dress. Fresh ones daily.) and hung or folded or draped, she sits in her corset at the dressing table. I notice she has a mole in a triangle of olive skin above her collarbone and that her face looks tired from the day.

I unpin her hair and pick up her brush. It's just like the one in Gertrude's room, but the hairs stuck in it are darker. My heart stutter-steps again, but I pull the brush through the dark thickness of her hair, breathing with each stroke until I'm steady.

The widow eyes me in the dressing table's mirror. "So quiet? No more tales of learning embroidery at your mother's knee?"

I clean the long hairs from the brush while I decide how to turn the conversation. "Well, ma'am, you certainly have an advantage over me. Not only did I share the loss of my mother, but I imagine it was impossible not to have overheard particular details of my personal life"—here, I let an expression of grief flicker across my face—"when my employer put me in my place earlier today."

She waits a moment to say back, "A lady does not attend the private conversations of others." It's a good sign. She's moved on from barbs.

"I appreciate it," I say quietly. "I should have known a fellow mother would show such decency."

The widow doesn't quite meet my eyes in the mirror, but her face says my words landed.

I place her brush on the table. Under my breath, I tell her, "I won't let the men touch that room down the hall. Just want you to know." The widow gets still at the mention of the shrine to her dead daughter. It's like a held breath in the room, the widow, me, and Little Rose, all of us still as stone. Did I go too far?

Then all at once the widow exhales, and we snap back to life. "My nightgown's in the drawer," she directs, as if nothing happened at all.

Little Rose crawls over the duvet, nestling into the bed. I get them both tucked in and then call to Bridgeman. He's to sit outside the widow's door for the night, allowing me some rest. But just as I'm leaving, the widow stops me. Her brown eyes meet mine. "Thank you," she says, the words barely more than a whisper. Inside, my heart thrums with this small gain.

In the library, where I'll be sleeping, I undress myself. I've commandeered a basin of water and soap from downstairs. I give myself a quick wash, just arms and face, right there in the library.

I pat myself dry and change into my nightdress. As I do, I turn and startle to see myself reflected in the library window. Dark as it is outside, the window has become a looking glass. I don't recall the last time I've seen my whole self in a mirror.

I think of the mole in the triangle of the widow's collarbone. Her daughters know that mole. Her maid knows it. Her dead husband. Her traitor lovers. They know her whole handsome self. Who knows my body? Almost no one. Hell, it's been so long since I've even seen my body, I hardly know to claim it as my own. I stare at my reflection, seeing pieces making up a grown woman—eyes, hair, shoulders, legs—but nothing familiar enough to call *myself*.

"Kate," I whisper at the image in the glass. "Kate Warne." It doesn't feel like me.

"Mary Kate," I whisper. "Mary Kate Heaney."

Just saying my old name summons pictures out of the deep. Dirty, twisted turnips on a kitchen table in a turf cottage. My mam at my bedside in a long blue skirt singing a lullaby. My pap's arms warm around me, his voice soft in my ear. *My bonny hen.*

I remember bodies, lying right out by the road sometimes. My mam covered my eyes the first time we passed one on the long walk to town from our farm. I saw it through her fingers in the ditch. It was alive, the body, a roiling black mass. Before I could cry out, it broke apart into the air—a host of crows. Below them, clean-picked bones.

I remember after weeks of hunger, the dog from a neighbor's farm, once a fine red setter, came up the road. It was just skin on bone, one ear newly torn. It came right up to our door, whimpering and whining. But when I came out to sooth it with a pat—a pat I'd given a thousand times—that farm dog snapped and lunged at me with such savagery Pap finally had to drive it away with stones. I felt in that moment that to die was not the real terror. It was to die last. No one to stone the scavengers away.

I never saw Pap eat. Those dirt-cased turnips, a crow he snared—he gave those things to me, his only child. I ate them from his hands, eagerly, greedily. Pap didn't take one mouthful. He became an old man. Bent and broken and no more than thirty.

It was Pap who got the cough first. Fever followed. He was gone in a few days. Too weak to throw off a new misery.

Then my mam started coughing. The day came when she couldn't rise from the bed. I knew I must go out and find food, but I couldn't leave her side. I was young enough to believe any nightmare could be vanquished by crawling into her bed, her lips warm against my ear, singing her old lullaby.

But finally, there wasn't a choice. I dug through empty fields looking for an overlooked root. Waited outside the church for handouts begged off those luckier than me. Rummaged through rubbish piles behind the houses in town until their owners drove me away, their pity worn thin by the unrelenting stream of human grief. I became the scavenger.

But I ate. Then I returned to our cottage and fed my mam, using a spoon at first, later my fingers, to push a mouthful of whatever I scavenged into her mouth.

Sometimes in the night the red setter returned with three or four other dogs. They were once domesticated, but had become something else. The rule of the desperate: the strongest survive. They scratched and pawed at our door, giddy with the smell of us inside. I barred the door and crawled into bed beside my mam. By this point she was little more than a rasping, bony hump in the bed, but she was what I knew of comfort, of love.

"Go, mo chroí," my mam begged in hoarse whispers. "I'm going soon."

"I'll go with you," I whispered back, singing her lullaby with words I barely remember:

Hush now, grá mo chroí, hush now.

Is the worst thing dying, or is it surviving?

It was a neighbor from down the road who found me. He called me by name and told me he was a friend of my pap's. Mr. Sullivan. He said he had a sack of meal at his home and four daughters just like me. There was supper if I'd come. He went on about the iron pot bubbling on his stove until finally I followed him down the road.

They were packing, the Sullivans. They had an indenture contract with a ship's captain to take the family to America. Cotton mills wanted big families—children were more labor, and cheap. A few days later, I boarded the ship with them.

I remember as we left, the red setter was standing in the road alone. The other dogs were gone, but it remained.

In the widow's library window, I see the eyes of a little girl looking back at me. A girl whose dead have no portraits, no memorials. They lie in an unmarked grave somewhere. Not even a stone to remember them.

And when I die? Will someone keep a portrait of my face? Will anyone make a marker for my grave?

Suddenly something taps against the window of the widow's library, startling me out of my thoughts. It's a light little tap, like a pebble hitting the glass. Like a signal. It comes to me that backlit by the library lamp, my silhouette—a woman in a nightdress—must be visible from outside. And someone not aware of the widow's arrest might just mistake me for her.

I peer into the garden below but can't make anything out. Quickly, I dash out the door, past Bridgeman on watch in the hallway, into Gertrude's room. From this side of the house, I can see Dennis Mann, now on duty outside, leaning easily against the carriage house, showing no awareness of any trouble. Probably nothing, the tap. A night insect drawn by lamplight bumping against the glass.

But then I see the upper carriage house window. There, in its frame, is a male silhouette: Benjamin Early, the groom. His body is tense, trained on something in the widow's side garden.

I run back to the library window. After looking hard, I finally see them: two dark figures hiding in the hedge.

I go and whisper to Bridgeman where he's sitting in the hallway, guarding the sleeping women, "Weather's changing." He stands right up, on the alert. Together we listen at the widow's cracked door to discover if anything's afoot, but only sleep noises issue from inside. Not a sound comes from the Miss Mackalls in Little Rose's room.

"You got the goods." I nod toward the bedrooms. Bridgeman nods back, and then I'm whipping down the stairs to tell the others.

Tully and Scobell are in the kitchen. Pinkerton is there, too, returned from his errand.

"Widow's got callers," I tell them. "Two men. In the hedge outside the front parlor."

Pinkerton's brow furrows with anticipation. "Let's pay them a visit."

It's not three minutes later that I'm back standing at a window, this time in the parlor, right in front of where the men in the hedge are hiding. I recreate the same picture from upstairs: a backlit woman's silhouette. I wait a few seconds so I'm sure both figures in the hedge are likely looking at me and that Pinkerton and the others have had time to get into position.

Then I light the flash paper.

Even closing my eyes against it, I feel the brightness. When I look, the two men outside are covering their eyes, momentarily blinded. While they're stunned, Tully and Mann dart in and handily seize the smaller of the two men. At the same moment, Pinkerton grabs the larger man from behind with his short, powerful arms. But without so much as a pause, the larger man bucks backward, slamming Pinkerton against the house.

There's a heavy thud as Pinkerton's head hits the wall. Pinkerton slides off the man's back and onto the ground, senseless. Then Scobell rushes in from the side.

Scobell jabs at the man, but he's a fair piece lighter than his adversary, who is plainly an experienced fighter. And Pinkerton still hasn't risen from the ground. Scobell's alone.

"Watch it!" I call involuntarily. The man gets Scobell backed up against the hedge, dodging punches. I can't help but wince and swerve along with him from where I'm standing, useless as the window dressings. But then I see it: Scobell's shuffling to the side, dancing the man around. Scobell turns their fight so he's the one backed up against the house. It doesn't make sense; it gives the larger man a clear path to flee. I'm readying to call for Bridgeman upstairs, to get him in to help, when it happens.

Benjamin Early, the groom—and his shovel.

Just two swings and the large man falls. Scobell and Early gag and bind him. Pinkerton rises groggily. In the distance, I can just make out Tully and Mann holding the smaller man, already gagged and bound.

I watch Pinkerton shake Early's hand. Not long after, Early has the carriage hitched to drive Pinkerton and the two captives to the Union camp for interrogation. Scobell, Tully, and Mann watch the carriage go. Mann's got a hand on Tully's shoulder, easy like. Scobell turns and says something softly that makes Mann smile. I watch them watching, alone in the quiet dark by the window dressing.

— *Eleven* —

I pad back up the stairs in my nightdress. "All's good," I whisper to Bridgeman at the widow's door. He slides down into his chair with relief.

Back in the library, I look over my options for bed fixings. Nothing besides a cushion from the desk chair and the rug.

I lie down, but my body's still edgy from watching the fight. Were the men in the hedge conspirators coming to relay or collect a message? Pinkerton will get it sorted directly, but it doesn't mean I'm not itching to know. And Scobell. I'm thinking on him, too, and the hits he took.

My hips rest uncomfortably on the floor even though the rug is a thick Turkish-style affair. I turn on my back, then onto my other side, but sleep's never going to come.

I wish I could just check on Scobell. That's not wrong, is it? Just check on him, see how he's doing after the fight.

I slip out of the library and downstairs to the parlor where Scobell's spending the night. I tap at the half-open door.

He looks up, surprised to see me.

"You hurt?" I ask.

He shakes his head. "Got lucky." His body seems coiled, tight—a foot jiggling against the couch where he's sitting. I try to read his face but can't. Was it foolish for me to come? Maybe I should go.

He removes a silver flask from his breast pocket and offers it.

I waver, then go on and take it, perching at the far end of the couch. The flask is bourbon, sweet and smooth.

We sit quiet a moment. "Was the groom the plan? Or a happy accident?" I ask.

"Maybe something in between," Scobell answers. "He was ready for it. I took Early's interview today. After, I told Pinkerton: keep a watch on the carriage house"—Scobell smiles—"but maybe don't lock the door." He takes another sip of bourbon. "I tell you, I saw him holding that shovel and was ready to sing out 'Glory, Glory Hallelujah!'"

I recall our game in the library, naming books. "I might've sung 'For He's a Jolly Good Fellow' . . ." I look back at him.

He sees my aim. "There we go. How about 'It Came Upon a Midnight Clear.'"

". . . 'Au Clair de Lune,'" I offer.

His foot stops jiggling. "'Joy to the World.'"

"'Hark the Herald Angels Sing.'" I'm already running out of songs.

"'Oh say can you see, by the dawn's early light.'" He's so quick on it that unless he's bluffing, he has me.

I cast about for another one. "'The Dawning of the Day.'"

Scobell gives me a hard look. "Never heard of it."

"Sure you know it." I hum the chorus.

He shakes his head.

I suck my cheek. "Maybe it's just an Irish song."

"We both got to have heard of it or where's the pleasure?"

"I know it. Again, you have me beat." I glance at his buttonhole where I put the flower earlier today, but it's empty. Must have been lost during the fight.

He passes me the flask. "How come you don't talk about Ireland?"

I focus on the liquor. "Nothing to talk about."

"When'd you leave there?"

"Young."

His eyes stay on me. "You remember your parents?"

"What's the good in remembering?"

"Part of who you are," he says. "I guess I'd like to hear it—don't care if it's not pretty."

"What you've had to live is far uglier," I tell him.

"It's not a contest," he says. "Will you sing the rest of the song?"

I tell him the truth. "I don't know if I can recall all the words."

"I've had a hell of an evening, Katie. Will you just sing it?"

It takes two tries to get the tune right, but then there it is.

It's strange how songs stick in you. I can say the name "Amazing Grace" or "Mary Had a Little Lamb," or even a song I haven't heard since my mam sang it back in another land, and all at once, I hear it in my mind. As I sing to Scobell, I'm suddenly wishing I could hear my mam's voice the same way I recall the song's melody. That I could say her name and hear the song of her voice.

The tears come upon me before I can do a thing. I turn away so Scobell won't see, but when I look back, his eyes are soft.

I try to jolly the hurt away. "You didn't even hear the words right. I muddled them all."

"There's something true in it anyhow," he says. "Even without words saying it. Something of you." He wipes his eye. As he does, his coat pulls to the side, and I see something peeking out of his inner vest pocket. The flower. Tucked away for safe-keeping.

He follows my gaze. Then he looks back up and holds my eyes, like he's looking right into the heart of me.

I move closer, reach out and place my hand on his cheek. He lets it stay there a moment, but he doesn't reach for me.

There's a sharp twisting in my heart. My hand falls. "Is it your wife?" I whisper, but somehow I'm sure it must be me. Us. He regrets what happened.

"Kate—" He stops, then starts again. "My wife is a good woman. But she wants to live a quiet life. Doesn't matter other folks are still in bondage. She doesn't want to fight and maybe lose what she's got." He struggles a moment with something inside. "I can't blame her for that. Or for not wanting any part of a man who's chosen to do things different. She doesn't owe me anything." He's quiet another moment. "And I am who I am. My heart wants what it wants." He looks at me then with plain love.

I reach for his cheek again, but he catches my hand and brings it down.

I don't understand. "Why don't you want me?" I whisper.

He shakes his head. "How can you ask such a thing, knowing what it would mean for me?"

And then I grasp it. "Oh." So quickly I forgot the divide between us, the world we live in. But he doesn't have that luxury.

"Oh?" His hold on my hand is light despite the hardness of the words that come out. "I could be strung up, beat to death, cut like a pig. And those are the quick forms my demise might take, I get caught with you." He lets go of my hand, gets up and walks the length of the parlor. "I'm not a man and you a woman. We are not two people with feelings for one another. I am a Black man and you are a white woman, and those are the only two facts there are."

"I'll go," I say quickly, shame at my ignorance itching across my chest. I start for the door.

But before I get to it, he calls out softly, "I don't want you to go."

That hangs in the air a good, long moment. It doesn't make sense, him saying that after all he said before. But we're more than one thing, and at times our parts stand in opposition to one another. How do we encompass such contradictions without splitting apart? Who says we don't?

He blows out the lamp. I shut the door. He crosses to me, takes my hand, and places it on his cheek. Then he pulls me close.

We fumble with each other's clothes, and soon my body is against his. Until today, we had never touched, and now it's knees and arms and hips and bellies pressing skin to skin. His breath becomes mine as our faces bump and nudge in the dark. How often have I seen the soft curve of the chin now brushing against mine? The fingers running across my collarbone. The sparse hair of his forearm grazing my breast.

We ask soft questions. Give small assurances. We shift clumsily, moving, finding one another. And then there is the short, astonishing moment near the end when we shudder and strive to fit our disparate rhythms to each other's. My previous encounters were so altogether different: quick acts of physical release. Me, alone in a tunnel of my own self. It seems foolish to say, but before the act was not intimate. Now, for the first time, I feel joined with another. It's like finally seeing a place I've been told about a thousand times, but never been to. Or returning to somewhere I didn't know I remembered. What I know is that, here in Scobell's arms, on a couch in the widow's parlor, I'm home.

After, we're quiet, just lying there in the dark. The words from the love letters come unbidden into my mind.

I love you and will sacrifice anything on my own account.

It feels right out of a book. Someone who'd follow their lover into hell. It's so easy in a story, so easy to cheer for those who risk everything on love. But the living truth of it is nothing easy. The Union captain who called on the widow that night a week back? Pinkerton followed and arrested him after he left. But before Pinkerton could interrogate him, the man slit his own throat with a pen knife in his cell.

Ever yours.

What place is there for Scobell and me? Scobell is a Black man in a country at war over whether he should be named a man at all. Wherefore art thou Romeo and all.

I break our silence. "I guess this can't ever be something. Us two."

I can't see his face, but I feel a change in his body, a pulling back into his own skin where for a moment we were one. "Guess not," he says.

"Like you said before, it's too dangerous for you."

". . . Right," he says slowly. "Though that's my choice, isn't it?"

I feel a shake in my heart. Something too open, too raw. "We can't," I say quickly.

"But Katie—" he answers softly, his fingers brushing down my cheek.

It hurts. It hurts too much. The possibility of him right there before me. And the possibility of losing him right there on the horizon. I pull back. "And we got to put the work first. Can't jeopardize it or have any liabilities, you know that," I say.

He eyes me through the dark. "You're Pinkerton's own, aren't you?" He sighs. "And here I am, just human." All at once, there's a distance between us a mile wide.

And I can't stand it. I want to say something to bridge it. To bring him back to me. But before I can, the door to the parlor opens, a dark figure appearing in it.

We're caught.

The door closes as quickly as it opened, whoever it was retreating into the hallway. Too late, Scobell pulls away from me, grabbing for his clothes. Too late, I jump up, moving away from him. There's no hiding what we were doing.

"Who was it?" I ask tightly.

"Looked like Tully," Scobell answers, a shake in his voice. "I'm a fool."

"He won't give us up." It's a prayer, not a surety.

"I'm a goddamn fool," Scobell says again and goes out the door.

Alone in the parlor, my mind runs over each and every terrifying consequence that could await Scobell. Pinkerton might only fire us if Tully tells him, but if Tully tells others . . . There's been laws against dark- and light-skinned people doing what we're doing since before the country was founded, but that's nothing compared to what happens outside the law.

Scobell slides back in the door but stays beside it. "It was Tully. He won't say nothing."

"He swore?" I ask.

"He did."

"You believe him?"

Scobell's quiet a moment, then says, "I do."

I exhale heavily, a whimper on its tail. "I'm so sorry, John."

"Don't." His voice is flint. "That's not what I need."

Old words come through my lips. "Mo chroí," I whisper, but he's already slipped out the door again.

Upstairs, I sit in the library in hell, knowing how close he came to harm. We can't ever be something—not if he's going to keep out of danger.

My heart's pounding like horse hooves. I walk the length of the room over and over, staring at the library walls. After what seems like hours, I'm finally too weary to go on. I lay on the floor and try to sleep, but sleep still won't come.

I go to Gertrude's bedroom. I don't know why, but that's where I go. The shadows of the dead girl's things are all around. No color to them, just silhouettes. The portrait on the mantel. The dress draped over the clothes horse. I run the silk through my fingers. I go to the canopied bed and look at the book laying on the nightstand. With some surprise, I read its cover: *Uncle Tom's Cabin* by Mrs. Harriet Beecher Stowe.

I pick up an open perfume bottle. It's heavy like I imagine gold coins, its glass thick and smooth. I place the bottle against my cheek and breathe in the scent of a girl now gone. To grow up with such things around you. Thick and smooth. Heavy as gold. The armature of ladyhood. I feel a spike of envy. What must it be like to be daughter to such a woman as the widow? Her fierceness and allure. Her surety in the world. Tell me, Gertrude, does it make you inviolate to the dirty, failed lives of the rest of us?

I ease down onto Gertrude's bed, my angles sinking into her flowered duvet. I saw a child once, asleep sprawled out on her back. Her arms were loose up over her head and her legs were akimbo, like a full-blown flower. What must a child's life be like to engender such sleep? Little Rose sleeps like that, I'd wager. The dead girl, Gertrude, did too, no doubt. To sleep, my body wants to be folded up, pulled in, locked tight.

I curl into the bed, despite the heat, clutching myself close. For a moment, I smell Scobell's scent on my body and the raw hurt comes back.

I hold myself tighter. I'm who I've got. That's it. Everyone else in my life leaves one way or another, and they leave badly. Scobell wouldn't be any different. I got myself. Myself and my work. My heart eases a little.

I belong as a Pinkerton. I'm safe as a Pinkerton. I've become who I need to be: Kate Warne. My heart eases a little more. I search for Scobell's scent again, but all I find is the dead girl's perfume and behind it, beaded in my sweat, the sterile bite of soap.

— Twelve —

I wake just after dawn. My body feels tight and ragged, the dregs of a dream still rattling around. I step out of Gertrude's bedroom into the dawn-lit hallway. Bridgeman's sitting outside the widow's room, drowsy after his night's watch. He perks up when he sees me, eager to hand over care of the ladies so he can finally rest.

"Give me a minute first?" I ask him.

Downstairs, I use the water closet. I hear sounds from the kitchen and peek in. Scobell is already at the table eating a bowl of porridge. Tully's there, too, stirring a pot on the stove. Scobell glances up at me, then goes right back to eating. His look is mild but blank, and his body looks slack, like how he was with Little Rose when she came into the library. It hurts like hell. But I guess this is where we are now. I guess this is what I wanted.

I climb back up the stairs shakily and duck into the library. I hear Bridgeman at the widow's door calling after me. "Your watch started at dawn!"

"Coming!" I call. I quickly grab the desk chair and sit. I change into the second of two dresses I brought. Lace up my boots. Smooth my hair into a bun. All the while, I'm trying to calm my ragged breath, the tremors in my heart.

I finally relieve Bridgeman. "You look terrible," he tells me.

"And you look like fresh roses," I spit back. Bridgeman gets a little pout about the mouth, like he's not accustomed to women speaking to him so directly.

I gather myself and knock at the widow's partly opened door. I remind myself we've got a narrow window of time. I can end this war if I do my job right.

The widow nods me into the room. Little Rose is just waking. The widow herself looks poorly rested too. No surprise given the circumstance.

She collects fresh dress shields from a drawer while I gather linen underclothes from another. After those are on, I get her corset laced. The room's already warm—never cooled off over the night. Next is her hoop. After that, I open her clothespress, a warren of pillowy black shapes inside. She directs me to a different dress of black silk.

As I drop it over her head, we both smell the stink of old sweat, fresh dress shields and all. "Could the laundry be done?" she asks, her voice crisp and aloof.

"By whom?" I ask.

"I bring in a girl. Laundry needs doing," she adds pointedly. I look if she's directing this at my person, but she's surveying her bed. What with the captain's late-night visit a week previous and a female's propensity to throw out blood and sweat with only a modicum of predictability, I wager her sheets are rank. Of course, Pinkerton won't allow laundry going out or a girl coming in—too many opportunities for the widow's arrest to be noticed.

"We'll need to get it done ourselves," I tell her, an idea coming to me. Laundry's a burdensome chore, and sharing such a burden might breed gratitude and, just maybe, companionship.

The widow engages in some calculation. Decorum, she likely concludes, prevents her from asking the Miss Mackalls for help with her dirty clothes, regardless of the exceptional circumstance. And while playing at domestic humility, I remain her captor; I won't be undertaking the laundry alone. I imagine *Beadle's Dime Book of Practical Etiquette for Ladies and Gentlemen's* instructions on the subject:

CHAPTER VII. HOUSE ARREST: *Etiquette for the Hostess*

The widow considers a moment more and then agrees. "We'll do it after Little Rose's lessons. And my maid will assist us."

I finish buttoning up the widow's dress. "Oh, everyone's being sent away this morning. The servants. The Mackall sisters, too." After I speak to Pinkerton, it won't be a lie.

I can see the effect on the widow. A subtle decline in her spine. She'll have no one left. No sympathetic heart in the whole house. No one but her eight-year-old daughter. And perhaps me.

I bring the widow and Little Rose to the dining room for breakfast. Pinkerton's arrived from his hotel by then, and I explain my plan. He gives me the go-ahead. I break the news to the Mackalls, then search them well and good before they leave to ensure they don't transport any messages out of the house. Tully and Mann will take them in a covered carriage back to the Mackall residence where Mann will remain to keep them sequestered. Can't have them communicating the widow's arrest to others.

To my next business: I take the narrow stairs down to the servants' quarters in the basement. Lizzie's packing her affairs into a round bandbox. Someone already gave her the news.

"It's likely just a few days you'll be gone," I tell her.

She bangs a story-paper into the box. In a mood, Lizzie is, her body telling me all about it. "If you wanted to be friendly, should've been before announcing I was moving to the carriage house."

"It's the room above you're moving to, and it's outfitted for sleeping."

"Next to the groom's lodging!" She's all cut and sneer as she tries to close her bandbox, but she's got at least three dresses coming out the sides.

I reach to help.

"No, no, no, and thank you very much." She moves the box away from me. "I can pack myself, can't I?"

She can't. She's shoving the dresses inside the lid with her fingers.

You'd think a maid would know from folding clothes. I sit on the bed and watch.

Lizzie's got a pale yellow ribbon she's trying to tie around the whole box to keep the lid on. Wouldn't you know, the box being circular, her yellow ribbon's going to slip right off. Thing's got Lizzie beat, but she doesn't see it yet. She looks up at me. "Isn't there enough suffering in this world without you coming to make more of it?" She finishes the ribbon's bow and lifts the bandbox triumphantly.

Like a charm, the yellow ribbon slides off, the box spilling out all over the floor. Three dresses, two aprons, a pair of bonnets, a comb, at least three story-papers, more hard candies than any one girl should consume, and a compensatory family-size jar of tooth powder.

I'm placid as a pool.

"You can help me now!" says Lizzie in a fury.

I pick up a dress that shows reworking—a widow's hand-me-down, most likely—and fold it up tight. I can fold a dress to fit in a bandbox. I can't guarantee the wrinkles will ever acquiesce to an iron after all's said and done, but I can fold it to fit. Lizzie's scrabbling after a candy under the bed. It comes out in a dandelion puff of dust. They weren't even wrapped. She starts picking off the dust. "Don't eat that." I take the candy and throw it back on the floor. I get the second dress in fair form and move on to the third.

Lizzie kneels. She stacks the stories and comb. Plops them atop the folded dresses. Looks at me and says without prompt, "The widow is a good woman. I don't know politics, but I can tell you what type of woman she is, as I'm the one who dresses her and minds her daughter and what have you. And what I see is a woman who gathers people at her table." Lizzie stands right up. "I'm not calling her a peacemaker, she's never that. But she's not squirreling herself away only seeing and talking to those who favor her opinions, is she now? No, she's not. She'll quote you the law right off by heart as if she were reading it. And you see it in their eyes, them as come to her table. She's not running about in bloomers, playing the fool. She's just bringing them round with words and reason. You don't like what she says, fine. But can you not credit her for saying it as she does?"

She lives in her heart, Lizzie. If it wasn't in her words and her surfeit of hard candies, it's in her manner; she's fairly pushing her chest out at me as she rails. Bodies are nothing if not honest. I'm still about that placid pool when I tell her, "Any person endeavoring to preserve the institution of slavery can have no redeemable aspect or quality."

"Oh, and if that didn't come straight off a pamphlet." She falls back on the bed like a fire died down. "You turn your eye from what she is and see only what you choose. My, but you're the narrow-minded one." She goes on. "You'd not be saying such things had you seen her as I have. Oh, but that Little Rose is cherished like she's made of gold. And I don't have to tell you that's a rare find in this world. Did your mother make you feel like gold? I'll tell you mine never did, to be sure.

"And her daughter Gertie—those two would get into it proper. Arguing like politicians, the girl for your abolition, the mother against. A high-spirited one, Gertie, ever going her own way, but the widow loved her all the more for it. You never saw a person tend an ailing child with more care than the widow did her Gertie, no regard for herself." Lizzie's working herself up again, thinking as she is on the dead girl. "And looking after her other daughters, getting them to safety. And then back she comes to Washington, because her home's here and her blood's here, and isn't she the most doughty one you ever saw?" Lizzie kneels down to the bandbox, jamming the last bits in now there's space from my tight folding. "Other ladies are hiding themselves away." Her head pops up, and she waggles a finger. "Not our widow. Not like you, Kate, with your spying and such. That's not even your true name, I'd guess. A sham, you are. Just like Dennis Mann and his ham!" So much for the honeyfuggle.

She gets halfway out the door before coming back for a pair of boots under the bed. She comes right at me as if to shoulder past, but I don't move because, as I said, the girl lives in her heart. Won't venture into physical violence. And so it is, her sleeve brushes mine is all, but I feel the heat as she goes out the door to the carriage house. It's under my breath that I say, "Best of luck to you, Lizzie."

I'm set to return to the widow when I see Minnie Ann's door. Impulsiveness, it is, my knocking. There's a wary "Yes?"

I push open the door. Minnie Ann's on her cot, the same as last time I saw her, fanning herself.

"May I come in?" I ask.

"You're already in," Minnie Ann says in a way I can't distinguish for alacrity or irony.

"I wanted to see how you're getting on, ma'am," I tell her.

"I'm about to lose my place." Her fan quickens. She's not as level as yesterday, but still miles from Lizzie.

"Well, I was just seeing how you were getting on, ma'am."

Minnie Ann looks at me. "I'm getting on to thinking I should be out looking for a new place." Her tone is sharp, but her body's at ease except the working of her fan. She's pure head, Minnie Ann.

I told you Pinkerton put me in charge of the female bureau, tasked with hiring women agents. I say to Minnie Ann, "You know, a person who could learn the affairs of an employer could do some good in these times."

Minnie Ann acts like I haven't spoken. "Would you pen a letter for me if I tell you what I want to say?"

"We could find you a place, ma'am. Maybe in Baltimore, among the rebels?"

Minnie Ann's voice gets taut as a wire. "I'd like to post a letter at my church asking after a new position."

"You'd be doing important work, ma'am."

"Stop calling me ma'am!" Minnie Ann cries. Everything stills. Her fan. Her face. Mine. We look at one another. "I don't know what your *ma'am* is aimed at. Whatever it is, I don't want it. I want"—she takes a breath—"you to pen me a letter." There's a heavy moment, then slowly, slowly, her fan starts back up.

I'm passing back through the kitchen when I come upon Tully, lately returned from dropping off Mann and the Mackalls.

(Did I write Minnie Ann's letter? I did. Distracted the whole time, wondering over what misstep it was I took with the woman. "Hell is full of good meanings and wishes" and all.)

Bridgeman's at the table now, shoving his face full of porridge like he's never eaten. Tully's sitting beside him. I try to forget Tully is the one who caught me and Scobell last night. I try to act as Scobell did earlier: like nothing happened of any import between us. I compose my face into the picture of a steady agent. "Any news on last night's callers in the hedge?"

"Got their names," Tully answers. "Hope to have more soon."

"Spies?" I ask.

"Couriers," says Bridgeman through a mouth of gray sludge. Not high level enough to possess a cipher key, but likely able to finger other members of the spy ring.

"It's been a busy night and morning, as *you* know," Tully says pointedly. I shoot him a hard look.

Bridgeman sits back from his empty bowl, breathing like he just finished a sprint. "Tell her about the letters."

Tully smiles blithely. "We got a probable identity of Mr. H, our love-letter writer: Senator Henry Wilson of Massachusetts, chairman of the Committee on Military Affairs."

If we wanted a source for the intelligence the widow furnished to the Confederacy, the intelligence that contributed to the improbable triumph at Manassas (and the widow's liaison with a United States Army captain was considered insufficient), well, we got one. If we wanted a scandal to shame the entire cabinet of President Abraham Lincoln, we got that too. Henry Wilson's an abolitionist.

Scobell comes into the kitchen carrying dirty dishes from the widow and her daughter's breakfast. The picture comes into my head of him and me together in the parlor last night. My breath gets tight. "Any difficulties with the Mackalls?" I ask Tully to get the picture out of my mind.

"None to speak of. The younger girl was relieved to be back with her mother in her own home, even with Mann staying on," he recounts. "But the older girl was a mess, weeping and carrying on like a goose."

"You mean the younger. She's the weepy one," I correct him.

"And I'm talking about the older," Tully says back. "Clinging to her stitching, saying if she had to leave the widow, she needed a token of her dear friend."

I get still. Scobell must feel it—he turns from the sink and watches me close.

"What happened to the stitching?" I ask.

"We finally let her take the damn thing," Tully scoffs.

Lily, the older Mackall, would only be weeping for one reason—subterfuge. "You're dead certain it was the older?" I ask.

"Why're you stuck on this?" Tully snaps.

The hearts and flowers pattern the widow drew for the border of the embroidery. "You only need two symbols for Morse code."

Tully pales, guessing my fears. "Oh, damn it all to hell."

Scobell gets it too. "You're going to need the carriage." He's out the door in a moment.

Five minutes later, the carriage is flying along Sixteenth Street toward the Mackall house, Scobell at the reins, me in the back. It's midmorning, time for social calls among the lady-types in Washington, dozens of carriages like ours clogging up the road. Blood's thundering up the back of my neck with my fervor to get there.

We pull up outside the Mackall house. As I step down, I glance around. Outside the neighbor's house, another carriage has just deposited a lady in green for a visit, all done up in corset and hoops. She looks over at me, takes in my working-girl attire, and her brows start to knit, wondering what low-class woman is calling at the Mackalls' this Saturday morning. I give a polite wave, all calm and composed, while my heart's just pounding.

"Whistle if I've got an audience," I say low to Scobell. He gives a nod.

I knock at the Mackalls' door, two sets of staccato raps that Mann, who's keeping them sequestered in their home, will recognize.

As the door opens, Scobell starts whistling an easy tune, telling me the lady in green is still watching from the neighbor's porch. Goddamn it.

"Is Miss Lily Mackall at home?" I call mildly.

I hear Mann's low murmur, and then Lily appears framed by the door. I give her a look over, noting a subtle bulge in her pocket. I'm betting it's the encoded embroidery. She's keeping it close.

Next door, I hear a maid greet the lady in green. In a moment, she'll be inside, and I'll be free to do whatever I need to. But then Lily, too, notices the neighbors.

"Mrs. Ames!" Lily calls quickly. Next door, the lady in green turns. "How fine to see you this morning," Lily goes on. "Visiting Mrs. Dickinson, are you?"

Mrs. Ames answers, "I am, my dear." She still has an uncertain eye for me. "Is all well over there?"

Lily's face settles into a smug smile. She steps farther out of her house. She knows witnesses are to her advantage because I can't use physical force in their presence. I see Lily sizing it up, figuring maybe she can slip past me while I'm hamstrung by Mrs. Ames in her green dress. Maybe she can get that embroidered message to someone in the widow's spy ring and alert them that the widow's been compromised. I'm about to lose it all.

"Mrs. Ames, is it?" I call to the lady in green. "Could you call Mrs. Dickinson? I'd have her hear this too." Lily's eyes narrow. A second woman comes out of the house, joining Mrs. Ames on the front step. I address them both: "My dear ladies, I suspect you have no idea the true character of this young lady before me."

Lily's body tightens, readying for flight. Mrs. Ames and Mrs. Dickinson look wonderingly between me and Lily.

I go on. "Why, Miss Lily Mackall is none other than . . ." I turn to Lily. "An angel of mercy."

Lily looks at me sharply.

"The item concealed in her pocket," I tell the ladies. "Is an embroidery she has lovingly stitched to brighten the children's ward I oversee at the Georgetown Poor House."

There's a cluck of admiration from the listening ladies. Hell if I'm going to lose anything to Miss Lily Mackall.

Lily glances back at her front door, assessing her options. Mann's just visible, blocking any retreat.

I continue, "When you now pass me that carefully stitched work of yours, Miss Lily, please know you are improving the life of at least one orphan this day." I give a broad smile.

Lily hesitates, looking over at Mrs. Ames and Mrs. Dickinson.

"Why do you pause?" I press. "Would you prefer to accompany me to deliver the embroidery yourself? That could be arranged."

Stiffly, Lily reaches into her pocket and offers her stitching. I take it. "Thank you, my dear." I nod to Mann. Lily retreats back inside. With a wave to the neighbors, I walk back to the carriage. For a moment, my mind rests clear and easy. I remember the thrill of being a Pinkerton. The pursuit of your suspect. Knowing what others don't. Doing whatever needs to be done.

Scobell's waiting at the carriage door. I give him a quick wink. Another rebel beat in the name of the Cause.

But Scobell barely meets my eyes. "Ready, ma'am?" he playacts for the neighbors.

" . . . yes, thank you," I say back. It makes me want to retch playing that I'm his employer, but I tamp down what I'm feeling. Close it up. Lock it tight. Ride the rest of the way back to the widow's house bound in that silence.

In the widow's kitchen, Pinkerton receives the contraband stitching. He slaps my back hard enough I stumble forward. "That's my girl!"

I don't have Scobell, but I've still got the agency.

Pinkerton glances toward the wall, beyond which the widow, now alone but for her daughter, sits. "It all rests on you, Kate."

— *Thirteen* —

The widow's demeanor has been sobered by her friends' departure. That's her frame of mind as she settles in next to her daughter in the front parlor. The girl's lesson books are stacked before them, but the widow's eyes are on the girl herself, adjusting a starched cuff here, patting down her dress there. Little Rose wears a crinoline under her skirt. Ruffled apron on top. A ribbon rosetta at her neck. Books aren't even cracked yet, and the widow's already imparting lessons, pressing the girl into the shape of a lady.

I sit with my needlepoint on a chair by the door. Clouds have broken the sun's strength today, but the air's heavier. I take a look at the girl's lesson books. Here's the books I *don't* see:

McGuffey's First Primer
The Heman's Young Ladies' Reader

Here's what I *do* see:

An Abridgment of Lectures on Rhetoric
The Young American, or, Book of Government and Law: showing their history, nature, and necessity

Little Rose is put to reading from the government book first. After a couple pages, the widow stops her. "That's fine, Rose. I would now have you compare the child's role in a family to that of a citizen in a society. Gather your thoughts." The widow nods to a blank paper and lead pencil sitting ready.

Little Rose sets to writing. She pauses once to give her privates a good hard scratch.

"Little Rose!" scolds the widow.

The girl looks chastened for about a second, then returns to the page. As the girl continues, the widow's arm comes around her with an ease that says they once shared a body. Little Rose pushes back against her mother to straighten herself in her seat. Pushes against her mother like she's a wall or a stone, sure of her steadiness. Would I touch my mother so had she lived? Would she have given me lessons in cuffs and ribbons, in books and essays? I feel the same pang of envy I did in Gertrude's room.

Little Rose's pencil lead drops to the table with a clack, thoughts gathered. "A child in a family," she speaks aloud, "is required to obey her parents. For example, coming to supper when called, telling the truth, and behaving in good and natural ways. It is from obeying in a family that a child understands the necessity of obeying laws in society."

"And how does—" begins the widow. But Little Rose stops her.

"Mama!" the girl says, an intensity coming into her eyes. "Mama, is everyone someone's child?" The truth and enormity of her discovery are all over her face. Suddenly she turns to me, and I see the shift as she perceives that even I am subject to this truth.

The widow barely glances at Little Rose. "Everyone is someone's child, yes." Her tone is light, saying none of this is revelatory. Little Rose reads that tone. Tempers her awe in relation to it. I see the change on her face. She reconsiders. Comes down to thinking, maybe it's not such a big thing, her discovery. The widow sets the girl on to her next assignment.

While she works, I think on the girl's words. *Everyone is someone's child.* I remember being young enough to have that kind of revelation. Young enough that every feeling seemed to explode within me. Each discovery possessing the grandeur of a true epiphany, seeming to crack the world open.

My revelations mostly came by way of Consider Pritchett, the Quaker I knew at Tremont. Consider was in her early twenties when I knew her. She could have been a handsome girl, but she wore high-necked dresses and pinned back her thick dark hair in a simple bun. Her whole self was like this: almost handsome, but too pinned back. The other Yanks called it a pity that such beauty was wasted on a strait-laced Quaker who devoted all her time to "causes" like the Anti-Slavery Society and the Women's Suffrage Campaign.

Consider always had an eye out for me. I don't know whether it was her interest in causes (wasn't I the perfect cause: a poor paddy orphan?) or if she truly liked me, but she became the closest thing I had to a friend at the mill.

It was Consider who invited me to join the labor union. It happened one day in Spinning Room No. 2, just before dinner break during the spring I turned twelve. I was tall. Tall enough that I had recently graduated from changing bobbins to working as a spinner.

I had just turned off my spinning frames when Consider appeared at my side. I was wary; Yanks didn't casually socialize with Irish. She plainly wanted something. But she had been kind to me in the past, so I listened when she tilted her head to the side and asked if I would consider joining the Tremont Female Labor Reform Association.

In Irish opinion, labor unions were a Yank preoccupation that only invited scrutiny from the mill owners, which we Irish already had aplenty. Consider saw me hesitating. "Maybe just join us at a meeting to try?"

I gave a vague nod, figuring that would be the end of it. But then Consider held out her arm. I didn't recognize the gesture. She was offering her hand to shake. It was a Quaker gesture, she explained, a gesture of equality and friendship.

I was taken aback. No Yank ever touched a dirty paddy if they could help it. And here, one was offering me her hand. I felt special, seen. I took it and shook.

Consider must have noticed the shift in me, for she said, "The Irish have never joined the union, but you seem like you might be more forward-thinking than the others."

I didn't even hear an insult. As if reading my heart, Consider added one more thing. "You might find you belong with us." The words hit their mark, though in truth, I had already been persuaded. People who live in their heads and hearts can be convinced by words and sentiments. Those of us who live below are only persuaded by actions. To change, we must be pummeled, jostled, pressed into another shape by lived experiences—we must be *moved*. Consider's handshake had done just that. I agreed to attend a trial meeting a few days later.

The union meetings became the highlight of my week. Through them, my world opened up. I began to view my life in new terms, terms like mutual assistance and fair recompense. I began to question the conditions we worked in, and whether there were alternatives.

While the other Yank union girls never fully embraced me, not as true friends, they were civil. Once as interchangeable as machine parts, those Yanks became individuals. They became Julia Warne, the union secretary, and Harriet Coots, member-at-large, from Erin, New York.

Consider also introduced me to the things she read: William Lloyd Garrison's *The Liberator*, pamphlets on the Rights of Women by Elizabeth Cady Stanton, *Narrative of the Life of Frederick Douglass*.

I had often dreamed about where our cotton went after it passed through our hands: Buenos Aires. Paris. Peking. I imagined girls in foreign cities wearing dresses of cotton that I had spun. When the girl in Peking touched her skirt, could she feel the echo of my hand? I liked to believe so, that there was some trace of me traveling out of the mill with the cloth, traveling safely across the ocean all that long way to the girl in China. I imagined a bond between us, such that if I saw her, I'd know it was my spun threads she was wearing, and she would know it too. But before Consider Pritchett, I never wondered who had the cotton before me. What was in the past worth looking back at? Ocean voyages of a different sort.

After meeting Consider, I began thinking a lot more about the girl who had the cotton before me, the enslaved girl who had picked it. I began to imagine a piece of her coming along with the cotton to me. A little piece of her story traveling through my fingers. And a piece of her also going on to Paris, Buenos Aires, Peking. A little piece of her and a little piece of me woven into every bit of cotton that traveled on, our stories buttoned around the Peking girl's waist each day as she dressed in our cotton.

I found myself emulating Consider. The way she tilted her head before she spoke. The open manner with which she greeted whoever entered the room. Her frank handshake. I admired how she didn't seem to care about her looks, as if she was above such trivialities. I even began to accompany her to the Improvement Circles arranged by the Mill Girl Betterment Committee.

I already knew, by this point, how fictions got marked on us by others, like Nabby Fife calling me a dirty paddy. But with Consider, something new occurred to me. Something wondrous. If one person can write a story on another, why couldn't I do the same? What if I could shed my old stories like too-small boots and write myself anew?

In Consider's company, I began this revision. Rubbing out the girl from before. Crafting a new story of a confident Yankee raised to keep pace with New York forests and New Hampshire mountains. My Irish brogue slid into new contours, flattening into middle-of-the-mouth American English. During this time, I even left off using the name Mary, answering to just Kate, so people wouldn't know me straight-away for Irish.

It was a morning a few years on, in March 1856, that we mill girls found a notice on the factory door advising us that, as of that day, wages would be cut, machines sped up, and spinners would tend four frames instead of three. I was seventeen years old.

The same night of the notice, there was an emergency meeting of the Tremont Female Labor Reform Association. Girls were packed into the community hall, so thick you could hardly see through them—

members and nonmembers. Everyone had come looking for an answer to the notice.

Consider stood at the room's center. Her voice was quiet as she took us through what we might do. She told us of mill girls a decade before who had "turned out" in protest. They had left their very machines to gather in the mill yard in unified resistance. In so doing, they had successfully opposed wage cuts.

Then, Consider said this: "We might take our misfortune as an opportunity. An opportunity to advocate for honest pay for honest work in healthful conditions for every girl, be she Methodist, Quaker, Presbyterian, or Catholic, hailing from here or abroad, originating from a good family or none at all. We will stand as one." That is what Consider said.

This is what I heard: Beginning that day, every girl would belong. I would cease being a paddy or an orphan. We would bind ourselves together in a radical act, an act of transformation, that would change every mill girl into a sister. It came to me as a revelation.

There in the community hall, I looked at the girls around me. Could we do it? Remake the world so it was not the strongest who survived, but all of us together?

I remember I called out in agreement with Consider's proposition. Then I did more: I took up the hand of my neighbor. She was inspired, in turn, to take the hand of her neighbor. Soon every girl in attendance was literally joined. In this propitious posture, we decided: We would turn out to protest in solidarity against the mill owners.

The next morning, we arrived at the mill in a stream of sisters, gravel crunching under our boots. My limbs felt light and my heart was pounding.

I climbed the stairs to Spinning Room No. 2 and took my place at my spinning frames. It was only minutes before the morning bell—our signal. When it sounded, we would not reach for our machines. They would not thunder into action. It would be my voice instead of the clamoring spinning frames that filled Spinning Room No. 2. I would sing the classic song with Consider's reworked lyrics:

Come all you weary factory girls,
I'll have you understand,
We're going to leave the factory
If we don't receive what we demand

Others would join in singing, and together we would walk out the door, stepping down the stairs as one family. Our great tide would flow across the grounds toward Consider, awaiting us on the canal bridge. We would stand behind her as she asked the overseers to see us not as workers, employees, and adversaries, but as daughters, sisters, and mothers, and to treat us with as much dignity and care as such kinship warranted.

And then it happened: the bell rang. A silence of held breaths followed. My voice broke through. A strange and lonely sound.

Come all you weary factory girls

My eyes met the girl's next to mine. I sang louder. She smiled back apprehensively and joined the refrain.

I'll have you understand

"The bell rang!" shouted the overseer.

I looked to a second girl. She looked from me to the overseer. I sang louder still.

We're going to leave the factory

"You!" the overseer brought his mouth to a girl's ear. "Machines on! Or I'll walk you out of this mill, never to come back!"

The girl called out "I'm sorry, Kate," and her frames rumbled to life, first, second, third, fourth.

If we don't receive what we demand

The other girls looked at me miserably, voices faltering. I screamed the next verse against the pounding of the spinning frames.

May friendship reign throughout the whole

Outside, Consider was waiting. I beckoned to the rest of the girls and started toward the door. I could not bear to look behind me at how many were following. I could only walk, hoping, trusting they would be there.

As sisters let us unite

My screeching song—I was still singing!—bounced off the spiral stairs. I climbed down, listening for steps behind me, unable to hear over my voice and the machines that shook the very mill. I was almost at the door to the yard. When I crossed through it, I would reach behind me for the hands of my sisters and lead them to the bridge. Ahead, I could see dawn's light through a crack beneath the door, and I could not resist; I turned and looked back.

And there he was: the only one who followed. The overseer. He clapped me on the back and shoved me into the light. The grounds were empty. Where were my sisters?

The overseer muscled me across the gravel yard. I was weeping, but still singing. I couldn't stop. But it was the original words of the song that spilled out my lips:

Come all you weary factory girls,
I'll have you understand,
I'm going to leave the factory,
And return to my native land

A sudden fury flooded my heart. I turned on him, the overseer. I lunged for his face with my hands, grabbing hold of the loose flesh at his neck with my nails. He boxed my cheek, then got a hand under my chin, shoving me away. I rushed him again, but he hooked a finger into my nose, driving it up, while his other hand grabbed for my ear. I fell back, low and crouched. He ran at me, catching my jaw with his fist. I landed hard on the ground. He flipped me and dug his knee into my back. He called out to someone I couldn't see. I heard footsteps as my face pressed into the gravel.

Moments later, I was wrenched up by more man-arms and dragged out of the empty mill yard. Crossing the canal bridge, one of the men tread on a piece of paper, already brown with boot prints. On it, I recognized Consider's handwriting. Her speech. Was she dragged away like me? In my mind, I saw Old Peg the ragpicker gathering the paper into her sack of lost and broken things.

I sat that night in the Tremont jail. They released me the following morning. The overseer was too embarrassed at being attacked by a seventeen-year-old girl to bring a charge against me. Two days later, I was on the train to Chicago to find a job in meatpacking. I never saw Consider again.

In the widow's front parlor, Little Rose puts down her pencil. Her mother reads over her work. It's better, I think, for the widow to temper Little Rose's revelations now, so she doesn't have to learn the hard way like me.

After the failed protest, Consider's revelation fell away like scales from my eyes. I had opened the floodgates of my heart, believing I could be joined to the other girls. But I had forgotten love's opposite: loss. You'll say the opposite of love is hate, but I don't agree. You can't love without fear of loss and you can't have truly lost unless you have loved. Two sides of the same coin. The world flows with both. Great, terrible floods of loss—and the current, the thrust behind it? Love. It wrenches lovers apart, divides families, pulls loved ones from one another. Every love story, truly, is just the story of loss. Who wants a story like that? Better for the widow to protect her child.

The widow kisses Little Rose's head as she reads over the girl's writing. "Very good," she pronounces. Then she straightens the ribbon rosetta at the girl's neck.

— *Fourteen* —

It's finally time for laundry. I'm still hoping the shared work will lay enough common ground that I can worm into the widow's trust. That's all I need, just a little bit of trust. If I get that, I can get this job done.

We gather Little Rose's stained dresses, drawers, and stockings. The widow walks ahead of me into her own bedroom to pull the sheets from her bed (suggesting lurking evidence of her indiscretions on them).

"May I gather your garments?" I ask from beside the hamper.

"Mm," she agrees.

Soon each of us has a whole heap of dirty clothes. At the top of the stairs, the widow pauses. "I'd like to collect an item from the library."

I nod in answer. Of course, I tail her in there, me and Little Rose and all the dirty laundry.

Scobell's up the ladder, still searching the books. The widow's body stiffens when she spies him there, but she turns with a smoothly composed face toward a low shelf of magazine volumes. She pulls out the stack of *Godey's Lady's Books*.

Scobell pushes himself along the ladder. All at once, it clunks against the desk chair stuck in its path. He curses under his breath before remembering us. "Apologies," he mutters. The widow pretends he's not there. Scobell climbs down and moves the desk chair out of the way. I was the one who left the chair in the ladder's path when I dressed this morning. I flash him an apologetic look, but he doesn't spare me a glance.

The widow holds up one magazine in triumph. As I start to leave, she asks, "Have you no items to launder?" I hadn't considered she'd allow my low-born drawers to boil in the same waters as her own. Devil can surprise you now and again. I gather my things.

Behind the kitchen is the room set aside for the sole purpose of laundry. Water comes out of a pipe in the wall, and there's even a stove to heat it. There's also a long table for the soaking tubs, so our backs will be spared the bend. In the corner is a big old monster of a contraption, a standing rotary mangle, like's advertised in the papers, with a turning handle to wring out your larger items. It'll be a blessing come time for the bedclothes.

The widow works at pinning a thick apron on herself. I reason by her clumsiness the woman hasn't pinned on an apron in a decade. This leads me to wondering if she has any more knowledge about laundering clothes than I do. If she doesn't, we're in a fine predicament because I know all of nothing. (And that mangle's about big enough to gobble up Little Rose whole.)

Before I can wonder more, the mystery of the widow's library detour explains itself. Little Rose, from a perch on the table, reads from the *Godey's Lady's Book* aloud. It's an article with instructions for best laundering practices. Praise the Lord.

The girl reads one word to the next, linking some words and pausing before others, with no regard for punctuation, in the way of new readers that leaches away half the meaning: "'Make a lather by boiling soap and water throw in a handful of salt previously to putting the articles into it.' This is for muslin. Are they muslin?"

"They are linen," rejoins the widow.

"Mine are muslin," I come in. The *they* is drawers. Perhaps mine will not debase hers after all. But like the widow, I am in ignorance, awaiting Little Rose's instruction as to the particular washing techniques of linen and muslin.

Little Rose's eyes rove the page. "I think it's the same," the girl concludes. "Wait!" she cries, spooking me halfway to reaching for the soap. "Are there stains on the drawers?"

What an awkward moment that now transpires between the widow and me. What intelligence would we two adversaries care to share with one another concerning our most private encounters with man and Mother Nature?

"What solution is suggested?" asks the widow, bypassing the awkward. I notice the perspiration on her brow has already grown from dew to trickle. The August heat is pressing on the walls, just pressing the spirit from every living thing. The stove under the boiling tub raises the heat even more. Why'd we wait until the middle of the day to begin the washing? I see our error now.

"'A paste of French chalk may be laid on the stain it shall be left to dry some hours then lightly scraped,'" the girl narrates.

The widow utters something under her breath, I wager something along the lines: This is why we hire a girl for the laundry. And what she means is a *poor* girl. A Black girl, most likely. Certainly someone who can't get anything else but such work.

"I'll fetch that chalk," I say, hoping for respite from our Turkish bath. Then I spy the damn chalk on the shelf directly above me, along with something that looks to be starch and laundry blue both together in one.

"May I go outside?" Little Rose moans, waving the *Godey's* in front of her. Kids don't ever have a feeling that approaches slow, do they? Their every sentiment is a fire-alarm breaking out of perfect calm. Little Rose kicks the table for emphasis.

"Little Rose!" her mother says, low and sharp. A voice to be reckoned with. "You will perform your share of our duties. Now, come off that table and assort these articles." The widow eyes her daughter until she moves.

"Yes, Mother."

The girl reads her mother better than she does *Godey's*. The widow's backbone, held rigid when she returns to mixing soap into the tub, tells the girl she's on a short leash. "By cotton, linen, and silk, you sort them," the widow directs. Her spine softens some. "This day we'll learn together the difficulties of the duties we bestow on others and better appreciate their labors by our own." Well, look at that. Maybe there's some Christian heart under all her layers somewhere.

I set out a second tub of soapy water, a third for rinsing, and a fourth for the blue and starch combination. I drop the widow's bedsheets in the first tub. The widow's working the French chalk onto her drawers, so I go on and get to scrubbing.

I make a poor fist of the business. It's not half the hour that's passed, and I've rubbed the skin from both knuckles. You can't conceive how much my knuckles sting in the suds. You'd think a factory girl could stand up to a bedsheet and come out on top, but it's been nearly five years I've been gone from textile work, and I feel it in every raw knuckle. I'm short-breathed, and I haven't finished the first sheet. Who're these girls doing laundry? Titans.

"Are these the same fabric? They're not, are they?" Little Rose holds up two soiled table napkins. I couldn't care if it were two poisoned vipers she were raising up, asking which to set on me, I'm so hot and fatigued.

The widow wipes her neck on her apron. She's got a creek of sweat running down her head. "They're both linen, dear."

"Yes, Mother, but this one's shiny." Little Rose holds one cloth up for the widow.

"I'll take a closer look." The calm of the widow's voice is worse than a harpy's. I try to blow a sweat bead I can feel hanging from my brow, just threatening to drop into my eye.

"I thought only silk shimmered so," the girl continues their interminable debate.

"Well, it may be the way the cloth is treated," the mother goes on.

I can't keep quiet any longer. "It's that one's plain weave linen and the other's satin weave linen." My voice is not nearly as tranquil as I might have hoped.

The widow looks over to me at the tub. I can nearly see the snide remark creeping toward her mouth, and I gird myself, knowing it will take all of heaven's mercy for me to keep from biting her head off in return. There they are, her words, ready to melt out. "I've finished with the chalk if you'd like to attend to your underthings, Kate."

My name's strange in her mouth. I swallow down my burst of temper. "I'll just finish this bedsheet first." I dig back into the washing like it's easy as eating pie. Finally, I pull the sodden thing from the first tub with a clothes-stick and place it in the second.

I turn to my drawers, a sad little pile at the corner of the table. The French chalk's a fine white powder that I sprinkle on the part you'd think I might. I don't know why I'd go and reveal another personal detail like knowing different linen weaves.

My drawers need a moment for the chalk to set, so I'm back at the first tub working on a second sheet. Little Rose's done with her sorting. She's looking agitated again, like she might launch into a good, loud whine.

"You know what would help mightily to pass the time?" the widow asks. She hands the girl the edition of *Godey's*. "Would you select a story to read aloud?"

Little Rose swells with purpose and gets situated. "'The Relentless Seas,'" she begins. "'A lady in the prime of life sat twilight duskily falling around her.'" Hell, we're back to her monotone narration. "'Her husband was absent these many weeks at sea her only comfort was her dear daughter but the comfort was short-lived one day the daughter grew very ill—'" Little Rose's head darts up, in her eyes the sort of deep compassion you see only rarely in the young. "Let's read a different story," the girl says in a careful way, as if unsure her mother has yet noticed the story's unfortunately familiar turn.

"Certainly," the widow says lightly, feigning ignorance. "Though I remember reading this story, and I believe it grows less somber as it continues. Why not skip to the following chapter? An aunt arrives, I recall."

Little Rose turns the page. "Aunt Cora!"

"There we are." The widow lifts the sheet from her tub with the clothes-stick and brings it to the boiling tub. The dress she wears is soaked in a perfect line across her upper back where her corset ends. I can see her ribs straining at it as she pushes the sheet down in the roiling froth. In this heat, with such a task, she wears her corset. Another animal, ladies, I tell you.

Little Rose reads on. "'The grief-stricken lady's Aunt Cora arrived like a holly berry in a bare winter landscape you must rise from your couch exclaimed Aunt Cora you have suffered the worst a woman might suffer yet you must rise.'"

The widow determines the first sheet has boiled long enough. She lifts it with the clothes-stick, but isn't it a burning, steaming pile? I haven't a clue how to help her, except to stand in front of the girl so she doesn't get scalded as her mother brings her burning load to a rinsing tub. The widow, occupied as she is, notes me shielding the child. The woman misses nothing, I'd wager. No thanks does she give, but she saw it. The girl is looking over my arm, oblivious to harm, watching her mother push that boiled sheet down into the new tub. Little Rose has surely never seen her mother at menial labor, which accounts for her rapt attention.

Gradually she returns to her page. "'The dear wise aunt guided her beloved niece to a neighbor's house wherein a number of ladies had gathered together knitting taking her Aunt Cora to the side the grieving lady confided I am like a specter I cannot feel the sentiments of the living.'"

Parsing the girl's text manages to keep my mind off my labors at the bedsheet, even if the story's the saccharine kind of Goody-Two-Shoes drivel these magazines regularly afflict on their readers. The widow moves her sheet from the rinsing tub to the starch-and-blueing.

"'Said Aunt Cora what if I told you that the dear lady in fawn were six months a widow and that sweet girl in the lace collar lost her sister last winter and that lady knitting the pink stockings lost a daughter as you did not one year ago I would say spoke the lady their joy must be as counterfeit as a poor miner's pan rattling with fool's gold.'"

It's a two-hander, the mangle. Seeing the widow readying for it, I leave my bedsheet to feed hers through the roller while she works the crank. Twice through, then onto the drying rack. She's strong enough, the widow. Tall, and ate better than me while growing. We get that first sheet hung, and it's a poor celebration we have. Just a sigh between us knowing exactly how much it takes to do the one, and then knowing how much is left to do. But when the widow says something under her breath, it's not a complaint or even a reference to the work we've set out for ourselves. It's altogether different, prompted, it seems, by the read-aloud story. She nods to her daughter. "Too young to have witnessed such as she has."

The girl's still at her plodding oration, but I'm feeling more chip than I have since walking into this hellhole, because what she's just uttered is a confidence. It's a tit-for-tat game, just like with Mrs. Maroney. Pinkerton provided my confidence to the widow in the remonstrations he ensured she overheard. The widow has now returned her first confidence. A bona fide sign of progress.

Little Rose is still ekeing her way through the deadly Aunt Cora story. "'The women's cheeks were alive with natural blush and their eyes filled with honest sentiment why I cannot conceive how but they possess a true joy admitted the lady Aunt Cora replied the task with which they occupy their hands is knitting items for poor orphans.'"

It's good I got my proof of progress because the story's getting to the place you want to gouge out your eyes for its cloying inanity. I might tell you the rest of how it goes; it'll continue with platitudes about suffering together and sharing burdens. There'll be mentions of "Good Samaritans" and "thinking of others before ourselves" and "Christian duty." All of it whipped up into a sugary confection by some lady writer and her editor. But you tell me if a person who ever lost another person—someone stuck deep in their heart—you tell me if that person ever took solace in reading about someone else knitting socks with a twinkle in her eye. I'm thinking this bitter-coffee sort of thought when the girl looks up from the page and says straight to me, no games, no peevishness, as if she's seen into my head, "Let me stay with my mama."

It hits me in the gut.

The girl says, "I'll go to prison. I'll go anywhere. Just let me stay with her." Through the girl's eyes I see her thinking on her dead father, her dead sister. The other dead babies her mama lost. Thinking on her living sisters shipped off to safety outside this war-bound city. This girl, she sees herself down the road the way you do when you've lived some. She sees herself here with her mama doing laundry, reading aloud in this hot, hot room, and knows it's a time she may feel lucky for soon.

From somewhere in my heart comes a lullaby.

Hush now, grá mo chroí

All at once the close air of the laundry room's unbearable. I reach into my pocket for my kerchief and give a small yelp as something bites into the flesh of my palm. A red bloom spills across my apron as my hand begins to bleed. It's the arrowhead, the one I took from Little Rose.

The widow hands me her own kerchief. I quickly press my cut flesh. It's trembling, my hand. Trembling like I'm a little girl. I tell myself it's the blood and not Little Rose's words.

"Let me wrap it," the widow says. She uses the same tone she used to tell Little Rose to put on her nightdress. I still my hand, best I can, and let her bind my palm. I can see the widow's hair close up, a few stray grays peeking through the brown.

"You need to trim your nails," she says absently to me as she tucks the edge of the kerchief around my hand. She seems to catch herself. "I apologize," she says quickly. "Habit from being a mother." Something flickers across her face.

I feel another tremble in my guts, but this time it's from something different: a notion that's just come to me. Maybe I've been wrong— maybe it isn't the dead daughter I should be concentrating on. Maybe it's the daughters who are left. The two far away in Utah territory and the one here, begging to stay with her mama. Maybe they're the key to it.

The shake in my guts gets worse. I squeeze my bleeding hand. The sharp sting pulls my attention away from my trembling. Pulls it back onto the girl and the widow and the work I've got to do.

— *Fifteen* —

The widow is sitting at the dressing table in her bedroom. It's night. We didn't finish the laundry. I probably don't need to tell you that, seeing as you can't have less knowledge of the task than the widow and me put together. You surely foresaw the job unfinished before we even began. There you go. Got through the bedclothes and the drawers, that's it.

I place the dress I just removed from the widow to the side. Cold, her body reads to me.

Little Rose is on the bed nearby, eyeing me as coldly as her mama.

"Have you made an account to your employer of our day?" the widow asks me. So that's the cold. While she dined on her supper of cheese and crackers, she correctly surmises I took the time to recount our day to Pinkerton.

In the kitchen, he listened to my report: the widow's small advances in trust, the girl's plea to stay with her mother, my suspicion that her living daughters were the aperture I needed.

"So, offer her that," Pinkerton said. "She sees prison on the horizon. Promise her her daughters."

I was taken aback by his willingness to concede anything. "Can we make good on that promise?"

"Of course not," Pinkerton spat back at me. "Are you quibbling over something that might give us an advantage in this war?"

"No," I said quick, and hurried back up the stairs to the widow waiting in her bedroom.

"I gave my employer my report," I tell the widow. "But he understands less of laundry than me, and little of women." I remove two apples from my pocket and offer them to the widow and Little Rose. The girl eases right up and into that apple. The mother puts the fruit to the side.

I get to work on her corset, picking at the tight little knot I made myself this morning. Splits my nail without giving way, the damn thing. Strong enough to rig a sail, corset laces.

"These dress pads should be burned," the widow says, unsticking them from her pits. "Else you'd like to launder them." She gives me a hint, just the hint, of a smile.

I smile back, but reserved. The Good Servant.

"Brush my hair?" she asks while she pats her cheeks in the mirror.

I take the bristles through her hair. She's handsome. I'll give her that. I wonder what it would be like to be armed with beauty like hers? Hattie Lawton is pretty, but men have betrayed their country for the widow. *Men*, plural. What is it about her that commands such devotion? What drove Mr. H and the Union captain to sacrifice *anything*? What could I do with such beauty?

The widow glances at me in the mirror. I close my face. It must be a common thread in her life—the envy of other women. When she has her supper parties, men's wives must sit at her table, looking at her, seeing her glamour acting on their husbands, but seeing through it . . . what do they feel? Hens waiting to pick the outsider to bone.

But then again, the Mackalls are devoted to her. And her daughters too. Their hearts are joined. How does the widow manage it?

"Fetch my nightdress, would you please?" the widow asks. "The second drawer in the chest." I find a neat stack of cotton nightdresses, starched-and-blued and ironed smooth by more experienced hands than mine. "You'll take one for yourself," she adds.

I look right at her with surprise.

"Isn't yours still to be laundered?" she reminds me. "I wouldn't think you'd have brought many."

The air tastes sweet as I pull a second nightdress from the chest. "Thank you, ma'am."

Little Rose is gnawing at her apple core, now and again checking on her mother. When I undo my wrapper dress, the girl's eyes leave the apple to pore over me in my underlayers.

I pull the nightdress on. Its starched thickness runs along my skin, smelling of blueing and crushed lavender blossoms. It takes a moment to feel the widow's gone furtive. When my head pops out of the nightdress, she's over at the bedside into something. I'm thinking of the heavy brass candlesticks up on the mantel I might go for, need be, when she turns holding what? Nothing but a big bottle of brandy.

"I thought we deserved a reward for our work. That is, if you partake."

"I hope it won't count against me," I say, my hands out to receive the bottle. I remember Tully checked it earlier. She produces two glasses, also from beside the bed.

While I pour, the widow helps Little Rose with her nightdress. She's a whirl of girl-limbs, white cloth waving like a signal flag as she elbows into it. I survey the widow and Little Rose and me in our matching dresses—could you tell us from one family?

The widow and I clink glasses full up with brandy. I wait to hear what words she might utter in toast. "To a woman's labors, always underestimated," she says.

I let her drink first, out of habit. She takes the brandy down, less a tipple for Little Rose. I follow suit in draining my glass and pour again.

The widow sips this time. She nods at me but speaks conspiratorially to Little Rose, "Look at her hair. May you never allow yourself such a nettle patch." Little Rose guards her own reaction until she can gauge her mother's intentions. Her mother guffaws. After heat like today and heavy labor during it, a glass of brandy goes straight to the head. "Come here, girl," says the widow. And she's talking to me.

A row of turtles on a log, we are, one behind the other, right along the side of the widow's bed—Little Rose plaiting her mother's hair, the widow plaiting mine. Plaiting my very hair.

"May I ask you something?" says the widow. We're on our third glass of brandy. "May I ask what it is you find so distasteful in womanly things?"

"I wouldn't say I do, ma'am." I wince. She's braiding with such rigor, I have to lean forward against each yank-twist just to remain upright.

"Excuse me, but you do." She employs her mother voice again, the one she uses on Little Rose, like she's turned me into a makeshift for her absent older daughters. "I've seen no decoration save one brooch. You pin your hair with an indifference as to your company. Your garments are ready-to-wear, and you've made no alterations for your figure." Yank-twist, yank-twist.

"I prefer simple things," I say in reply. "Natural inclination since childhood."

"Oh, don't give me that moonshine." Yank-twist.

"Ma'am?" I turn to read her face.

"Bad as Little Rose, keep your head still." She guides my head back. "I've raised enough daughters to know when someone's laying it on. Quit pandering, and speak candidly. Why do you despise womanly accoutrements?"

Why do I? I suppose it comes from reading, if I'm honest. I got my first subscription to the Tremont Circulating Library when I was ten. Reading wasn't permitted in the mill rooms during work hours—on pain of losing your position—but for six cents a week, I had as many books as I could cram into the corners of my days. The librarian directed me to the "girl stories."

The History of Little Goody Two-Shoes
Aunt Kitty's Tales
The Wide, Wide World

Here's how they mostly ran: A girl orphan is taken in by relations, a terrible encumbrance she is on their charity. The girl grows up delicate featured but pretty. She comes to grief through her association with a man of dubious circumstance. Whether her virtues outweigh her flaws tips the outcome toward tragedy or happily-ever-after.

You'd think given the kindred circumstance of my own bringing up, I should have adored such stories. But I never managed it. Maybe it was knowing my flaws (such as a poor temper or not being pretty) would consign me to a tragic ending. What I did know was that the heroines all seemed namby-pamby and thin-skinned. None had a secure wage job. And none got her family back.

I quickly discovered I much preferred story-papers and adventure tales, like Pinkerton's. In short, "boy stories." They had their own conventions and implausibilities, but their heroes determined their fate not through good manners, but through things like wrestling bears. Those heroes never hurt. They never wept. They were never lonely or abandoned. I tore through those stories, every one the library owned. You can't help what stirs your blood. And in your own mind, you're ever I—not she, her, he, him, what have you. Just I.

I suspect it was because of those books that I became a "tomboy," dressing in simple, ready-to-wear dresses. Wearing functional, low-heeled boots. Adding no decoration or embellishment to my clothes or hair.

Once I became a Pinkerton, it seemed a good approach—a safe approach. People notice every little thing alluring girls do. Being attractive becomes your whole story. Fair Helen. My Bonny Blue-Eyed Girl. How could I tail a suspect if I attracted attention? How could I steal someone's secrets if they saw me coming? I preferred to be Ulysses, not Helen, shape-shifting as I liked. And what choice did I truly have in it, after all, with a face as plain as mine?

I answer the widow as boldly as I imagine a daughter of hers would. "You know my profession. Womanly frills and contrivances are costume pieces I add to become someone else."

"Mm," she considers doubtfully. "A female detective is a lonely life, outside the security of conventional womanhood. Perhaps you were drawn to the profession because it fit your natural eccentricity. Or perhaps you simply reject the emblems of those who have rejected you."

My plaits pull right out of her hand when I turn, feeling naked under her scrutiny. "That's not what I said!" The "ma'am" arrives late, tacked on the end, and don't we both hear it.

Her look is all challenge. "Tell me, then."

"Well, to start, maybe the circle of what's womanly should get wider instead of me trying to fit myself into it."

The widow glibly takes up my argument. "Yes, and why must we distinguish between woman and man at all? Or old and young, Black and white, rich and poor, criminal and honest? Why should we endure any distinctions? Why are we not simply all the same?" She drops the mockery. "Because we aren't." Little Rose is still perched behind her mother, holding on to her hair like puppet strings, but the girl's the one pushed and pulled along as her mother's head nods and shifts with talking.

"You want to pretend difference doesn't exist?" the widow continues. "You're playing the fool. On my passage through Panama to San Francisco, I saw a culture of people where women were no more than beasts of burden. Truly, they lived in an antediluvian state in that disease-ridden swampland. There is a brutalism in the very poor—I suspect you know it well. Why must I lie about knowing it too? Should I sacrifice the world of culture and art and philosophy that raises us from beast to human—Shakespeare and Mozart, Franklin and Jefferson—on your altar of human uniformity? There are people who are better than others. And I am proud to live in a time that allows the exceptional to rise. And, as our forefathers brilliantly discerned, for exceptional souls to shepherd the less able. Now." She refills both our glasses nearly to the rim. "Don't yes, ma'am/no, ma'am me. I want your best counterargument." She takes a long sip.

I'm already talking. "Maybe the exceptional rise if everyone starts out the same, but some started out on fertile Virginia plantations, stolen from Indians, with money for seeds and slaves for the work, and some of us were dumped off a boat in Massachusetts with famine bodies and an indenture contract, and some came with far, far less than that. You're the one mistaking uniformity. I believe we're different, yes.

And I certainly believe some of us are better souls than others. But it doesn't fall along the lines people draw: rich or poor, white or Black, American or Panam-Panamia—"

"Panamanian," the widow provides chiply.

"People aren't one thing. The lines you're drawing are lines in the ocean. You can put a line on a map and call one body the Pacific and one the Atlantic, but the truth is open water. There. My counter-argument." I take a long pull of brandy.

She stares at me a moment, then allows a smile. She pulls Little Rose around onto her lap. "But you still haven't said why you hide yourself under this drab little facade."

"I don't! There's no facade!" I don't even try slipping a ma'am in there.

"Indeed, you do. Plain Jane, the detective. Don't tell me there's not more to you underneath."

My blood is pounding. "And I already answered you, didn't I just?"

"Is that—" The widow pauses. "Is that an Irish accent I hear?" My brogue weaseled out with my anger. "You are hiding things!" she says in mock surprise.

"I certainly am not!" I say in crisp, Yank English. My heartbeat's clamoring in my ears.

The widow wiggles herself over Little Rose onto her haunches, sticking her back up like a cat. "You look ready for a fight." She picks up a plump pillow. "You're a fighter, I can see it." She is utterly ludicrous. "You know you want to fight me." Her pillow hits me in the chest.

Indeed, I want to tuck my fist and hear my knuckles crack across her face. I smile demurely. "No, ma'am, I do not want to fight."

"Did you see that, Little Rose? See her jaw tighten? I think she's dying for a fight." The widow launches another pillow. It hits me square in the nose, and isn't another right on the tail of that one. And then don't I throw one at her, hard as I can. How can I help it?

She lets go a huge cackle, and rushes at me with a long bolster. The bolster hits me chin to pelvis, and her on top of it. It's jammed between us, her body pressed on me like a cougar. Her face is just inches from mine, laughing like Hecate. Hell if I can tell if we're still playing.

"Ladies against Plain Jane!" she calls to Little Rose. I hear the door open, see Mann's eye in the crack. The widow laughs wildly as the daughter whips a pillow at my feet. Mann shuts the door. It's just pride that keeps me from calling him back. The widow's strong as hell. Her heat presses around the bolster as I roll us to the side, stuck like wrestlers. I'm already panting with holding her off. "What. Is. Your. Aim. Ma'am?!"

The widow laughs again, but now it's banded with exertion. "Ladies are stronger than you guessed," she pants. I try to roll again. "Come on, Little Rose! Defend your honor!" calls the mother, and doesn't the girl just launch herself atop us in a rain of bony elbows and knees. It's playing. The girl means it's playing. My urge to crack my knuckles across the widow's face cools. That's all it is, a game. The long game. Here we are. The widow's mad. Attacked me with a damn bolster.

My body slackens. Hers follows. Her face is still inches from mine. I'm breathing in her breath, hot and sweet, and something else at the back of the brandy. The sour of alcohol. The supper of cheese. Something gamey, animal, underneath it all. "What a tussle!" she says with glee. Then, she rolls to her back.

We lie next to one another, the bolster between us, just breathing. For a moment, our breath finds the same rhythm. Twin breaths. When the widow speaks, it's quiet. "My daughter Gertrude and I, we would tussle." She waits a moment, then goes on. "Lord, but Gertrude was a . . . she was just an imp. She always could rile me right up, Gertie. So contrary. Flying in the face of convention. Anything I said, she had to go the other way. Society. Politics. All of it. Pillows were my last resort." She turns her head and looks at me.

And it's like time has stopped, or we've stepped right out of it. Here we are in our twin nightdresses, two women looking at one another. The widow seeing a missing daughter. Me, a mother I never had. But also seeing ourselves. Two women who share an occupation—no, a *vocation.* Wrestling for a place in the world with our whole selves. Breaking rules of female propriety—in our jobs, in our beds—and doing it because something in us won't allow otherwise.

The widow whispers, "Who truly understands women like us?" And it doesn't feel a sham. It doesn't feel like she's playing her game and I'm playing mine. It feels true.

We hang in that truth for about a breath.

And then I pull myself back. What am I doing having any kind of sympathy for this woman? I roll over. Survey the shambles of the bed. Set to straightening things. Games have rules to order them. I feel for the framework of mine. I remind myself who I am: the Good Servant. The Makeshift Daughter. The Pinkerton detective closing in on her target.

The widow watches me from the bed. "It's a uniform. Lace and trimmings. Jewelry, ornamentation," she supplies. "A uniform, as much as personal taste." She refills my brandy glass.

"Army of the American Woman?" I say, taking the glass.

She looks at my hair, sucks her teeth. "All my work undone." She points me to the bed, and we're back in our row of turtles.

The brandy has loosened her tongue. "No one treats girls well unless it's demanded of them," the widow says, yanking and twisting once again. "When people regard my daughters, they say, 'look what care has gone into her hair and dress. There's people looking out for this one, watching how we treat her.' That's what the uniform does." A girl in careful plaits and starched cuffs. Cherished like gold. "I teach my children how to live in this world," the widow finishes. "Every girl deserves that of her mother."

I can't help it when I pull back. It's the tiniest of tugs, but of course she feels it. I curse my sloppiness. The brandy's getting to me too.

"Little Rose?" the widow says lightly. "Get a thread from my sewing basket to tie these, would you, please?" Once the girl trots out, she says delicately, "In truth, I didn't hardly have a mother." Of course, she remembers my own mother passed away. That's why she's making her delicate remark.

Maybe I can make it serve now; help me wedge on into her heart a little more. "Tell me about her," I lead.

I can't see the widow's face, her holding my hair as she is, but I do hear the slow inhale. "Five daughters, my mother had. And after my father died of his own foolishness," she says matter-of-factly, "it was too many mouths in the family and too many of them girls' mouths." She laughs, but it's bitter.

Little Rose is dawdling on her errand, so I push, "How'd it happen?"

"My father?" The widow is all scorn. "Killed by our slave's hand. My father fell off his horse and hit his head while blind drunk. The slave finished the job so he wouldn't be blamed for the injury."

"You must hate the man," I say.

"The slave or my father?" she asks, and then Little Rose returns with the thread. The widow ties off my plaits. There's a lightness at my back where, for a moment, we were tethered. "Use the pot," she tells Little Rose, and the girl disappears into the water closet. The widow turns back to me. "We were sent away after his death, my older sister Ellen and I, to our aunt's house. Ellen became my mother."

"Your aunt wasn't a mother to you?"

"My aunt was not a . . . motherly sort. She didn't want children, and reluctantly took us in. And I was at an age that I needed direction."

My laugh is real.

"I did," the widow protests. "All those fascinating creatures in the boarding house: men. I tell you, one evening Ellen caught me in the laundry looking at their drawers, sticking my fingers through the flies." She fills her glass up with brandy, tipsy enough she forgets mine. "I had the devil in me. Ellen took it upon herself to educate and culture me. She warned how the city girls would look on us country girls, and the prettier we were, the worse it'd be. Ellen taught me a girl with no name can still thrive if she's got a fine mind and a stainless reputation." Her sister's shadow flickers across her face.

The widow drains her glass. She looks at the mantel, at the miniature portraits of her daughters. "Florence is all the way in Utah Territory. And Leila? Why, she's making the Panama passage alone probably this

very week. I won't have word of her safe arrival for another month."
She holds out a hand to Little Rose, who's standing uncertainly by the
water closet door. "To have them so windblown . . ."

The girl comes over and crawls onto the bed near her mother, owl
eyes in a little worn face. "I marvel that I now find myself in circumstances so akin to my mother's. Widowed. Though thankfully not five
daughters. Only f . . . " She gets utterly still. "Only three."

Four daughters is what she began to say. It's on her face, in her ears,
the absence of that word's sound filling up all the space in the room.

> I have a daughter.   I have a mother.
> I had a daughter.   I had a mother.

Such a minute difference in sound. What a devil of pain. I watch as
the widow looks into that pain. I swear, I see her do it. Dares to look
and find her lost daughter in it. "A family tree is a poor metaphor, isn't
it? Trees grow up and out, but we grow back down into the earth." The
widow presses her cheek against Little Rose's head. "When my mother
passed, I was lost. I had become the trunk of the tree, no one between
me and the ground. You feel the weight on you when you get to that
place. It's a true weight, being the one to bear the rest up." She stops.
"I was there feeling so sorry for myself, the trunk of the tree and all,
frightened I was next for the grave. But then." She pauses. "But then
I wasn't next, and that's when I was reminded there's something worse
than leaving this earth, and that's someone else leaving first." She takes
a breath. Catches it, more like. "I don't know your situation." She says
this like an apology, like she doesn't want to presume.

But again, she knows it. Pinkerton made sure she thought I lost
a child.

Tit-for-tat. "Mary Alice," I say, giving my mother's name as if it's
my lost child's.

"Mary Alice," repeats the widow. "She was your only one?" It hurts,
her saying the name. The whole thing hurts, doing what I'm doing.

"Just the one." I feel my mam in my chest. "I was left behind," I whisper and then cover my lips with my hand. But when I look at the widow, it's her who's weeping. Caught up with her own ghost: the girl she dared to see.

"I blame myself," she says, and then sobs start coming hard, grating up out of her like each one is clawing its way out. "My Gertie!" It's a girl who screeches the name, not the widow. Not the woman I've come to know, but a girl slamming her fists against the woman she's trapped in, the woman who lives in a world where such grief can happen. Her body heaves, utterly overtaken by Gertrude's ghost, unformed sounds and moans spilling out, her eyes streaming, joined by spill from her nose.

And I take her up. I gather the widow's body into mine, holding her together. Little Rose lunges into us, knee cracking on her mother's jaw, awkward and desperate, wanting solace for her sadness at seeing her mother weep. I rock them. A lullaby coming out on an exhale, without me even thinking to do it. I'm rocking myself, too. And my mother. She's here in my arms as well. I rock us all back from hell.

———

We're tangled in on one another, a heap of starched white that breathes lavender. The widow reaches out a hand and picks up the end of my plaits again, its gentle weight joining us. "You have the same fine hair as Gertrude," she says.

Her tears are spent. Little Rose's too. So wholly spent is Little Rose, in truth, she's snoring atop my leg.

It's time. Time for me to crack her open. For a moment, Scobell's voice is in my ear. *You got one hard heart, Mrs. Warne.* I push that voice away.

I look into the widow's eyes, a deep concern in mine. "Ma'am, why are you still here in Washington? Now's the time to look to your blood. To go to the daughters you have left."

The widow's breath gets jagged with feeling. "It's too late."

I lie. "It's not too late. The men—my colleagues—will do anything for your cipher key." I get still. "Their plan is to take your little girl away. Force your hand. They think it's the only way. Tomorrow morning, they're going to take her like they did the Mackalls." I can feel the fear rippling off the widow. "But I could help you. Please. I know what it's like to lose a . . ." I let my words hang a moment, then I go on. "I could help you work your advantage. I can convince the men. Arrange to get you and Little Rose out of the city. Bring you to your other daughters in Utah Territory."

The widow looks at Little Rose snoring her little snores, her arms loose about her head.

"You don't trust Pinkerton," I whisper. "But you can trust me. All I need is the cipher key, and I can make it happen." I say it softly, knowing full well the moment she hands it over, we'll have the evidence to put her before a judge. Most likely she'll be hauled off to prison immediately. "You're the tree that must shelter your girls from harm."

She takes a sharp inhale. "I can trust you?"

"Yes."

She's staring at Little Rose, but her thoughts are somewhere deep inside herself. "Thank you." Her words are no more than whispers. "Thank you for . . ." She takes a quick breath and looks around as if realizing where she is. "You're sleeping in the library? It's hardly suited for sleeping." She pushes a pillow toward me. "Stay here tonight." The widow looks at the bedroom door, her eyes betraying her trepidation at the men beyond it. "I'll feel safer knowing you're with us." It makes sense with what I've made her believe. The widow starts tucking herself into her own pillow, readying to sleep.

So, I lie down where I have been offered. All I smell is lavender. I glance over at the widow. Her limbs are folded in around her, locked in, curled tight. Little Rose is still snoring. Soon the widow's sleep sounds join hers. Tucked into the bed with them, I feel a swell of feeling. Tears threaten to well up in my eyes, I don't know why. Maybe it's because I have won.

— Sixteen —

I sleep a dreamless, drink-heavy sleep. No, there was one dream. My mother, in the bed, as she was the last day I saw her.

"Leave, mo chroí," my mam whispered. "I'm going soon."

"I'll go with you," I whispered back. "We'll be together always."

In the dream, she rose and cut me down like a tree. Felling me at my roots.

In the widow's bedroom, I stutter into waking, shaking the dream off. I've won, I remind myself.

The widow and Little Rose are just stirring when I duck out of the room to gather fresh clothes from the library. No one's on guard outside the widow's door. With me inside, it was unnecessary.

Scobell is in the library, already back up the rolling ladder, still hunting for the cipher. "You look like an egg meringue," he says.

My thoughts are dull and plodding after last night's indulgence. My nightdress, he means: like a billowy, white meringue. Sweet liquor is the worst. "Right."

There's a little spark in his eye, like he's about to say something else. But then he seems to think better of it and closes up his face. He turns back to the books. It cuts me, even just a little thing like him turning away.

"I did it," I whisper. I want to prove I was right—us separating was necessary not just for his safety, but for the work. "I broke her."

He freezes on the ladder. "You have the cipher key?" he mouths.

"Getting it this morning," I say. I push away any misgivings at my lies to the widow. It's not my job to think about that.

Scobell sighs. "Thank the Lord."

Then two things happen at the same time.

First thing: I go to change into my other dress over by the library fireplace and notice the hearth stones are warm. More than August-morning warm.

Second thing: Scobell slides the ladder along the bookcase in celebration. There's a clunk as it bumps against the desk chair, once again in its path.

"Goddamn it," he mutters.

I sort of half turn toward him, my thoughts still on the fireplace. "It wasn't me left the chair in the way this time," I defend. "I was in the widow's room all night."

He sucks his teeth. "No one else has been up here, and I'd know if I moved the damn chair."

I'm not listening to him. I'm looking at a tiny pile of ash underneath the fire grate—which is also warm. Very warm.

We both get there at the same moment: someone besides us has been in the library. Scobell's eyes get wide.

"Oh hell," I whisper.

"But you were with the widow last night?" Scobell asks hotly. "All night, yeah?"

"All night."

Scobell nods, but then hesitates. "There any way she could have left the room without you waking?"

A drink-heavy sleep.

Oh Lord. The hair. The nightdresses. Crying over her daughter.

She was laying common ground.

Then she got me drunk on brandy and heartache, wedging herself right into my heart.

Sleep here tonight, she told me. Wagering if I slept in the room, no guard would be posted outside the door. Once I was asleep, she must have snuck into the library and burned what we hadn't yet found. The cipher key.

I believed we were playing a tit-for-tat game. And we were. Hers. I thought I was acting the part of a lost daughter. But she was acting too.

I trusted her. And she beat me.

I stalk into the widow's bedroom. She's just rising from the bed. I back her up against it until she's forced to sit.

"Why, Kate," she says, as cool as the first moment I met her. "Distress does your complexion no favors."

Everything, the heartfelt confidences, the promise to hand over the cipher key, it was a performance staged to convince me I had broken her. Goddamn, but I'm a fool. "Shut up," I snap.

Little Rose is near the bed, wearing a pair of her mother's slippers. She's frozen now, eyes on us.

"You believe I'd trust you?" the widow says calmly. "You lie about everything you are. Your Irish accent. Your humility. I doubt you bore a child. And you certainly haven't lost one or you'd never have the indecency to use my loss against me."

"Shut up!" I say louder. I hear footsteps in the hall, know them certainly for Scobell's.

She smiles easily. "Poor thing. Outplayed at her own game." She's still in her nightdress, her hair in the messy plaits Little Rose made. "You think you're a ruthless spy, but you're weak and wanting in every way. No family, no society, no looks, no husband, and now that you've failed with me, not even your apish spymaster. Just a sad little stray."

"Shut your mouth!" I scream. Fury roars up through me. I will show her how ruthless I am. In a moment, I'm out the doorway, running to a dead girl's bedroom.

The widow guesses where I've gone because suddenly she shouts, "No!" and it's not her smooth, managed voice any longer. It's something raw coming up out of her. "Please, no!"

But I'm already in Gertrude's room. And the lamp's smashed to the ground, spraying shards out across the rug like shattered ice. I swing the chair like an ax, finding the dressing table, perfume bottles spilling the dead girl's scent all over the floor. I take up a splintered chair leg to smash the bristle brush and its long brown hairs. I tear at the drawers, pulling them clean out of the chest, flinging their contents to the floor. Needles of glass tumble with linens and silks. And finally I take up the portrait of the dead girl, bringing it down atop the bedpost, the torn canvas like a crown of thorns.

Because she cracked me open. Last night and again just now.

The memory that stirred my dream last night comes to me, clear and sharp. The final day with my mam back in Ireland. I woke that morning, but the bed was cold—my mam no longer beside me. My heart seized with terror that the dogs had finally come. That they'd dragged her away. But I found her just outside our home, leaning against the door.

"Come here, my heart," she whispered, her whole body heaving with the effort to speak. "You must leave if you're to live."

I clutched at her legs. "I never will."

"I know it," she said and cupped my little face in her hand. "Fetch me a drink?"

I ran to the well and started to turn the handle to raise the bucket. Behind me, I heard the door shut. And the bar fall into place.

I scrambled back to our home, my heart thumping against my rib cage. I pulled with my whole strength. But the door wouldn't move; she had locked me out. My own mam, barring me from her side.

I scratched and dug at the wood, kicking and snarling, trying to claw my way back to my mam. I screamed. Screeched her name. Wailed. Wept. Wherever she was going in our little farmhouse, I wanted to be with her, warm in the bed, sailing off into the unknown together. She was all there was of love. The rest was feral teeth, scavenging, surviving. My fingers bled, slivers driven under the nails. Was the worst thing dying, or was it surviving alone?

The widow named my terror and my failure. I am still a broken little girl, and those I love will always abandon me. But if I can destroy the widow, I can destroy that truth too.

I hear the widow's heavy, catching sobs from the doorway. I turn, but it's not just her. Little Rose is there, too, beside her mother, looking at the wreckage of her sister's room. Her eyes meet mine, her face open in terrible sorrow.

My breath drops out. The girl looks to me, the question all over her face: How could I do such a thing?

I can't bear her eyes on me. I run. I run for the door, bumping against the widow in my haste, but hardly caring. I need to get away from the girl's look. I make it out of the room, and then Scobell is there and Pinkerton, and they've got me by the arms as I kick and scratch, desperate to get away from a little girl's pain.

Part Two

— Seventeen —

August ends. In September 1861, the fighting moves into Kentucky. The rebels take Lexington. The Union waits for Major General McClellan to make his move. They wait and wait. Then they wait some more.

In Washington, white army tents fill every open space, like mushrooms after a rain. Fortifications, gun batteries, and rifle pits surround the city. At breakfast and suppertime, smoke from army cookfires casts a haze across the horizon. Nighttime, the streets are raucous with Union Army soldiers on the drink. They tried to shut down the sale of liquor in Washington, but you can't keep people from a golden goose. Liquor's sold out of every back window and false wagon bottom.

Bawdy houses, too, have sprung up across the city, providing "horizontal refreshments" (along with the clap and the pox). All manner of Ladies Aid Societies stalk the streets with signs warning of the dangers of such sin. Indeed, for every woman offering to succor a man's body, there's another directing his soul to salvation.

It's a changed city. Yet alongside the changing landscape and looming threat of attack, threads of normal life persevere. Late summer fruits need preserving. A child outgrows a pair of shoes and needs new ones. Someone has a birthday. A bugle reveille startles a goat foraging in the muck on Pennsylvania Avenue. A maid carrying eggs for a wedding cake skirts around a newly dug rifle pit. Life carries on, as it must.

As for me, after what I did in the dead girl's room, I'm just a broken mess, not anything solid enough to make up a person. Pinkerton fixes his eyes on me: "Bangs."

Scobell helps me out of the widow's house to the carriage. As we walk, I wonder if this is our last moment together, him walking me out. New terror charges into my heart. *God, don't let this be it.*

Benjamin Early drives me to Pinkerton's hotel. He tells the hotel manager I'm suffering from "female fatigue."

I lie in Pinkerton's hotel room for two days, just staring at the ceiling. Pinkerton stays elsewhere. It's a small, plain room marked by the woody scent of Pinkerton's hair oil. There's no amenities other than a feather pillow, a lamp on the bedside table, and a wooden cross nailed to the wall.

I lie in the bed trying to think on anything but the widow's words to me. On anything but Little Rose's grief-struck face. Every time I close my eyes, I see a dead girl's portrait torn apart. I hear a bar falling into place on a door in a dying land so many years ago. I clutch myself tight, wishing it were Scobell's arms around me and wonder how my heart hasn't split apart at the seams.

The second night, I finally fall asleep. I wrestle through dreams filled with dogs scratching at the door. They bark and snap and scrabble against the wood until suddenly, with a sharp splinter, they're inside. Hot, sour breath is against my skin. Panting all around. I try to fight them off, but two get hold of my legs and pull me from the bed. Others lunge in. My mam calls out, "Mary Kate!" I scrabble back across the floor to her, but a dog has my leg and is pulling me away. I look at the dog and its face is the widow's, olive skin glowing. The door slams shut between my mam and me. I hurl myself at it, trying to get back to her. Then it's Scobell behind the door, and I'm fighting to reach him. Suddenly a snarl comes out of my own lips. I look down and realize with terror that I've become the dog.

I wake in the morning with a startle, wet with sweat and my breath heaving. It's an overcast day, dull white light coming in the window. I can smell myself where I lie. Sweat-stink and unwashed skin and the faintest whiff of lavender. That's what finally gets me up.

I go down the hall to the little bathing room and fill the tin tub. I undress and sink into the water, trying to work out what all's happened to me. I guess I tried to take the sad, wounded little girl I was and rewrite her over as a hunter. *The rule of the desperate: the strongest survive.* But it didn't work. I thought I could erase my old story, replace it with a new one, but it's all still there: a jumble of lived stories and longed-for fictions, scribbled atop each other.

The widow found that girl beneath the surface and teased her out, loosening a history of longing, envy, loneliness. A soft heart at my core. The terror at what she opened up was too much. It turned to hate. It turned to fury.

My fury did its job; it swept me out of the feelings crushing down on me. It burned the ache to ash. But it left me with something worse. The shame of a little girl's sorrow. The truth that I don't know who I am. Hunter or prey? Pinkerton Kate Warne or the poor paddy orphan Mary Kate Heaney? One thing I do know: I'm still alone.

The bathing room is just a bare-walled little closet. There's a stool for undressing, two hooks for clothing, and a tiny ledge with a lamp, a bar of strong soap and a brush. I take the soap and brush, and I scrub my every inch. I scrub off the stink. I scrub off the lavender. Then I scrub more.

It's like I'm trying to rub out all my past stories with the dead skin. But there's so much on me: The years trying to prove myself to Pinkerton. My betrayal of Mrs. Maroney. The failed protest with Consider Pritchett.

I scrub until my skin is as red and raw as uncooked meat. I don't stop. I want to grind it all away. Nabby Fife calling me a dirty paddy. The piled minutes of the cotton mill. The Sullivans who I lived with when I came to America. The last lingering images of my mam and my pap.

The only one I don't scrub off is Scobell. I keep him locked up tight in the back of my heart. He's the only story I don't want to give up.

At long last, I rinse. Wipe myself dry. I return to the room.

I lay on the bed naked, my skin burning, wishing I could be just this: a bare human. Not prey or a hunter.

Not a mill girl or a Pinkerton.

Not an immigrant or a Yank.

Not an orphan or a daughter.

Not soft-hearted or hard-hearted.

Not Mary Kate Heaney or Kate Warne. Just a bare, human body. A blank page.

———

Pinkerton comes to see me the following day. He pounds on the door like a landlady wanting rent. I prepare for a tongue-lashing. I prepare to be fired.

Pinkerton walks past me into the room, his hat still on, and says quietly, "We need you."

I stay where I am, seated on the bed in my plain dress, eyes on the cross nailed to the wall. "I failed" is all I can answer.

"She beat you," he agrees solemnly. "Same as she did Lewis." His tone is altogether unlike him. No hollering. No fury.

"What is it?" I ask, suddenly alert. "What's happened?"

He takes off his hat and holds it at his chest like at a funeral. "Newspapers made the story of the widow's arrest. Same morning she burned the cipher key."

We were too late. Even had I got the cipher key, the rebels would have received the news of the widow's arrest and changed it. But it still doesn't reason that he's so calm. "I let you down. I thought I could—"

"You think you let me down?!" he erupts. "You put a fear in her! She was in a proper state over what you did to that dead girl's room. Couldn't put two words together after it. She's not trying any more foolishness." He shakes his head. "Didn't think you had it in you. You proved yourself, girl." He puts his hat back on. "I'm sending you to Richmond. I got a job for you at the Confederate White House."

I can't hardly believe what I'm hearing. I figured I'd be let go. Instead, it seems I'm promoted. And for what I did to Gertrude's room. A cold sweat of shame runs down my spine. Can't he see the Kate Warne who did that is a sham? Just a trumped-up fiction to disguise all my weaknesses and failings.

And yet here he is giving me everything I always wanted. Pinkerton's no fool. A *rare specimen*. Maybe I'm the one who's got it wrong. Maybe this is what strength feels like. My unease is just the growing pains of finally letting go of the past and becoming someone new. "What's the job?" I ask tentatively.

"A note came through McClellan's office. Someone claiming to have access to the Davis family home and intelligence to share. A potential source," he finishes.

"Or a trap."

"Exactly. You won't know until you meet them. Varina Davis is holding a reception for the Orphan Relief Society in two weeks. She's carting in children from the Episcopalian orphanage to show off her generous Confederate heart. There'll be musicians, provisioners, decorators, orphan minders . . . it'll be a regular circus."

"Surely there'll be security," I say.

"Surely," he says back. "But it may be the only time the contact knows they can meet. Might be a slave." In Richmond, enslaved people need a pass just to cross the street. "Hattie and Webster are well known in Richmond. I need an unfamiliar face—who's not afraid of the risks."

It's risky to be sure. The Confederate White House isn't just Jefferson Davis's home. According to Webster's intelligence, it's also Davis's office and meeting place—the tactical center of the Confederacy. The value of a source with access to that house is immeasurable. My heart's already thumping, the heaviness of the last two days burning away with anticipation. This is the work I always hoped for. This is who I've aimed to be. I guess I'm accepting the job.

"You won't know what you're walking into until you're there,"

Pinkerton warns. "You'll travel with one of our couriers. He'll be your help if it goes bad."

I nod. I'm half hoping he assigns Scobell just for a chance to see him and half praying he doesn't, for Scobell's safety.

"Well?" Pinkerton prods.

"I'll do it," I tell him.

"Then be in the office tomorrow morning!" he practically shouts. He goes toward the door, then turns and waves his hand at the bed. "And I want my room back!"

— Eighteen —

A little after dawn the next morning, I arrive at Pinkerton's wartime offices. George Bangs, the manager, is already there. Bangs is as fastidious as they come. An indoor cat, so to speak. He wears a neat little tie and a neat little shirt, into which he tucks a neat little napkin each day for lunch, which he takes at his desk. He keeps himself pulled in tight, viewing the world as if through a glass window. He greets me reservedly, eyes flitting up and down my dress, taking in my traveling boots and bag. "I've brewed tea," he offers.

"She can take her tea while we talk!" Pinkerton barks from the back room.

I follow the voice to find Pinkerton at his desk; Tully is seated opposite. So, Tully's my partner on the job.

"Cheese makers," Pinkerton announces as I sit next to Tully. Bangs pours my tea. "A married couple with a cottage industry. You began making your own, but now you collect cheeses from widows and homemakers in the region of Washington, Maryland, and Virginia, and sell them in the city market of Richmond." He unfolds a map showing the enemy lines and our route. "You carry a small, perishable load, so you make regular border crossings. You're a public good because you're supporting war widows and the like on both sides. And you're unsuspicious because there's a woman involved." Pinkerton, Tully, and Bangs look at me. "You got to cover ten miles a day to make it in time for Mrs. Davis's reception."

"And once we get to Richmond?" I ask.

"Cheese delivery for the reception is your pretext. We don't know who the source is. Your job is to find them and decide if they're trustworthy. If they are, establish a drop site where they can leave intelligence. If it's all a ruse . . ." Pinkerton gives a long, slow exhale. "Tully will have the wagon waiting." He looks me in the eye. "Listen to your gut, and be ready to run for it."

I nod.

"And Tully's not just transport," Pinkerton goes on. "He'll be making the drops for the field agents from now on." Tully has often done courier work, leaving supplies and picking up intelligence. "Three drops: one for Webster and Hattie, one for Lewis, and one for Scobell."

"Scobell?" I say, as light as I can manage.

Pinkerton nods. "I've posted him to Richmond too."

The next morning, Tully and I are on the road. We travel by steamboat down the Potomac to Aquia near Fredericksburg. From there we continue by horse and wagon.

Wagon travel proves laborious and uncomfortable. Traveling with Tully even more so. He's poor-tempered in the mornings, driving the wagon sullenly beside me, until the dregs of sleep finally fall away. Then it's fits and starts of sociability, always studded with his nasty little jibes. But we cross the Confederate line with little trouble. The guards look at our pass, poke around under the canvas sheet covering our load, while I fret over the day's heat ruining our cheese. The graybacks wave us through, eyes already on the next wagon coming into rebel territory.

"It was always thorny," Tully tells me, once we're well clear of the line and back on quiet road again. "Me traveling alone, as a courier," he clarifies. "I used to pose as a railroad map publisher. Bringing maps to train depots and stations along the line from Fredericksburg to Richmond. One time through, I was given a proper interrogation, rebs rifling through my bags, all of it. And there I was, sweating like a pig, because the messages I was transporting were worked right into the maps. All it would've taken was one border guard with an instinct for code-breaking." Tully shakes his head. "Much safer this way. They hardly bother if there's a woman present, so long as she isn't a looker."

"Shut it, Tully," I snap.

He sucks his teeth. "You should feel fortunate. Can actually do your job instead of men pawing after you day and night. Girls think pretty is a gift. Not always." His eyes are staring at the road, locked on something in his past.

I wonder if Scobell is on the road too. I imagine him crossing the border, making his way to Richmond. I wonder what his disguise is, praying it's good. Whatever danger there is for us, it's tenfold for him.

Tully interrupts my thoughts. "Did you hear how the widow did it? Got the message to General Beauregard that won them the battle of Manassas at Bull Run?" Poor nature aside, Tully's a bit of a gossip. "Dairymaid." Tully raises his eyebrows in a lewd expression. "Some young cousin or friend of the widow posing with a cart of milk jugs. The Union sentinels let her cross over the Potomac. Not a one giving her a moment's thought. She drove that milk cart right up to the Confederates, a message tucked into her hair." Tully nods with satisfaction. "That's why Pinkerton wants you on this job. No one notices a woman."

At night, Tully and I share a room since we're playing husband and wife. I wonder the first night if he'll give me the bed and take the floor. He doesn't. We sleep head to toe as I once did as a girl with the Sullivan family.

Tully doesn't snore, but he does call out in his sleep. Shrieks and cries nearly every night in a voice years younger than his. His morning sullenness starts to make sense. Still shaking off past ghosts come to call in his sleep. We never speak of it. He doesn't offer, and I don't ask. Not about his cries or if I do the same.

It's seventy miles, give or take, between Fredericksburg and Richmond. Our horse, Peanut, is a beast of an animal. Tully says he's mild as horses go, but all I see is fifteen hundred pounds of muscle with hooves like hammers and big yellow teeth. I steer clear of him, letting Tully handle his hitching and unhitching. One morning, walking to the wagon, Peanut gives a big snort right near my head. It startles me half to death.

Tully laughs at my jumpiness. "You haven't never been around horses?"

"Tremont Cotton Mill didn't offer lessons in horsemanship," I snap.

I climb on the wagon, and we get started. We've been fortunate with weather, but it's still slow going. Peanut's pace is not what you'd call fleet. "Can't Peanut go any faster?" I gripe.

"Peanut's pulling the both of us, plus the cheese, and you should be grateful. He's not a machine."

"I wish he were."

"You know," says Tully, "how a person relates to animals reveals everything about their personal character." He looks knowingly at me. "Your relations to Peanut, for example. Fear. Antagonism."

"That's a bunch of horseshit," I tell Tully back.

"Come on, didn't you never have a cat or a dog? I had a fine cat once. A fine mouser, she was. Would curl right up in my lap too."

The only people I knew with pets in my life were the boss's wives at Tremont. Had little pampered dogs and the like, bred for nothing but their curled ears or long fur. We'd pass the wives in their gardens as we walked to and from our dinner break, their dogs shivering nervously among the flowers, mustering the occasional shrill bark. They were better cared for than us mill girls, to be sure. The wives brushing their hair, feeding them meat, adorning them with ribbons and collars. I once asked another mill girl why anyone would waste a ribbon on a dog. She told me it was in case they ran off. People would know they belonged to someone. People would know they were precious. Like a ribbon rosetta at a girl's neck. My thoughts go back to the widow's words to me. *Sad little stray.* I wonder if she regrets saying those words now.

Tully takes my quiet as proof of his point. We ride on in sullen silence.

We arrive in Richmond the day before Varina Davis's orphan reception. Tully and I divide the agent drops between us. I leave news and money for Pryce Lewis with a hotel manager, collecting his field report from the last few weeks. Tully visits a tobacconist who serves as Timothy Webster and Hattie Lawton's drop. Tully and I meet up in the afternoon. "You want to do the last one?" It's Scobell's. The drop's with a cook at a rough sort of tavern.

I hesitate. "You ever see him at the drop?"

"Sometimes," he says. "We might pass a minute together."

"You do it," I say. It'll be too hard to see him. And I don't need any distractions from my work.

I spend the afternoon at a teahouse, making myself useful listening to the talk. Three people mention the upcoming reception at the "Gray House" as they call the Davis home. It sounds like it'll be a whole song and dance. I know the kind. At Christmas in the mills, the boss's wives would make a show of coming by and donating their castoff clothes and toys to us workers. Some mill girl would be pressed into making a speech of gratitude, even though it was our sweat that allowed those wives luxury enough to spare castoffs. Varina Davis's reception seems about the same. The reception will begin with speeches by the wealthy ladies of Richmond, after which the orphans will sing a song. Singing for their supper and all.

The biggest gossip is Varina Davis's audacity at hosting a party while visibly with child. As if she, a mother three times over and first lady of the Confederacy, should just hide out in her room for half a year. Despite such grievous impropriety on the host's part, the reception remains the social event of the month. A big crowd will be safer for me. But it could make it harder to find the source.

Tully returns from Scobell's drop. He doesn't say anything about it. I pretend I'm not aching with interest. We drive the wagon in silence down K Street past the Davis house. I take in as much as I can. The house is three stories with thick columns all across the front. A fence rings the property. There's a gate to an outbuilding kitchen at the side of the house. That'll surely be where provisions are delivered for the party.

Meanwhile, Tully's surveying the roads, looking for the best escape route if I'm suspected. "I'll need to keep the wagon a little ways out," he concludes. "Don't want to get stuck in among the carriages coming for the reception." He settles on a spot about a quarter mile away. I recall Pinkerton's words: *Be ready to run for it.*

"How fast can this horse go if pushed?" I ask.

"I'll take care of Peanut," Tully snips. "You take care you're not discovered."

The following morning, I can barely get down any breakfast, I'm so edgy with nerves. Midmorning, Tully and I take one last pass by the Davis House. The gate near the kitchen is open, and there's already people afoot making preparations for the midday reception.

Tully parks the wagon alongside the house and helps me unload a fifteen-pound wheel of cheese. He's about to go, then stops. "You want me to pass on a message to someone, in the case, you know . . ." He pauses. " . . . it goes to hell?"

Scobell comes into my head. I push him out. "I don't have a someone."

Tully nods. "I'll be waiting down the road."

I cross through the gate to the outdoor kitchen, carrying my cheese. A few maids and such are moving between the kitchen and the house, ferrying platters and dishes. I stay to the side of the flow for a moment, taking everything in. This is the difficult part. I need to attract the source's attention but not raise any alarm.

I shift the cheese in my arms. The thing's heavy, even for a former mill worker. I watch the servants going to and fro. Some are household slaves, some look to be hired Irish. The source will be searching for a stranger, and, not being a professional spy, probably won't be clever about hiding their attention. A few of the servants throw me a quick glance, but no one's eyes linger.

I make my way to the kitchen door and take a peek. Inside is a steaming clamor. Three cooks are furiously working. Handing off pans. Calling out directions. Cursing one another.

"I got a cheese," I call out, knowing it sounds inane but needing a way to test their interest.

"Bully for you!" one of the cooks calls without so much as looking up from her cookpot.

The others give me hardly more attention. Not a cook.

Leaving the kitchen, I nearly bump into a woman coming in. She's young, in a maid's apron. "Who are you?" she asks baldly.

I lift the cheese in answer.

"What's that?" She eyes me.

"It's a donation," I say. "For Mrs. Davis and her Orphan Relief Society."

She considers me. "A donation?"

"And maybe if Mrs. Davis likes it, she'll buy from us in future times." A little self-interest makes anything less suspicious.

"Oh." The maid's face opens up like my presence all seems perfectly reasonable now. "Mrs. O'Melia receives all donations," the maid says, picking up a platter of cold meat. "She's the housekeeper. This way."

I shift the cheese in my arms and follow her toward the servants' entrance to the house.

"And what do I call you?" the maid asks as we walk.

"Ellen," I say back. "Ellen the cheese girl will do."

She laughs and leads me through the threshold into the house. She takes me to a small office just inside, its desk piled with ledger books and receipts.

"I'll nip up and fetch Mrs. O'Melia," says the maid, gesturing her meat platter toward a narrow staircase up to the main floor. Jovial chatter and sounds of music filter down from it.

I wait in the housekeeper's office, trying to calm my banging heart. I imagine the Confederate officers two floors above me in Davis's office, planning the very next moves of this war. If we could get a spy with access to this house, it could change the whole thing.

But of course, those same officers could sniff me out. Haul me off to prison. Or worse. I hear steps on the stairs and peek out to see who's coming down.

It's a ruddy-faced, middle-aged woman with broad cheekbones and curly dark hair under a housekeeper cap. A circle of keys hangs from a cord at her waist. She marches smartly into the office, placing her hands on the desk possessively. "And what's this now about a cheese?" she asks in a strong Irish accent.

I show the wheel in my arms. "We heard about Mrs. Davis's generous reception for the orphans."

She sizes me up. "I haven't seen you before, have I?"

"My husband and me, our dairy's up by Fredericksburg. This is my first occasion to the Gray House. My, but it's a fine house," I say, wide-eyed. I glance to the cheese. "It's not much, but we wanted to, you know, do what we could for the Cause."

She seems to accept my story. "You can place it here." She pats her desk. "Or rather . . ." She pauses and licks her lips, thinking a moment. "Perhaps . . ." She considers some more. All at once, her face pulls into a taut smile. "Mrs. Davis will want to thank you for your generosity. Why don't you wait here while I see about it."

I weigh her change of mind. Is she just overwhelmed by reception preparations? Or is she suspicious and planning to alert someone? She's already bustling out the door. Hell, I don't know what to do. "Stay right there," she calls back.

I put the cheese on my hip and go into the corridor. A quick look says the rest of the floor is servant quarters. I plant myself by the back door so I can surveil the premises better—and so I'm well positioned if I need to run.

A tall servant comes in from the outdoor kitchen with a tray of cakes. He sidles by me and up the stairs. I hear him murmur to someone else coming down. It's a woman holding an armful of empty cloth sacks like tailors use to cover dresses. The woman glances at me as she leaves.

Then she stops and returns to the doorway. She looks at the cheese and back at me. "That for the party?"

"Yes," I say. "Came to town just to deliver it."

The woman looks around her. She's Black, with full cheeks and bright round eyes. She seems to be about my age. "I dropped off party dresses earlier from the seamstress down the street. They let me stay

THE WIDOW SPY   171

and enjoy a cup of punch with the servants." She's lingering. She could definitely be my source.

I say back: "The tailor down the street must be a fine place if it's used by Mrs. Varina Davis herself."

"It's frequented by her and many other fine ladies." The woman goes on carefully, "We're always very busy, wish we had help with deliveries."

It's her. It's certainly her. "Seamstress down the street," I repeat.

She glances around her again and then sticks out her hand. She looks at me keenly. For a moment, I don't grasp what she's doing. Then I remember Consider Pritchett—she's offering me her hand to shake. It's a sort of test to see if I'm the right person. I reach out, grasp her hand, and squeeze. Something small and soft comes into her eyes: hope. "Ask for Mary," she says, then turns and goes.

I make to go, too, when a voice rings out from inside the house. "Hold up just a moment!" It's Mrs. O'Melia, the housekeeper, coming down the stairs.

I confirm that my source is safely gone, then look back into the house. I can just make out a backlit figure coming down the stairs behind the housekeeper. "I've fetched Mrs. Davis to thank you!" she calls.

She's lying. No heavily pregnant woman is stepping down those steep stairs to thank anyone. Whoever the figure is behind her, they're not coming with good news.

"Can't stay. Apologies!" I rush out the door.

"She ran!" I hear behind me.

There's a servant carrying a tray of custards coming toward me. I launch the cheese at his knees as I pass, causing him to fall in front of the doorway with a crash of glass and pudding.

As I tear around the corner of the house, I look back to see a man in Confederate uniform just clambering over the fallen servant to chase after me.

I'm almost through the gate. Up ahead, I can see all sorts of fancy people arriving for the reception. Carriages already jam the road. Street vendors, too, drawn by the crowd.

All at once, I realize the stupidity of Tully's plan. There's a quarter mile of road between me and the wagon, and the man behind me isn't running in a dress. I'll need to lose him in the mess of people and carriages out front of the Davis house.

I make it through the gate and into the road. I dart behind an empty parked carriage and peer through the wheels back at the gate. The Confederate officer comes out. He takes in the jumble of people with dismay. But then he starts into the melee, headed in my direction.

Just then, a man vending candies steps up to the very carriage I'm hiding behind. "Bonbons," he shouts. He'll see me in a moment and wonder what a woman is doing crouched down.

I start to move, but then through the wheels, I see the Confederate officer skirting around the carriage next to mine. He's almost reached me.

The vendor is suddenly right at my side. I look up to beg him not to say anything and get a hell of a surprise.

It's Scobell.

"Bonbons!" he calls outward, while he nudges me with his foot under the carriage. I drop to the dirt and roll underneath. I watch the officer's boots come around the side of the carriage where I was lately hiding. "Candies, Officer?" Scobell calls to him. The boots keep walking.

I'm not one for prayer, but I pray now in thanks for Scobell. He squats and sticks his hand under the carriage. I grab it, and he hauls me out.

"Stay low," he whispers. He leads me through the warren of coupes, carriages, and shays: me, crouched, holding up my skirts, breathing hard; him checking for the Confederate officer. When he signals, we dash across a bit of open road and turn the corner. "Tully's too out in the open," Scobell says. "I got somewhere for you."

I don't know where he's got; it's all fine houses and stately manors around us. Scobell walks ahead of me. I brush the dirt from my skirt shakily and hurry after.

He takes me down a small lane behind one of the great houses. "Wait here a minute," he directs, then jogs back the way we came. He returns a moment later. "No one's following. Come on."

I trail him farther down the alley. I'm eager to ask what all he was doing outside the Davis house. How'd he know to come? How'd he see the trouble I was in?

We stop at a carriage house. "Wait here," he says again. He gives a knock on the door and disappears inside. I hear murmurs. A moment after, a groom puts his head out. He's an older man, skin a deep black, a full beard on his chin. He sees me and curses under his breath.

He goes back inside. I hear his and Scobell's voices again. The groom's tone is sharp and wrathy. He swings out the door, shaking his head. "Not too long," he calls to Scobell. He doesn't look at me at all.

Scobell waves me inside the carriage house. It's warm and smells like hay. There's not much light, but I see a carriage filling up one side, two stalls with horses in them on the other. One of them snorts softly.

There's a small stool in the corner by the stalls. I drop onto it. My legs are shaking. My hands too.

"Did the officer see your face?" Scobell asks quietly.

"I don't know. Maybe," I answer. "The housekeeper sure as hell did." I sit on my hands to stop them from shaking. "What were you doing there?"

Scobell leans against the horse stall but keeps watch on the carriage house door. "Saw Tully at my drop yesterday. He told me the plan. Sounded risky. Thought you could use extra eyes."

"What you did was risky!" I whisper back. "What if that officer suspected you?"

"I don't hear a thank-you," Scobell says with the hint of a smile.

The man's joking. And not ten minutes after we lost a Confederate tail. "Maybe I'd rather you in one piece," I snap.

"So you do care?" He turns to me.

"Of course I care!" I hiss.

"You've got a way with misdirection, Mrs. Warne."

"You saved me," I tell him. "And I'm just trying to protect you."

"I didn't ask for you to protect me!"

"And I didn't ask for you to come to the Confederate White House and get yourself caught up in my danger!"

All his breath sighs out. "It's been so long since I seen you. I don't want to fight." He checks the carriage door again.

We're quiet a minute. A horse stomps. Scobell reaches a hand over the stall door and pats its nose.

I look at him. His eyes are gentle as he gives the horse a scratch. It fills something up in me to see him. "How are you?" I ask lamely.

He looks back at me. "Boarding house has bedbugs. Itch like hell."

I laugh at the everydayness of it.

His eyes return to the horse. He scratches down its neck. "Saw my wife."

"Oh?" My heart clenches.

"She's got someone. New man." His eyes stay on the horse.

I gird myself and ask. "It hurt?"

"We married young. A lot's changed since. Us both, and, you know, the world. So." He's still looking at the horse. He clears his throat. "I guess it's hard, even if I prefer it this way." The horse lifts its nose to Scobell's. Scobell gently pushes it away. He smiles, but there's grief in his eyes. Loneliness too. "I think on you," he says simply.

I take an uneven breath. "I think on you."

There's a whistle from the carriage door. I startle, but Scobell shakes his head. "That's Henry. If it were trouble, he'd already be gone. He just doesn't want us to stay too long."

I start to get up.

Scobell motions me back down. "Henry can wait." He looks me over like he's learning me. "Passed a man selling fruit the other day. Wondered if you preferred cherries or apples."

"We got so little time, and you're talking fruit?"

"Luxury is talking little things with someone. Don't you think?"

In truth, I don't know. Like I told Tully, I've never had someone. I shake my head. "Everyone likes cherries best."

"Now that's just wrong," Scobell says back. "A good, crisp apple?"

There's another whistle, then a rap on the carriage house door.

Scobell sniffs. "I guess we got to be moving."

I stand, and for a moment we're face-to-face, our bodies maybe a foot apart. I feel the pull between us, both of us wanting to do something, but unsure. I want to reach out so badly, but I just can't bear the cost.

"I found the source," I say, breaking the pull between us.

"Oh," he says. He gathers himself. "Good. That's good."

Another rap comes at the door.

"Coming," Scobell calls out. He looks back at me, but I don't trust myself to meet his eyes.

— Nineteen —

It takes me a while to cut back to where Tully's waiting with our wagon, but I get there. "Fuck, fuck, fuck, fuck!" Tully chants as I climb in. He whips the horse into a trot. "What took so damn long?" Tully checks over his shoulder to be sure no one's following.

"Scobell happened," I say.

"He wasn't supposed to be here!" Tully ejects.

"I know it. But he got me out of there. I might not have made it otherwise."

Tully checks behind us again. "And the source?"

"Seamstress shop somewhere near the house."

Tully nods. "Hattie can go. You shouldn't show your face here again."

We ride a moment in quiet. My insides are still roiling. It's the exhilaration and terror of the Davis house and all the feeling brought up by seeing Scobell.

Tully drives us back to our boarding house to pack. This evening, we start back for Washington.

An hour or so later, we're on the road, heading out of town. "Don't we need to make a drop to tell Hattie about the source?" I ask Tully.

"No indeed," Tully smirks. "Guess who's staying at the inn with us tonight?"

I look at him in surprise. It's a rare thing to see Webster and Hattie. They've been deep undercover for almost a year now.

"Rebs are sending Webster on some business out of the city and it so happens he and Mrs. Webster"—that's Hattie's disguise—"need to stay over the night." Tully raises his brows. "Webster's in so well with the rebels, he was offered a position as captain in a Confederate regiment. Pinkerton's angling him to become a double agent."

We've got a few hours of travel to the inn. My mind keeps turning back to Scobell—thinking on him and wishing there was some way things could be different.

"What's got you so puckered?" Tully gripes at my mood.

"Nothing," I say, brushing him off.

"Then quit pouting and give us a chat."

A distraction would be good. "You know, I was the one who hired Hattie," I say.

"Mmm," Tully murmurs approvingly at my subject. He's thinking on her soft blond curls, her pretty blue eyes and button mouth.

"Pinkerton asked me to find a second woman for the agency, and I put out an advertisement, and who comes in but Hattie." Tully settles into his seat at the prospect of some good tittle-tattle. "She sat in Pinkerton's front office, acting all chip and plucky. Endeavoring to present herself as the very picture of firm self-possession."

"But she wasn't?" prompts Tully.

"She was trying. She explained she had worked as an actress."

Tully gives me a dirty smile. "Actress, was she? Oh, I bet she was." Actress is about a half step away from prostitute in most minds.

I ignore him. "She took the tea Bangs poured her like men served her hot beverages all the livelong day. Told me she was looking for better pay, and how she had tried at the police department, but they wouldn't hire women. Oh, she was doing her best to be bold, but there was her teacup, held directly in front of her heart." I hold my hand at my chest like a squirrel clutching a nut. "She didn't move it through the whole interview. Not an inch. Didn't take a sip, just clutched it right there in front of her heart like the world's tiniest shield."

"Hah!" Tully cackles. "You read her like a book." Just as Pinkerton had done to me, years before. "Did you tell her?"

"I told her she was telling stories she didn't intend. She thought I meant about being an actress. But then I showed her how her cup betrayed her. She told me she'd be powerfully good when it came to the work. And I said, 'It's always the work.'"

Tully grunts in agreement, then raises his brows. "She say anything else about being an actress?"

"No," I say to dampen his prurient interest. The truth is we did talk on it a little. "At times you might need to play that you're married to another agent," I told Hattie. "That a problem?"

Hattie brushed back a yellow curl. "When you're an actress, miss, you get plenty of practice playing *all* types of roles." Her teacup was now on the table. "I don't shock easily."

I had another question. "There going to be any men from your former 'roles' coming to the offices sniffing after you?"

She shook her head.

"Husband?" I asked.

She shook her head again.

"Father?"

She snorted. Then she said, "And what about your employer?"

"What about him?" I said back.

"Will he be sniffing after me?" she asked bluntly.

"No," I snapped.

"Are you with him?"

"He's married." Hattie's eyes stayed on me like I hadn't answered her. "And he's not the type."

She gave me a look that said: Every man's the type. I guess when you're as pretty as Hattie is, they might be.

A week later, she was a detective. A Chicago paper published an article about Pinkerton's female agents. In it, Pinkerton referred to us both as widows. He also said Hattie had a "spotless character" and that I possessed the masculine attributes of firmness and decision-making, despite being a female, that lent themselves to covert operation in dangerous circumstances.

It was bold of Pinkerton to hire women. Most people in this country view the wage-earning female as straying outside a respectable woman's province (and miles beyond a lady's). And female detectives? We're hardly better than actresses: exposed to the male world, sure to be sullied. Calling us widows helped. It said our virtue didn't require excessive precautions. Unmarried women are a dangerous element, like a cocked gun or a rabid dog. Something's going to happen, sooner or later, and it's going to be bad news. And a married woman has a husband meddling in her affairs. Saying you're a widow, it's almost like saying you've retired from womanhood.

And Hattie did prove powerfully good. She took to the work like a duck to water, playing roles with ease. I'd be lying if I said I wasn't jealous at times.

It's evening when Tully and I finally arrive at the Linden Inn, a fine family establishment with half a dozen rooms about eight miles outside Richmond. Tully handles Peanut while I take our bags inside.

As I pass through the inn's parlor, I spy Webster sitting, smoking a pipe. Hattie's nowhere to be seen. Still, my heart leaps just to see Webster. His dark hair curls around his face, and he's wearing a full beard and mustache. He doesn't acknowledge me, nor I him. He's Richmond society, and I'm just a plain-looking cheesemaker, but I know he's marked me.

I settle Tully and me into our room, then see about getting us some supper. Webster's gone by the time Tully and I tuck into our meal. But two hours later, once all the guests have retired for the night, the inn's owner leads me and Tully to a trapdoor around back.

It goes down to a root cellar. Two hanging oil lamps make so many shadows the room seems almost darker for them. The walls are stained with mold and seeping water, and the corners are stacked with musty-smelling vegetables. But sitting atop two stools in the center of the cellar are Hattie and Webster, and all at once that dim place feels as merry as a Christmas party.

I know Webster by his stellar reputation but have encountered him personally only a handful of times, and usually in circumstances like this. The two of us have never shared a formal introduction or an idle chat, yet he clutches my forearm in greeting, like a comrade in arms. It could not be more contrary to my childhood with its numbing tedium, its deep loneliness. I've dropped in on Webster's life from nowhere, yet his sloping blue eyes greet me as warmly as a friend.

Hattie stands when I turn to her and pulls me into a quick, hard embrace. "Kate," she says in brisk greeting.

She produces a bottle of whiskey and several glasses. "Are we raising a toast in celebration?" She lifts a pretty blond brow.

"We are!" I share the few details of our new source, while Hattie pours drinks all around.

"To Mary," Webster raises his whiskey. "May she prove the death of the Confederacy."

"And to John Scobell," I add. "For coming to my rescue."

"What's this now?" Hattie asks.

I explain Scobell's surprise appearance outside the Davis house. "Didn't need to do it, but he did." I take a sip of whiskey.

Hattie's drink stays in her hand. "He wasn't assigned to help?" She shakes her head. "That's some damn foolishness."

"He got me out of a situation," I say back quick.

"He's a fool to risk himself," Hattie returns. "It was your job to get yourself out of there."

"I know it," I say, feeling defensive of Scobell and me both. "And I might've done it. But he was looking out for me, and I'm grateful."

"Sounds like he's gone soft for you," she says mockingly.

I feel a rage starting to crawl up my insides. "Took guts to do what he did."

"Sounds like you're soft too," she says back.

Tully leans in with a grin. "You two going to fight?"

"Shut it, Tully!" Hattie and me overlap.

He holds up his hands innocently. "Just asking, wasn't I?"

Webster's nursing his drink on the stool. He shifts with a wince.

Hattie's attention darts to him. "Your joints?"

"Stiff." Webster brushes it off. Hattie's eyes stay on him. "They give me trouble time to time," he says to Tully and me. He looks back to Hattie. "Nothing warranting concern." Webster tries for a change in conversation. "Rose Greenhow—we heard about her arrest in Richmond."

Tully launches in, happy to spill the details of the "captivating widow." He tells them about the house arrest, and Lewis getting beat. He's just getting to my part when Hattie interrupts. "Pinkerton didn't use her daughter?"

Webster nods along with the question. "Why didn't he use the girl?"

"I threatened it," I explain. "But it didn't move the mother."

"You took her daughter from her or you threatened to?" Webster clarifies.

"Threatened."

Hattie sucks her teeth.

Tully points to Hattie. "That's what I said."

Hattie swirls the drink in her glass. "I would've taken the girl first thing. Purpled her eye. Pulled a tooth. Let the mother hear the girl screaming. She'd've started talking straightaway."

My stomach turns. I feel slivers under my nails. Hear Little Rose's voice in my head, *Let me stay with my mama.*

Webster drains his whiskey. "Sounds like Pinkerton's losing his edge." He offers the bottle around, but I don't hold out my glass. I'm not feeling like celebrating anymore. The others note my mood shift. There's an awkward moment of quiet.

Tully puffs his lips. "Well, this is a depressing party. Can't someone tell a story or sing a song?"

"How about the time Kate and I first met?" offers Webster. He gives me a conciliatory smile.

"Let's hear it!" Tully claps his hands.

Webster starts it off. "Pinkerton and I were investigating a counterfeiting ring back in Chicago. Trying to find where they were working out of. 1856, it was. We tracked the ring to a likely location, but we needed to surveil the place and catch them in the act. And that's where Kate came into the story." He nods to me to take over.

I try to let go of my pique. "I was rooming in a little establishment, run by a Mrs. Blumenthal. German-born. I was newly come to Chicago and looking for work," I start. "It wasn't a large place. You know the type: foyer, dining room, parlor—all the same room. So, I'm eating supper one night, and this fellow comes in the front door. Nice-looking fellow. He comes in and asks for a room for the week." I look all around. "Seems all right, you say. Nothing irregular in a person booking a room. But here's the thing: The boarding house was clean and all, but still the sort of place that didn't look askance at a foreign accent or a former mill girl who couldn't manage a week's rent all at once. And this man? His wool coat wasn't nothing special, but his shirt beneath? A high-quality, tight-weave linen with a ruffled edge. Something you go to specialty outfit for. And so I'm asking, what's this fancy fellow with his fine linen shirt doing in a boarding house like mine, asking after a room?"

"Mmm." Hattie nods along.

"The matron installs this man in the room above me," I go on. "And that's when things get odder still. It was a quick-made building, didn't keep out sound, and I could hear the footsteps above me when Mr. Linen Shirt crossed the room or sat on the bed."

"You getting to the good part soon?" asks Tully.

"I thought you wanted a story," I snip back.

"I just heard the Irish were natural storytellers and was wondering when we were going to be treated to that," Tully answers. Webster and Hattie both laugh.

"All right, all right." I quicken things up. "Mr. Linen Shirt spent the night watching out the window. I could tell from the shifting of his weight on the floorboards. Together with his rich clothes, it gave me a presentiment that something suspicious was afoot.

"Next morning, I told Mrs. Blumenthal. She had done me the kindness of taking me in, and I guess I thought it the right thing to do. She told me thank you, but that I didn't need trouble myself about it. And that's when I saw a man behind her in the parlor-foyer-dining room. A bear of a man with a black beard like a boar bristle brush." Hattie and Tully recognize the description. "His eyes were on me, glowering like the devil. Heard every word I had said about the man in the linen shirt.

"About an hour later, I hear hollers coming from the road. I check the window and see the same devil man and his fine-shirted associate dragging another man from the private residence across the street. I tear down the stairs to alert Mrs. Blumenthal, but she's there at the front door, watching the whole thing. 'Counterfeiter,' she says."

Tully nods. "I see where you got to. It was Pinkerton, the devil."

"And Timothy Webster in the fine linen shirt," I finish. "That was worth the wait, wasn't it?"

"It had a nice turn," Tully allows.

Webster makes a soft grunt as he adjusts himself again on his stool. Hattie's face tightens. "Let's get you to bed."

Webster looks annoyed but he doesn't argue, just stands stiffly.

Hattie offers him her arm.

"I don't need it." Webster waves her away.

Hattie gives a strained smile. "Let your 'wife' help you."

"You're not my wife," Webster says softly, but there's something behind it.

Hattie closes her face quick, but not before I see the hurt that flashes across it. They've been living as husband and wife for more than a year now. It wouldn't be hard for that to start to feel real. To start to have feelings for the person you're sharing your days and nights with. She accused me of being soft on Scobell; it looks like she's got experience with something similar. But maybe Webster doesn't feel the same.

Webster climbs the stairs awkwardly. She trails after him. "Safe traveling," she calls back to Tully and me, but there's no feeling in the words.

— Twenty —

Our travel back to Washington is plagued with poor weather. The mud alone delays us an extra two days. I felt such a thrill after making contact with our source at the Davis house. Such a swell of feeling at seeing Scobell. But it's gone now. I feel numbed by the autumn chill. Or maybe it was our night with Hattie and Webster. Is Hattie what I've been aiming for all this time? Is she what I got to become to be a top Pinkerton agent: someone who calls Scobell soft for risking himself for me? If he's soft, what's strong?

I know the answer. It was in her voice as she described what she would have done to a little girl to break her mother. A deadness hangs in my chest. I see Hattie trailing up those stairs after Webster. A shade following after Orpheus, certain never to reach him.

Tully seems as miserable as me, saying little as we approach the border between North and South. Once on the other side, he loosens some. Enough to gruff, "What's the matter with you?"

I don't know how to say it. "Can you be both strong and soft?" I finally ask.

"What tripe is this now?" Tully spits back. It's been raining without cease for the last hour, and water runs in little streams off the sides of his hat.

I pull my felted wool shawl around my shoulders and try to say it a different way—a way Tully can grasp. "There was this dog, back . . .

back before I left home." Tully knows about the Great Hunger. "There was a whole pack near our place, and then there were fewer and fewer. But this one dog survived. It was a mean bastard, but it got through. And I guess maybe I've always thought being like that dog is the way you survive."

Tully grimaces. "Eating other dogs?!"

"It didn't eat the other dogs! The other dogs starved," I snap, realizing for the first time that it surely ate the other dogs.

"Oh, they just starved, did they? Then, what, got buried in little doggie graves by their loving owners?"

"Forget the damn dogs! The point is—"

"And my point is," Tully cuts me off, "that the world is a nasty, nasty place. And you best thicken that skin if you want to come through it whole." He sighs, then mutters, "And maybe eat another dog if you must."

I don't try to talk to Tully about it anymore. We make it to Washington a day later.

Back at the offices, Pinkerton has news about Rose Greenhow. She remains under house arrest, but her home now holds a number of other women suspected of being rebel spies. The War Department has named it the House of Female Detention. The papers are calling it Fort Greenhow.

As for Tully and me, Pinkerton decides our cheesemaker guise is a solid gambit for crossing the border. He assigns us to continue as couriers for the Richmond agents.

I've got several days respite in Washington before we leave again. I walk back to my boarding house that evening along Seventh Street. Food stalls are abustle in the chilly evening, vending every which thing. Fried bread. Noodles from China. Long, skinny, brown-and-yellow fruits called bananas. I stop to get myself some supper. That's when I see a posted notice.

GREAT FAIR
In aid of the SANITARY COMMISSION
To be held in the evening at Willard's Hotel,

Washington Oct'r 5
Friends of the Sick and Wounded Soldiers make ready your
contributions for the support of this great and good work.
Let them be ever so small they will be thankfully received.
Please put this up in a Conspicuous Place

Notices of its kind are glued up all over town, enticing females to donate their time and goods in support of the Union army. I wouldn't usually give it any attention, but the man is taking a long time serving up my noodles, so I'm occupying myself with reading. Which is how I see a name I recognize at the notice's bottom.

Addresses to be given by
Rev. Dr. Bellows, Chairman, US Sanitary Commission and
Miss Consider Pritchett, Chairman of the Ladies Committee,
US Sanitary Commission

It stops me still in the street to read Consider's name. I haven't seen her since the morning of the Tremont strike five years ago. I stand there dumbstruck to discover her here, in Washington, and giving a speech in just two days' time. The noodle vendor has to call to me, "Miss! Miss!" to hand me my supper.

The Sanitary Commission is one of the largest aid societies, aimed at supporting sick and wounded Union soldiers all across the North. Fairs like this one are almost like conscription events, drafting an army of women to give money, food, medicine. To knit socks. To visit prisoners. To nurse wounded men in the hospitals. An army of women to put back together what the army of men has ripped apart.

I walk the rest of the way back to my boarding house thinking on Consider Pritchett. She came to the mill because her brother attended the Harvard Divinity School, and her father couldn't pay his tuition as caretaker of their Quaker meetinghouse. Consider was sent to earn the tuition in his stead. But the entirety of her time at Tremont, Consider was secretly saving for a second tuition: her own. She aspired to a degree from the Mt. Holyoke Seminary for Women. When she told me this, I didn't even know there were seminaries for women. In fact, I knew so little about Protestants, I asked if she intended to become a minister.

Contrary to all reason, at the mill, Consider found a place she could exercise her mind far beyond the limits of the isolated Pennsylvania farm where she grew up. The circulating library. The Improvement Circles. The labor union. Consider took every opportunity she could find to "better" herself, as she called it. And she had letters from her father back home, hundreds by the time I met her, all stacked up in a pink-papered bandbox under her bed. A correspondence. Think about that word: *to correspond*. While Consider was at Tremont Cotton Mill, she and her father, why, suddenly their two selves *corresponded*. I suspect their conversations never went two ways before she left for the mill.

I arrive at my boarding house. It's a tall, narrow establishment with a neatly inked sign in the front window: WOMEN ONLY. I climb the front steps and into the foyer. The matron is serving up supper in the dining room—I can tell by the foul smell wafting through the place. She's just a terrible cook, boiling her meat until it's a tasteless, colorless sop. Boiling everything else too, like she never heard of a fry pan. Biscuits so hard you could break a tooth. And she still charges twenty-five cents the meal. I look at the poor dupes waiting in the dining room and shake my head.

In my second-floor room, I dig into my noodles. My room's sparsely furnished. A bed and tin bathing tub. One table and chair. All quick-made furniture: no embellishments or extra comforts. My room's also situated right above the kitchen. The supper smells sneak up through the floorboards, haunting me with the ghosts of meals past and present. Overcooked peas alongside the meat-sop, tonight. And something acrid. Burned rolls?

Mrs. Sullivan cooked like that. Just awful. To be fair, she was cooking around an eleven-hour workday. Her meals were quick and to the point. Mostly giant pots of porridge, made in the morning and eaten the rest of the day with whatever seasoning she had on hand. Salt. More salt. Sundays were the only day she had time for anything else. She'd bake bread and sometimes a cake, if she had eggs. What a treat it was when I left the Sullivans and moved into a boarding house with a talented cook.

I stop a moment in my eating, while thinking on that moment. I was twelve when the Sullivans threw me out. This was a little after I became a spinner, but just before I joined the labor union. I still barely knew Consider, but she played a part in the story.

I had lived with the Sullivans since I arrived in America at age seven. As I said, they had been our neighbors back home. When my parents died, they took me in and added me to their indenture contract.

The other Irish on the ship called me fortunate, blessed, saved to have had such luck. But I didn't feel any of those things. All I felt was a hard fury sliding into my bones, deep as marrow. It was fury that my mam and pap had abandoned me. Fury that the Sullivans weren't my true family. Fury that I had survived. I nursed that fury all the five weeks to America.

There was a feeling in the weeks after I arrived like there was a place I was meant to be, and I was just waiting to go there. I couldn't shake the feeling, and no matter how many days I slept next to the four Sullivan girls, head to toe in the bed, it didn't ever feel like home.

We lived in a two-room apartment on the third floor of a tenement building. Born into a turf cottage, dug from the earth itself, our lodging seemed perilously high. I never could climb those stairs without a feeling of mistrust, like one day it might all crumble from beneath my feet.

The Sullivans tried to do their best by me. They were not cruel. They were not neglectful. But something never quite fit. Mrs. Sullivan mixed up all our names so no one was just Mary Agnes or Mary Belle. We were all Mary AgnBelle or Mary Jakate. But when she introduced us, it was a sure thing: this is my Mary Louise, my Mary Belle, my Mary Agnes, my Mary Jane—a breath—and this is Mary Kate, the possessive openly lacking.

And sometimes I heard Mrs. Sullivan griping to Mr. Sullivan, griping that I ate more than my portion of porridge or that she'd have enough for new shoes if it weren't five children she had to clothe.

When she said such things, Mr. Sullivan repeated some nice phrase about Christian charity and Jesus's sacrifice, then reminded her she had my wages each month against my keep.

Maybe it was that I didn't look like a Sullivan. Mrs. Sullivan was fair-haired and built like a duck, long in the neck and wide at the tail. Her daughters took after her to a close degree. Me, I was tall and narrow and plain, with brown hair and skin speckled like an egg—my blue eyes my most defining feature. It was like the story of the ugly duckling, only if she were never discovered to be a swan—just a plain little bird in a family that didn't match.

By the time I was twelve, the Sullivan household felt full to over-flowing. I'd say it was our growing bodies making the stuck-close feeling, the four Sullivan girls' and mine, bolting like weeds, but it was as much our personalities bumping against one another that made it feel so full.

One of the Sullivan girls was of an age with me. Mary Belle. By the time I was twelve, I already stood as tall as many men, tall enough to be moved up to spinning and a full wage. Meanwhile, Mary Belle still looked like a child as she hurried through changing the bobbins in Spinning Room No. 2. I spent my spare time deep in library books, lost in my own fantasies. Mary Belle found a nose in a book intolerable—an insult, even—when there were live people all around to talk to. She doted on boys and her looks, playing Who's Prettiest in her mind with every girl she passed. She had a jealousy simmering just below her skin, Mary Belle.

Well, one Sunday I was helping Mrs. Sullivan with the bread, when I heard a strange sound coming from the bedroom where Mary Belle was watching the littlest sister, five-year-old Mary Jane. I couldn't place the sound at first, so inconceivable it was. But then it came again.

Tearing paper.

The sound came once over. Then many times over. Laughter followed.

Recalling that none of the Sullivans had ever so much as looked in the direction of a book, I rushed into the bedroom, already fearful of what I'd find.

There, behind the curtain where we girls all slept was Mary Belle, little Mary Jane in her lap, both of them laughing so hard there were tears in their eyes. In Mary Belle's hands was a library book of mine. One I'd borrowed many, many times over the years because its story once touched my heart. I watched as Mary Belle lifted a page and Mary Jane ripped the paper clean out of the book with a shriek of joy. Pages were all around them like so many autumn leaves, dead book leaves, torn from their binding.

"Bastards!" I shouted, hardly knowing the word's meaning except that it was how Robin Hood described miscreants.

Mary Belle lifted another page for Mary Jane to rip, but stopped to squint at the illustration. "Why, Mary Kate's written on this one! Look at that: *grá mo chroí*," she sounded out with difficulty.

Something came out of me then, something deep and feral. I picked up a hairbrush and pelted it at Mary Belle.

Mary Belle struck back with words. "What're you writing such a thing for? You miss your mam, is it?" There were pages all about the floor, some ripped straight through the words such as wouldn't ever be repaired.

"You bastards!" I hurled a boot at her and scrabbled for more things.

"No one to love poor Mary Kate. No mam, because you're an orphan, no boys because you're plain," Mary Belle sang nastily.

"Bastards," I screeched, throwing another boot. Mary Belle dodged it.

"Curse all you like, we're the only family you've got. Except you're not true family. Just a Heaney." A dead name for a dead family.

Behind me, I heard Mrs. Sullivan drawn by the ruckus. "Mary B-Agnes! Mary Kat-Belle! Mary Jane!" I didn't care. I took up a heavy wooden horse toy and aimed for Mary Belle's face.

I missed. It cracked against little Mary Jane's temple. Blood shot out in red pulses. Both girls shrieked and cowered. I screamed once more, "Bastards!"

Mrs. Sullivan charged across the room. Mary Jane's cut wasn't deep, but the blood was just spurting out, as head cuts will, all down Mary Jane's face and dress, all across the quilted bedspread, making the whole scene a bloody horror. Mrs. Sullivan rushed to her girl and pressed her fingers to the wound.

"It was Mary Kate!" cried Mary Belle. Sprayed by Mary Jane's cut, it looked as if she was weeping blood.

Mrs. Sullivan surveyed the room, her bloody girls, the toys and boots and book leaves scattered across the floor. She tried to look at Mary Jane's wound, but the blood swelled right out again. "I'll have to stitch it!" Mrs. Sullivan cried. "And for what—a book? What kind of girl puts a book before a flesh-and-blood person?!" She turned to me. "Apologize!"

But I wouldn't. "It's Mary Belle who should apologize," I growled.

Mrs. Sullivan's hand came thwacking across my cheek. "You'll do it now!"

I refused. And something in her changed. When I saw the thing, that tiny shift, I tell you, a dread came right over me. Mrs. Sullivan said, "I've done my Christian duty by you and more, don't owe you a thing. You will apologize or you can walk right out that door!"

And weren't we all shocked still, me most of all.

My voice came out of the silence, "I won't apologize."

Mrs. Sullivan laughed in a great burst. "Then go, there's the door. When you decide you're ready to be a good girl and apologize, you can come back."

I walked out the Sullivans' door. A head down the hall poked out, took me in with my tears and red cheeks, then pulled back in like it had seen enough.

I sat all the rest of the Sunday evening in the hallway, not knowing half what to do. My cheek swelled where Mrs. Sullivan had struck me, and I suspected my eye was purpling. The swelling helped me thicken my skin, as I knew I must. Mary Belle had finally said what I'd always half known: I didn't belong with them.

The men came home from working on the canal at seven. They were dark shapes against the stairwell, paying me little mind, a lone girl in the hall. As one passed, the dark shape became Mr. Byrne. He looked at me, then to the shape that became Mr. Sullivan behind him. Mr. Sullivan said nothing, just took a deep breath and sighed it out. He disappeared into the Sullivans' door, a shard of lamplight in the dark, and all the other men disappeared behind their doors too, with their shards of light. Only faint yellow lines under the doors were left.

Looking back, Mrs. Sullivan surely believed I would capitulate. Wasn't hers the kind of threat parents make a thousand times? And wasn't I just a twelve-year-old girl with nowhere else to go?

And me? I think I believed she would give in. I was waiting for her. Waiting for her to reach out, to pull me back into her arms, into her home, to tuck me in beside her daughters. And that through her, someone else would come back. Someone from long, long ago. Demeter would find me in hell.

But no one came out of the Sullivan door to collect me. No heads peeked out to see if I was still here. I tucked into the corner of the landing. It felt cold because of the dark, and dingy because it was dingy. No one ever cleaned that part. It was no one's but the landlord's, and to be sure, he'd never been to the building for cleaning or anything else besides. What happens to the little bits that belong to no one?

I listened to the evenings passing behind the doors. Mr. Byrne scolding Mrs. Byrne for something about a shoe, and every now and again Mary Jane shrieking from within the Sullivans'. The sounds got softer as the evening wore on. All at once, the line of lamplight under the Byrnes' poorly hung door went dark. Not long after, the Sullivans' door went dark too. I was all alone in the blackness.

I woke because something ran over my leg. The rat got thrown by me standing up. I rubbed my hands down my legs to stop the itchy, dirty feeling of little claws along my calf. I felt dirty all over, little claws in my hair and under my collar. I brushed down my whole body.

It was a tomb, that hallway, like the little marble houses erected in the cemetery. Mam and Pap weren't in a tomb. There was no stone for them marked "Heaney." Just a common grave. Bodies in a ditch.

I could hear the rat on the other side of the hall. It was doing little things that rats do at night in hallways that are dark like crypts. I couldn't bear to sit back down, so I leaned against the wall. The mill bell would ring at half four. I needed only get to half four, and then it was a new day and Mrs. Sullivan must let me in again, mustn't she?

At the wake-up bell, I was still leaning against the wall. The doors were all quiet, but little lines of lamplight appeared beneath them again.

I heard Mary Agnes scolding Mary Louise for pulling too tightly as she plaited her hair. And then Mrs. Sullivan scolding Mary Jane about putting on clean stockings. I didn't hear Mr. Sullivan's voice a once, though he was surely there.

The door flew open at quarter to five. Mr. Sullivan nearly tread on me. The light behind him was bright and warm, and my belly ached from the lack of supper. Then Mrs. Sullivan came to the door. I saw her and felt a swell of longing for her to take me in her arms, to call me *my* Mary Kate. But there was so much anger too. An old, abiding fury for her being a Sullivan and not a Heaney. For never being the mother I wanted. It was up inside me, the anger, grinding like stones. All I could do was stare back without saying a word. Mrs. Sullivan shook her head and sighed. All the Sullivans filed out the door and after her down the stairs.

I was hungry and miserably tired as I walked to the mill. As I worked, I wondered if the overseer would let me sleep in Spinning Room No. 2. Would that be better than the hallway from the past night? The stove surely didn't stay lit all the night long for fear of fire, but at least there was a window in the mill room. I thought these dire thoughts all the way until breakfast.

Suddenly someone shook me awake. Consider Pritchett. It had not been a minute, I'd swear, but the breakfast break had come and gone, the thirty minutes elapsed in one heavy one. "Have you eaten?" Consider asked, and my eyes came full of tears. Consider went away. When she returned, she had a fistful of shell nuts. She poured them into my pocket. "Don't let the old man see," she said of the overseer.

I spent the next five hours wondering what I'd do when the dinner bell rang. Where would I eat if not at the Sullivans?

The dinner bell finally did ring, and everyone raced to turn off the machines and get home or to their boarding house because there was only one hour to get there, eat, rest a piece, and walk back.

Mrs. Sullivan turned to leave without a glance for me, her four girls following behind. Only Mary Belle looked back and only for a moment.

I turned around to find Consider there. "Come on, then," she said gently. She took me to Mrs. Brody's boarding house where she lodged. I suspected she just saw me as a charity case, a poor paddy orphan to tend with her Quaker benevolence, but I followed her anyway.

Inside the front door of Mrs. Brody's was an entryway for shawls and bonnets with a mirror. I took a look at my eye. It was purple indeed.

There was a large dining room set for twenty. Mrs. Brody herself was placing a great platter of chicken on the table. Like she sensed something amiss, she looked up dead into my eyes. I knew right then I never wanted to cross Mrs. Brody.

Mrs. Brody was British. There was talk she was transported to a penal colony and came up to New England from the Barbados sugar plantations. One girl said that before running a boarding house, Mrs. Brody ran rum on a gun ship from Providence to Bermuda. What's certain was there was a wealth of stories about Mrs. Brody, but no one had asked Mrs. Brody herself because Mrs. Brody was big and broad, with a nose hung to the side like a boxer. In truth, she looked a little like a boxer all over. And that's how she looked at you too, so no one who roomed at Mrs. Brody's house ever broached her except to say things like, "Yes, I will blow out my lamp as it's curfew" and "What nice cake."

"Can you add it to this week's board, please?" Consider asked Mrs. Brody as if she'd thought it through. Consider didn't advance until Mrs. Brody's nod, but nod she did. Then Mrs. Brody disappeared and returned with a plate and a stool. She set them at the table's corner near Consider.

I ate a large piece of fried chicken with gravy and a plate full of potatoes after that, with the same gravy. It was much more than I was accustomed to eating at the Sullivans, where I always split a piece of chicken, if I had one at all. And then after the chicken and potatoes, there was cake, which was nice indeed. I took a large slice and dug into it with relish.

Mrs. Brody stood a piece and watched me, like would be impolite in someone else, but in Mrs. Brody you just tolerated. She said, "I might have a compress for that eye" and came back with a damp pillow that smelled like herbs. I held it to my cheek as I finished my cake.

The girls all pushed back their chairs when it came to the hour's finish. Because the boarding houses were much nearer the mill than the Irish tenements, it was as long a midday meal as I'd ever had and as full fare as I'd eaten in a very long while. "Not to be made a habit of, Miss Pritchett," Mrs. Brody said. "Unless it's a new boarder you're bringing."

That afternoon, I felt better because of the food. When the bell rang for day's end, it seemed only moments since dinner. On the far side of Spinning Room No. 2, Mrs. Sullivan stood looking at me, hands at her hips, waiting. It was a sign. A sign that I could still apologize.

But I still couldn't.

All the spinners started to leave. I touched the cheek that Mrs. Sullivan had struck, pressing into the purple bruise. I reminded myself Mrs. Sullivan hadn't come for me when I needed her. She had left me in the hall the night through. She never even wanted me in her home in the first place. I pressed harder into the bruise. The pain flamed my fury, hardened my resolve. I didn't want to be a half member of the family, always wondering when she might order me to leave again. I would make my own way. I would close my heart to Mrs. Sullivan and Mary Belle and the rest.

I turned away from Mrs. Sullivan and followed the Yank girls down the stairs toward the boarding houses. I heard Mrs. Sullivan behind me spitting words of indignation and injury. It hurt like all hell, but I didn't look back.

That evening, I got a place at Mrs. Brody's. The next day, one of her Yank boarders left, saying she wouldn't lodge at a place that let to paddies. All Mrs. Brody said was "Glad to see the tail on that one."

Mrs. Brody gave me the boarding registry to sign. I carefully penned my given name:

Mary Kate Heaney.

I stopped and looked at my three names there on the page. Pictures came into my head, old ones and new: A name on a ship's manifest. Mrs. Sullivan screaming for me to leave her home. Mary Belle telling me I wasn't true family.

I told you I left off using the name Mary. This is the moment it happened. I looked at those three names, then I put the pen back to the paper. I scratched out my first name—the name binding me to my memories, the name I shared with the Sullivan girls, the name that marked me as a paddy. I scratched so hard the paper tore, but then it was gone. Divided from me forever.

I moved into Mrs. Brody's a new person: Kate Heaney.

And it was Consider Pritchett who had made it possible. Consider with her pinned-back hair. Her head that tilted to the side before she spoke. Suddenly, here in my boarding house room in Washington so many years later, I'm overcome with a longing to see her. She always seemed to know who she was. Maybe she can help me figure out my own muddle of a life.

———

Two days later, I head to the Willard Hotel. It's a grand place with velvet drapes on the windows and gas chandeliers lighting up the halls. The ballroom is packed with women of all kinds—rich, poor, and in between—all carrying sacks of donations. The knitting alone fills a quarter of the room. All these months of war, where have women spent their energies? In knitting, it would seem.

It sounds passive, sweet even. Who among us doesn't have an image of some kindly grandmother knitting a scarf for a grandchild? But what is knitting when it gets down to it? A series of loops. Coils. Twists. Stitches bound up tightly, one to the next. So many women with a surfeit of feeling—fear, concern, fury, zeal—all stuck up in them and no way out except through their knitting. Tense fingers looping stitch after stitch, binding up thought and feeling, coiling it away into miles of smooth, seamless fabric.

The audience takes their seats, and Reverend Dr. Bellows, chairman of the commission, comes to a lectern at the front. He's a compact man with a long nose and little pillowed bags under his eyes. He begins his speech with a prayer, bowing a bald head fringed with wispy white. I've never been much for religion. Mill girls at Tremont were required to attend services weekly in the Christian denomination of their choosing, but no one was exactly checking attendance.

After the prayer, he launches into a warmed-over sermon about Christian duty and womanly service. My attention wanders; I scan the crowd for Consider.

Reverend Dr. Bellows finishes his speech with another prayer. All the women in the crowd bow their heads again and give an "amen." The Reverend then looks to the front row and a lean woman stands. Even from behind I recognize Consider's straight back, her brisk step, the dark hair bound into a simple knot at her neck. She takes her place at the lectern and begins her address.

She looks older. Thinner. She must be thirty by now. I wonder if she ever made it to Mt. Holyoke. I remember her speeches from the Debate Society at Tremont. She was always a confident orator. Always a leader. A shepherd to the rest of us lost girls. So many of us were in the mills because they couldn't keep us at home. So many of us a younger sister or an unwanted daughter or with no family at all like me. And none pretty enough to be easily married. No one talked about that part—not us and not the Yanks.

Consider doesn't speak in Christian parables or platitudes. She talks frankly. Soldiering is brutal, bloody work, she acknowledges. But most every woman in the ballroom has also done brutal and bloody work. Most have lived through or attended a childbirth—ones that went well and ones that didn't. Most have nursed a dying relation, cleaned failing bodies, eased loved ones through pain and terror. "You are not the passive counterparts to your soldier husbands, fathers, and sons,"

Consider urges. "You are soldiers too. Your battles have been fought in the home. We call on your strength and your fortitude now." Consider doesn't talk long, but when she finishes, the audience erupts in applause. The Reverend Dr. Bellows stands and tries to get everyone to quiet down with a pinched look on his face. The crowd is much more voluble than they were after he spoke. Some ladies even stand from their chairs as they clap.

The crowd thins as people take their leave, but a number of women line up to meet and thank Consider. I wait it out at the back of the ballroom.

The last well-wishers finally leave. Consider must feel me looking on her, because all at once, her eyes flick up. I see the wondering look at she tries to place me, then a flash of joy with her recognition.

We have tea in the hotel parlor. It's a formal room with plush chairs and soft, warm light.

Consider sits forward in her chair, still vitalized from her speech. Her eyes walk all over me. "You see what I've been about these past few years." She waves in the direction of the ballroom. "But what about you, Ms. Kate Heaney?"

"It's Warne, now. Kate Warne. Changed it," I add, before she starts thinking I went and got married. I tell her about becoming a Pinkerton detective. "We're aiding the U.S. Army these days," I say vaguely.

"Mmm." Consider tries to take a sip of tea but nearly burns her lips. "Wasn't there a Confederate woman spy caught recently in Washington by some detectives?" She always was clever. "I read about it in the newspaper. Difficult work."

The widow's arrest is public knowledge, but I still feel wary talking on it. I fiddle with my teacup handle. It's so small and fine, my finger barely fits through. "I can't say much."

Consider blows on her tea. "Of course."

"It went bad." The words spill out almost before I can help it.

"Bad how?" Consider asks quietly. "If you can say."

I put it in general terms. "I tried to use her weakness against her, but she turned my own on me." The feelings well right back up. "For a moment, she almost got me to care—" I stop myself. I can't bear to admit I felt anything like care for a bigot like the widow. It's a betrayal of who I am. Of my work. Of the people I'm working for. "The short of it is: she beat me."

Consider looks confused. "But you arrested her, didn't you?"

"I didn't break her," I explain. "She never broke as a spy. And so I—" I don't want to tell her what all I did in her daughter's room. "I broke her another way, just for, I don't know, spite." I hear again Pinkerton telling me I had proved myself, and a heavy shame comes over me.

Consider waits to see if I'm done. She puts her teacup back on the table again. She folds and refolds her hands. Finally, she gets to it. "Before the war, I was working to make a unified women's labor union—white, Black, immigrant, all together—in New York City. We'd been trying for years but had never managed it. The thing holding us back wasn't fear of losing jobs. It was women not trusting women, hating each other, even. White women didn't want Black women in their union. Black women didn't trust white women to protect their needs. No one wanted the immigrants included. And on." Consider bites her lower lip. "If you want people to change their hearts, you can't fool them or fight them. You respect and listen to them—in the hope they'll do the same with you."

"I tried that."

"I'm talking about true respect," Consider returns. "Which it sounds like maybe you almost got to."

"I could never respect her!" I bite back. "She's nothing but filth."

"She's nothing but human. Broken, certainly. But who's not?"

"I know the moment I started to see her as human, she took advantage of me," I say. "That's why I failed."

"Oh, I fail nine times out of ten," Consider says with a laugh. It's an odd sound, her laugh. A sort of cackle, loose and sharp at the same time. I can't recall ever hearing such a thing from pinned-back Consider Pritchett. "I fail most every day," she goes on, a gleam in her eye. "That's my work. Heart by heart, I go."

"'True Love Wins?'" I jolly her. "I think I saw that in a *Godey's Lady's Book.*"

She raises an eyebrow.

"I don't have time to fix every bigot, one by one," I say. "And I don't care to."

She meets my gaze. "It's the only way that doesn't end in blood."

"They called for blood first," I snap.

Consider sucks her teeth and snaps back, "You answered."

She's changed, Consider. Lines have started to pull at her eyes, but those eyes are more alive. She's sharper and looser, just like her laugh.

She shakes her head at me. "You know those sappy ladies' magazines you despise sell ten thousand copies a week. All the women I work with read them."

"Doesn't make them true," I say. "Doesn't make me want to live in one of them."

"It's harder to love than to hate. That's why they read them." She looks keenly at me, the lines around her eyes deepening. "You know, I looked for you."

"What?" It takes me by surprise.

"I looked for you after the protest. But you left Tremont so quickly. I only found out you'd gone to Chicago from Mrs. Brody a year or so later. By then I was deep in my work. But wherever I traveled, I asked after you at the factories. Garment work. Textile mills. I figured you'd stick with what you knew. And wasn't I wrong in that!" Consider swats my arm. Her familiarity disarms me. "And now I learn you went and changed your name too! Why'd you do that? I'd never have found you!" She picks up her teacup and holds it up by her heart. "I missed you. There's times over the years . . . I could have used a friend." She tilts her head to the side as she used to do when we were just girls. I don't know why, but seeing it makes tears burst right out of me, jarring and messy.

Consider digs in her pocket for a handkerchief, but I'm already mopping the wet slop on my sleeves. She grimaces. "Oh, Kate."

"I always thought maybe I was just a cause to you. Certainly not a, you know . . ."

"A friend?" she says softly. "I *do* love a cause." Consider smiles, her eyes looking younger. "But it's always the people behind it, isn't it?"

I think back on losing my home with the Sullivans. Maybe it's not just a woeful story of a girl abandoned. Maybe it's also the story of a friend rescuing a friend: of Consider finding me, Mrs. Brody welcoming me, both helping me build a new home. I thought the lesson was I had to go on alone and sever ties with my past to survive, but maybe the lesson is also that there were people there for me, if I let them be. Perhaps all these years, I've been reading the story only one way when there was more to it.

We sit awhile longer. Two women in a hotel parlor, one quietly sipping her tea, the other messily weeping because life is people leaving. But sometimes they do come back.

— Twenty-one —

I keep thinking on Consider's words. How do we answer a world full of such devastating hate? I don't share her answer—I've lived too long in one way for her vision to become mine—but I see why she came to it. It's like how every star we see is a sun in its own sky. Her truth is one of those stars. I can recognize it for what it is: a light bright and true enough to anchor a world, even if it's not the one to anchor mine.

Soon after seeing Consider, I'm back on the road with Tully, ferrying intelligence to and from our agents in Richmond.

"I've outfitted cheese bells with hidden compartments in their handles," Pinkerton informs us at the offices before we leave. "Keep everything incriminating off your person and in the bells. Give them nothing to hang you by."

We make it to Richmond in good time. As before, we decide to split the drops. I plan to take Lewis's drop; Tully will take Webster and Hattie and Scobell.

We're in the middle of the city in the wagon. I'm just about to step down and head to Lewis's drop when Tully turns, contorting his rough face into an attempt at a winsome smile. "So?"

"So . . . what?" I ask guardedly.

"So, do you want me to take Scobell a message or not?"

"What message?"

"You know." Tully leans in. "Regarding your salacious passion . . ."

"Shut your trap!" I hiss. No one in the road is paying us any mind, but I still feel exposed.

"He risked himself for you," Tully whispers. "And I know you have feelings. I saw all your *feelings* hanging right out there in the open that night at the widow's house, didn't I?" He gives me a dirty smirk.

"It's too dangerous for him," I say.

Tully looks at me a moment, then nods. "It's your heart, but his neck."

I look away, hating the truth of it.

He picks up the reins. "Well, I'm going to tell him you're in Richmond . . ." He waits to see if I bite. I climb out of the wagon without looking back.

I settle into the parlor of the hotel where Lewis has his drop. I'll have tea as pretext for my being there, then swing by the manager's office for Lewis's parcel. The manager's a Union sympathizer and glad to help in the small way he can.

There's a stack of newspapers for patrons near my table. I pick through it, looking for something suitably bromidic for a supposed Richmond woman to read over tea. Before I'm halfway through the pile, a name on the front page of the *Richmond Whig* catches my attention:

LETTER FROM MRS. GREENHOW, A SOUTHERN LADY IN PRISON

I grab the paper and race through the article.

The *Richmond Whig* obtained, through one of Secretary of State William H. Seward's confidential agents, the following letter, addressed by a brave and noble woman to Seward himself. This letter of Mrs. Greenhow is the most graphic sketch yet given to the world of the cruel and dastardly tyranny which the Yankee Government has established at Washington. The incarceration and torture of helpless women and the outrages heaped upon them, as detailed in this letter, will shock many natures, and stamp the Lincoln dynasty everywhere with undying infamy.

It seems the widow secreted a letter out of her house through one of her guards. By this point, most all of us Pinkerton agents are working other assignments. The widow's house has been left to jailers. Detention doesn't require craft, just doggedness. Evidently not enough doggedness at Fort Greenhow.

The letter was purportedly written for Secretary of State Seward, demanding redress for the widow's treatment at our hands. But the letter's true purpose is plainly this: widespread publication to defame the North. Here's what she says about her arrest:

> We read in history that the poor Marie Antoinette had a paper torn from her bosom by lawless hands and that even a change of linen had to be affected in sight of her brutal captors. It is my sad experience to record even more revolting outrages than that, for during the first days of my imprisonment, whatever *necessity* forced me to seek my chamber, a detective stood sentinel at the open door. And thus for a period of days, I, with my little child, was placed absolutely at the mercy of men without character or responsibility.

It's fiction. But the kind of fiction that incites men to violence: a defenseless mother and child suffering in the barbarous clutches of enemy men. She goes on:

> these men boasted in my hearing of the *"nice times"* they expected to have with the female prisoners

She even mentions me:

> A female detective arrived. I blush that the name and character of woman should be so prostituted.

Lincoln's got to win this war not just on the battlefield, but in the hearts and minds of the people. A portrait like this is a big blow.

Pinkerton will have to answer for it. So much for looking the hero, not the lout.

I wonder if such publicity is maybe what the widow wanted all along. She had had the ears of presidents for decades, but when Abraham Lincoln was elected, she got shut out. She operated in a world that valued only certain things in ladies: beauty, marriage, wealth, reputation, sons. Her beauty was fading. Her husband was gone. She had no source of income. Her children were girls. All she had was reputation. How do women of a certain age prevent themselves from becoming invisible? . . . Beatification? So, she became a fiery, rebel heroine. The widow stopped herself from aging into irrelevancy. And she used hate as a tool to do it.

Tully finishes his drops and picks me up at the hotel. We eat a quick meal at our inn. Back in our bedroom, tucking in for the night, he hands me something.

"What's this?" I ask.

"Hell if I want to read your sordid bedroom chat," he says.

It's a message from Scobell. I take the paper over to the candle so I can read it. It's all unintelligible letters. "What's the cipher key?"

"He didn't give it to me, did he? Must have thought you knew it."

"Well, I don't!" I say, eager to get to Scobell's words.

"Calm your quim! He never mentioned anything? Something beyond carnal endearments?"

Caesar's shift—the cipher he once told me about. "Screw you, Tully."

"There's my girl!" says Tully and rolls over to sleep.

I bring the candle to the corner of the room where I can pretend I'm alone and get to work.

Caesar's shift is one of the simplest of ciphers, substituting each letter of the alphabet with one a fixed number of positions away. If A = C, then B = D, and C = E, and on. It's not so hard to break if you know the pattern. After a few tries, I've got Scobell's message.

dearest katie hear you are a cheesemaker married to tully my sincere condolences

im thinking of you in richmond so nearby would be glad if you wrote
me back yours john

I imagine him in his boarding house somewhere in this same city. Maybe lying in bed. His nightshirt rolled up over his arms. His hands maybe behind his head. Thinking on me just as I'm thinking on him. I feel the close distance like a tether again between our hearts, pulling on me with such force it's like a physical ache. I know writing him back is just drawing out the pain. There's no happy ending for us.

But I compose a message back all the same—knowing as I'm doing it that I shouldn't, and doing it still. It's just a quick message telling him I'm thinking of him too. I hesitate over the signature and settle for what he chose: *yours kate*

After, I lie opposite Tully on the bed, his gnarled toes offering a strong distraction from my thoughts of Scobell. When I finally sleep, my dreams are filled with dogs, scratching and pawing. I don't remember much else.

The next morning, Tully and I pack the wagon for our return to Washington, carefully tucking our contraband intelligence into the false tops of those cheese bells. My stomach is knotted with indecision about whether to deliver the message I wrote to Scobell. Tully is deep in his own morning funk, but he still senses my unease. "What's the matter with you?" he crabs.

I close my hands, running my fingers over the old calluses. "We got to make a stop. I have a message to drop at Scobell's tavern."

———

With late fall comes poor weather. Tully and I still make trips to Richmond, but fewer. When we do, Scobell and I exchange messages. At first, I just write little stuff, nothing so important you'd need a cipher for:

i walked up seventh street and bought breakfast at a food stall from a
man wearing the dirtiest apron i ever seen on a cook in public i asked

myself what youd say to that apron
will be in richmond by end of december its slow going peanut our
horse dont do more than amble

Scobell writes back pieces of his life:

one time i worked on a packet boat to fredericksburg for pinkerton
boat captain offered me forty dollars a month to stay on very good
money pinkertons lucky im loyal
if you grow tired of spying maybe you try sailing

Gradually, I start to answer his questions from long ago about where I came from. I find myself telling him things I've hardly admitted to myself:

figured it took bravery and guts to do this work
but maybe i came to it because its safer pretending to get close to
someone then ending it
i can push away like was done to me

Scobell answers:

its funny that our guts are our softest parts
if youve eaten heart you know its tough as hell and guts are just all
soft
i dont know why our softest parts are the bravest parts

It's easier, somehow, putting our lives down in code. Showing pieces of ourselves in words none but the other can read and sending them off, as if to a castle in the sky.

We reveal more. Scobell tells me how a slave owner called Theodore Scobell fathered two sons by his wife and then fathered Scobell.

the way i see it theres the same half of him in each of us sons

its just my father got to choose is it a glass half full or half empty
whats to the mans advantage adding a third heir to divide his wealth
or keeping a slave to make more of it
so im the half empty

I can tell the thing cuts deeper than the way he writes of it. Maybe straight through his heart. But we got to tell things the way we can.

We never say words of love, but they feel like love letters all the same. The two of us share the undersides of our smoothness. The rough and raw truth of us. As I do it, I'm finding parts of myself I forgot along the way. It's painful, I won't lie. It makes me think on Consider Pritchett and her endless capacity for love. I ask Scobell:

do you think we are meant to love everyone in this world
my head says we should
everybody is someones child and deserves human love
but my heart cant find a way to do it

He doesn't judge me. Just says,

you manage it katie you will save this world
maybe just work on stopping this war

He adds:

i know the glass half full is better
write again please i am happy reading your words ever yours john

I pore over his signature line, torn between wanting him safe and just plain wanting him.

We write so much I stop needing the cipher key to do it. It becomes a fluent second language only to us. But Tully still always makes Scobell's drop. I never go where we might happen to see one another. As much as I've revealed to him, I'm terrified by the prospect of seeing him in the flesh. The closer we come, the more it feels there is to lose.

One night, as I translate my life into a scrap of code for Scobell, something else comes back to me. I'm in the corner of the boarding room in Richmond. Tully is already starting to toss with nightmares in the bed. I'm describing the house where I was born, just the few details still stuck in me—turf walls, the wooden door with the bar, the old bed—and all at once words come to my lips. Old words. And all I want to do is tell him.

> my mam had a lullaby she sung i didnt know i knew the words till
> just now as im writing
> hush now
> gra mo chroi
> open your heart and i will fill it like a sail
> well be together always
> gra mo chroi
> the words are foreign to me now i think they mean my dear heart
> my mams come back to me in the words like shes with me here in the
> room i hear her singing—

And that's where I leave off for weeping. I wrap myself up in my own arms and hear a whisper in my ear, *Mary Kate*. And I remember that girl and the others I've been and wish I could go back and be a mother to those girls. That I could hold my different selves and sing to them. But since I can't go back, I do it now. Maybe Tully hears me from the bed, rocking and singing to myself in our room like I'm my own child. I don't much care if he does. For so long I've watched people leave my life, and I didn't see I've done something of the same. I tried to leave my old self behind, rub it out and start anew. But it didn't work. You can't erase your stories. You got to find a way to live with them. What Consider told me to do with the widow, I need to do with myself: take in a broken human and mend her.

We'll be together always, grá mo chroí.

Scobell writes back. It's a short message. Just one line.

i love you i want to see you

I make a decision. One more terrifying than the prospect of Lincoln's assassins in Baltimore. More terrifying than being chased out of the Confederate White House. Because the truth is inside me, plain as anything. I love him. I never fathomed a feeling could come upon a person so quick and stick so fast. We've barely known one another a full year. Yet it feels true and sure all the same. Like something that's been in me all my life, a seed or something, only now pushing into the light. I write back:

i love you

But before we can meet, something happens that stops our love letters for good. The dangers we've been fearing come true. Just not in the way either of us imagined.

— Twenty-two —

It starts in early February. Tully goes to Webster and Hattie's drop at the tobacconist, but there's nothing there. We wait an extra day. Still nothing. We report it back to Pinkerton when we return to Washington. He tells us to try again on the following trip. Maybe they got held up. Maybe they couldn't make it for safety's sake.

But on our next trip, the drop's empty too. The tobacconist has no information, just what we know: that neither Webster nor Hattie have checked in now for almost a month.

Tully and my return to Washington is grim, the two of us knowing something's wrong but not what. Bumping along in our maddeningly slow cheese wagon, I ask Tully, "What do you reckon?"

"They think the rebels are on to them, and they've gone quiet until they can get out." His face is as hard as carved wood. "Or worse." His eyes stay on the road ahead. "Something's turned bad, that's for sure."

In the offices back in Washington, Pinkerton makes an announcement: he's sending two agents to find Webster and Hattie and get them out of whatever fix they're in.

I'm on tenterhooks waiting to hear who he chooses, part of me wanting to go, part of me wanting nothing to do with whatever fix they're in, and all of me praying he doesn't choose Scobell.

Pinkerton finally decides. "It'll be Lewis and Tully."

I feel a full-bodied relief. But then I see Tully's drawn face at hearing the news and my relief goes.

Tully's set to leave for Richmond immediately. He's going alone on horseback for faster travel. He asks me to meet with him just before he departs. "I don't know what we'll find," he says grimly. "Could be they've got Web and Hattie and are holding them like bait for Lewis and me to walk into." Tully hands me a box.

"What's this?" I ask.

"For my sister." He sniffs sharply. "My next of kin, in case of the worst. There's a letter in there with her address and a token of . . ." He stops and blinks a moment, working to keep a handle on his feelings. "Our mother. If you would deliver it, need be."

"Of course, Tully," I say. "I'm sorry. I wish you—"

"Now, that's enough, Kate," he interrupts. "Save your tender thoughts for your own hopeless affairs."

"Good hunting," I tell him.

The next news we hear in Washington is more than a week later when a telegraph message comes through, telling us two Unions spies have been arrested in Richmond. We don't know which of them it is, but we certainly know the Confederate penalty for espionage is death.

Pinkerton hems and haws, then sends me south. My assignment is just to check in with Scobell and with the drops to see if there's any information that can help.

I drive Peanut and the dairy wagon across the rebel lines, this time alone. It would seem impossible two years ago: a woman traveling eight days by herself in a wagon. Staying nights in inns along the way. Hitching her horse with or without a groom's help. But now women alone are half the people I pass on the road.

It's not easy going. Each time an innkeeper asks after my "husband," I'm reminded of Tully's absence. Every mile I come closer to Richmond, my foreboding grows.

And Peanut. Goddamn Peanut seems bent on making it all the worse. Every other minute he's veering off toward some herbage at the side of the road, trying to eat like I've been starving the animal. Like we're on a pleasure outing and not hurrying on to dire business in Richmond. I haul on the reins with my full weight. I tell him he could be pulling a military cart instead of one woman and some cheese. I tell him fifteen hundred pounds of horsemeat would fetch a pretty penny in these times. But he senses my lack of resolve. It's a slow, infuriating journey.

Finally, I make it to Richmond. From Scobell's drop, I learn what news he's been able to gather. Webster fell sick, laid up in a bad way with rheumatic fever. Hattie was tending him in their hotel room. That was why they hadn't checked in.

Lewis and Tully found Webster and Hattie at their hotel, but while there, Lewis was recognized by a Confederate officer he had investigated back in Washington. He and Tully are the ones arrested.

Scobell includes a folded-up article from the *Richmond Enquirer* dated March the fourth:

Two Lincoln spies, giving the names of John Tully and Pryce Lewis, were arrested at the Monument Hotel on Friday last, and are now in prison. The proof of their connection with the secret service of the enemy is most positive.

Scobell writes that as far as he can tell, the Confederates have got Lewis at Henrico Jail and Tully in Castle Godwin prison. Separated, so they have no means of knowing if the other has confessed.

I lie in the same room where Tully and I slept head to toe all our nights in Richmond. I think of us agents, scattered around the city. Tully and Lewis in prisons. Hattie and Webster in their hotel. Scobell in his boarding house. We're within a few short miles of one another, but unreachable. Only Scobell and I can make contact with one another. And it's only to share bad news.

Back in Washington, Pinkerton contacts the war office, hoping to make a prisoner trade. The Confederates refuse. In late March, the Richmond papers announce Lewis and Tully's sentence:

Pryce Lewis and John Tully have been tried before the Court Martial now sitting at the City Hall, and condemned to be hanged as spies.

They will be the first Union spies hanged by the Confederacy. It is national news.

Lewis, English by birth, appeals to the British Consul for protection. Tully does the same soon after. The Consul denies them.

I return once more to Richmond. Scobell writes me:

gallows built at the new fairgrounds i passed them today praying for them both

Tully's box for his sister is at Pinkerton's offices. I recall her address was somewhere in New York. When I get back to Washington, I'll ask Pinkerton for leave to deliver it. I want to tell her about her brother's sacrifice in person.

And then something happens.

It seems at first a reprieve. Our best hopes and prayers have been answered: Tully and Lewis's executions are postponed!

I conclude the British Consul changed their mind and came through. Or that maybe Pinkerton finally managed a prisoner trade through his furious back-door bargaining. But on April 5, the very day after Tully and Lewis were meant to hang, the *Richmond Dispatch* announces something altogether different:

It is intimated, and we believe on good authority, too, that the condemned have made disclosures affecting the fidelity of several persons, one or more of whom have been apprehended. Rumor had it yesterday that one of the parties thus implicated was an officer holding a place under the Government.

The following day, a scandal hits Richmond, the size of which has never been matched in the war so far. Captain Timothy Webster of the Confederate Army and his wife are arrested as Union spies. Mr. and Mrs. Webster, the darlings of Richmond. It is a deep and true embarrassment for the rebels.

But of course, it's a thousand times worse for us. Because the writing is on the wall about as plain as it can be: Lewis or Tully—or both of them—betrayed Webster and Hattie. Gave them up to save their own necks.

I return to Washington as rapidly as I can with all the intelligence Scobell and I could gather. Webster is held in Castle Godwin prison. Hattie is most likely in a new prison converted from a tobacco warehouse they're calling Castle Thunder. Webster's trial is set for April the 25th.

Pinkerton already has the worst of it by the time I get back. The Confederate army practically telegraphed the news to Washington themselves: *Yankee Spy Timothy Webster Apprehended!*

Pinkerton is near out of his wits with sorrow. I know because he doesn't bark or snap when I walk into the offices, still coated in mud from my journey. He just comes up and pats my cheek. "Poor Webster. Poor Hattie."

He doesn't say a word about Lewis and Tully. Like me, he figures it was one of them betrayed the others. He tries again for a prisoner exchange, but Webster and Hattie have deceived too many of the Confederate elite for leniency. It's terrible knowing they're there and there's nothing we can do about it. Terrible knowing Lewis or Tully betrayed them.

I rest two nights at my boarding house off Seventh Street, but I hardly sleep. I keep thinking of them in their prison cells and me, safe as houses. The only difference is how Pinkerton assigned us. Had Lewis not been there to be recognized, had it been me sent with Tully in his stead, would any of this have happened? Dwelling on it doesn't solve anything, but I can't think on much else. I fold up, pull in, and hold myself through the night until morning.

I return to Richmond the day of Webster's trial, bringing the news of Pinkerton's failed efforts at a prisoner exchange to Scobell's drop at the tavern kitchen. The tavern's a ramshackle two-story building on the outskirts of town, painted a cheery yellow to hide its age. It serves cheap beer and mediocre food, mostly roast meat and cheese, to a motley assortment of low types. It's the kind of establishment where no one much bothers about a low-class woman bringing cheese, on occasion, to provision the small kitchen around the tavern's back. I leave a small parcel for Scobell with the cook.

I'm just leaving the kitchen when I feel eyes on me from the road out front. I look up to see Scobell, his lean body against a fence post by a bare cottonwood, one hand playing at a shirt button.

I don't dare greet him. I barely even glance his way, but my heart nearly jumps out of its cage to see him. Even at a distance, it feels like an intimacy, us setting eyes on one another after so much time. I want to reach out for his hand. But all I can do is walk on, the space between us as thick as earth.

The day after Webster's trial, the sentence is printed right across the front page of the *Richmond Dispatch*:

Yankee Spy to Hang!

It's no surprise, and yet it feels a fresh tragedy all the same. Webster's execution is set for April 29. Four days away.

I sit in my boarding house, overcome by grief. It's a lonesome feeling, and I find myself wishing I could see Scobell again. My only comfort is knowing he's out there and feeling the same.

I think on each of the four agents in prison. I wonder if Tully and Lewis heard the news of Webster's sentence. I wonder if Hattie did. And Webster. What must he be feeling?

Finally, I can't bear the waiting. I hitch Peanut to the wagon and drive past Castle Godwin where Webster's being held. I know it doesn't do nothing, but I can't sit idle any longer.

As I pass the prison entrance, I notice a line at the gate. It's mostly women holding baskets. Wives of prisoners, maybe. Or benevolent lady societies bringing food and blankets to the captive soldiers. All at once, I have a notion.

It's not much. Nothing that will save Webster. But I realize I, alone, of all our agents, might be able to get in to see him, under guise of womanly charity. I could offer to pass on words to a loved one, like Tully asked me to do. Or, I don't know, just bring him the solace of a familiar face.

It's a hell of a gamble. If he lets on he knows me, I'll be in a dire fix. But I can't bear four days of waiting while his time runs out.

The next morning, I line up with the other women outside Castle Godwin. A couple of the waiting women are wives, as I guessed. But some of the others are Quakers, bringing food and blankets to the prisoners. I offer my hand in the Quaker way to them. Suddenly they're asking which meeting house I attend, and how come they haven't seen me here before. I give them my cheese story, tell them I'm only in Richmond a short while, but Christian duty pulls me, and all that. They tell me they make regular visits to the prisons. It's from them I learn how it works. An older Quaker with thin blue eyes explains the baskets they carry are only partly for the prisoners. She lifts out a jar of buttermilk and packet of gingerbread. "For the lieutenant in charge." A *douceur* for entry. That same lieutenant will decide whether we're admitted or not.

We're not. We wait three hours before we're turned away. The wives are miserable, but the Quaker women don't seem puckered by it, which tells me this isn't the first time it's happened. But for me, it's one day closer to Webster's execution.

"Will you try again tomorrow?" I ask, keeping the nerves from my voice.

"And the day after that," the eldest Quaker answers chiply. "You're welcome to join."

It takes until April the 28, the day before Webster's hanging, before the lieutenant allows us in.

"Prepare yourself," one of the younger Quakers warns me.

The papers call Castle Godwin a "snug institution," as if it were some sort of hotel, but entering the brick building, the smell we're met with says different. Overcrowding, unwashed bodies, disease. The corridors are dark and narrow. The cells no more than closets with hardly a breath of air to be had.

I can't risk showing undue interest by asking after Webster, so I wait for fate—in the form of a sour, red-faced Confederate lieutenant—to decide if I get to see him.

He paws through our baskets (I brought cheese, if you can't guess), selecting what he wants for himself and checking the rest for contraband. He sticks his knife all through the biscuits the eldest Quaker carefully baked. Crumbles another woman's crackers to pieces just in the case she's hiding messages in them. Once he's done, he steps back like a hog after feeding and nods to a guard. "They can visit the ground floor."

One of the inmate's wives starts to quietly weep. I look to the elder Quaker. "The lowest-risk inmates are kept on the ground floor," she explains. "Drunks or disorderly types."

Webster's probably the most valuable inmate in the whole prison. I make to argue with the lieutenant, maybe get him to change his mind, but the elder Quaker quickly takes my arm. "He won't hear protests," she whispers. "Only get you thrown out or worse."

A wave of grief sweeps over me. My gamble failed. I made it into the very building—not a hundred feet, I'd wager, from Webster's cell—but I won't get to see him. The elder Quaker senses my sorrow and squeezes my arm. "Come on, we might still do some good today."

I swallow my desperate feeling and let her lead me down the corridor. There's four cells along the hall we're in. Some of the other women have already gone into the first several. The elder Quaker pushes open the door to the third cell.

Inside is Hattie.

Scobell told me she was most likely in Castle Thunder prison. But here she is in the flesh. She was arrested alongside Webster but hasn't yet been charged with espionage. A "low-risk" inmate.

Hattie's and my eyes pass over each other without any flicker of recognition. I let the older woman take the lead, sharing her biscuit crumbs and some clean bedding. When she's done, I step over. "May I pray with you, ma'am?"

"That would be a comfort," Hattie says back. We kneel together, face-to-face, near enough our murmurs won't be overheard. If the Quaker woman suspects something more than Christian concern over a prisoner's soul, she doesn't say it.

Close up, Hattie looks a wreck. Her hair's lank and tangled, her eyes red. But not, it seems, with weeping. She's all-fired with fury. "Was it Tully? It was surely Tully!" she whispers.

"We don't know," I whisper back. "You're the only one I've gotten to."

"They knew when they arrested us. They knew who we were." Her breath comes roughly. "You find who ratted. You find which one it was."

"They're trying for a prisoner trade," I tell her.

"Don't bother for me," she says, all bitterness. "They won't hang a woman."

"They won't hang a *white* woman," I correct her.

Hattie's fury flashes again. "They won't let me see him. They call me *Mrs.* Webster, but they still won't let me see him. They said maybe tomorrow morning before—" She can't say the words, but for a moment I see something in her face, all the feeling she's masking with her anger. Boundless grief. A bone-deep sorrow.

I clasp my hands around hers. "I'm sorry, Hattie."

Her face slackens, eyes softening. "I wish I could tell him . . ."

"What?" I ask.

"I wish I could tell him . . ." She looks at the words in her heart, then all at once her face closes like a snuffed candle. "I wish I could tell him I'll dance on the grave of the rat who did this."

I look at her. Here, at the very end of everything they've had together, and that's all she can say. "Hattie—" I start.

"Don't, Kate," she jumps in sharply. Whatever else she's feeling, she won't name it. Maybe she can't. And it's not my place to force her.

I embrace her quickly, giving her a reassuring smile. She gives me one back, a mask of strength to protect the devastating truth within her.

The next morning, I wake at dawn. Camp Lee, the military training ground where Webster is to hang, is west of the city. Despite Webster's notoriety, it's not a public hanging. I go to Scobell's drop and leave him a message, telling him I saw Hattie, that I tried to see Webster. I don't use their names, of course, in the case our messages are ever discovered, but I make it plain to him. In truth, I'm secretly hoping maybe I'll catch sight of Scobell again. I could use the solace on such a dire day. But he's not there.

I don't want to go back to my lonely boarding house, and, as rough as the tavern is, a woman can't loiter too long outside it without suspicion, so I order a breakfast inside that I can't bear to eat, and sit alone at a table in quiet vigil.

After an hour or so, I ask for the bill. When the man brings my change, there's a paper under the coins. A message back from Scobell.

Outside, I spy him leaning against the fence again.

I busy myself with the cart, looking for some pretext to return to the tavern kitchen. Eventually, I just pick up an empty crate and cross back behind the establishment.

There's some barrels and a pile of rubbish waiting to be burned. Nothing much for cover or privacy. Scobell arrives a few minutes after me. "Just a moment, ma'am," he says like he might to a provisioner. "Let me find the cook." He disappears inside the kitchen.

A moment later, he comes back out. "You can put that in the cold larder."

"Thank you," I say under my breath and follow him inside.

It's a tight little kitchen, not much more than a stove, bread oven, and table. The cook is there, glaring stonily at me as I slide past.

The cold larder is small and dark and smells of meat on its last day. A dressed hog hangs from a hook on the ceiling.

The door hasn't shut, and I'm already hugging Scobell because I just can't pretend anymore that I don't want to or that anything's more important. I press my face to his shoulder, breathing in the smell of him. I don't know how long we stand there holding one another. A good long time. Finally, Scobell softens his grip, but keeps me close.

"You know what's sadder than the two of us?" he asks gently.

"What's that?" I ask.

"That old story, what was it? Cleopatra and Mark Antony."

"Them?" I scoff, tears wetting my eyes. "Are they as sad as those other two, Tristan and Iseult?"

"Mmm," he says with bittersweet pleasure. "But how about Paris and Helen?"

"Orpheus and Eurydice," I say.

"Romeo and Juliet," he answers.

"You win," I tell him. "I can't think of anyone else as sad as us."

"But we got a little respite here," he says, squeezing me.

"I guess so."

He's quiet, but I can tell he's working on the words for something. "All that's happened with Webster . . . it made me think on what we do." I can't see his face well, but we're near enough I feel his breath with each word. "How every day in our work we're in heavy danger. Every day our lives hang in the balance." He gets still. "If they caught me, I wouldn't just be hanged . . . but I still do the work because it's what I believe. I don't think I can do otherwise knowing all the people who need this world to change. It's who I am, and the risk is worth it to me." He takes a breath. "And I'm not saying the risks of the work is the same thing as the risks of us loving each other, because it isn't. But I guess it made me wonder on risks being worth it."

"It's not worth it if I lose you," I tell him.

"It seems selfish of me, I'll say that," he says tightly. "Risking myself for something personal. But don't I get to choose that? In the stories, Juliet, Romeo, Orpheus, they got to choose. Why not me?"

I'm weeping again. "Because those stories are all tragedies."

I can hear him smile. "But they're also love stories, aren't they? I guess I'm saying, if I'm going to live the tragedy, I want the love part too." He says softly, "Who knows, maybe the two of us already lived the tragedy parts."

We both can't help but laugh, standing in a cold larder against a pig carcass, mourning the life of our colleague, and asking if tragedy might be behind us.

But my laughter turns sharp. "I want to say yes." I can sense his held breath. "I do say yes. I love you." I say the words I have never spoken. Words I've never imagined would be a part of my life. Getting to those words, that should have been the hardest part. But hard hasn't even begun. "I love you, but so what?" I say to him. "There's no way for us to be together. Carriage houses? Tavern kitchens? We can pledge ourselves to one another, right here and now. But then what? We've got nowhere, even if we're willing to take the risks."

I wait for him to answer. To find some way past our impossibilities. "Maybe after the war," he whispers.

I pull him to me, pressing my face to his chest. This is what love feels like. I stifle the scream of rage that wants to come out. He clutches me, squeezing back just as hard. Nearly squeezing the breath from me. We hold one another in fury at our love. Because love is never alone. Loss is its inseparable shadow.

Finally, we got to go.

"I guess knowing you love me has got to be enough," he says.

"Yeah," I say, because I've got no other answer.

We come out of the cold larder. We don't touch again. We don't say another word. As I climb into the wagon, I see him for a moment near the back of the tavern. This is it for me: the torture of knowing he's out there, knowing he loves me, but always standing just out of reach.

The next day, the Richmond papers announce Webster's death. He's a traitor to them, so they paint him as poorly as can be. Still, it's a grim affair. On the gallows, Webster asked the clergyman for Psalm 109, calling down vengeance upon his enemies. The clergyman refused. Then, the executioners bungled the rope. Webster fell hard to the ground through the trapdoor, in a half-hanged horror. "I suffer a double death," he was said to utter as they hauled him back up to try again. The second time, it stuck.

The papers say Mrs. Webster was allowed to see him the morning of the hanging. I wonder what she chose to say.

— Twenty-three —

Spring victories in the Virginia peninsula boost Northern morale, but then the Union hits a series of setbacks, mainly in the form of two Confederate generals: "Stonewall" Jackson and Robert E. Lee. The weather makes it all the worse, constant rain turning the road between Washington and Richmond into a seventy-mile mud pit.

Heavy as my sorrows are, the Union needs intelligence. Peanut and I slog our way back to Washington for Pinkerton's next instructions. We've come to a sort of understanding, Peanut and me. He doesn't disobey me so much anymore. Or maybe he's just too tired from the mud to fight. As we travel, I feel a strange sort of peace from the words Scobell and I exchanged in the tavern's larder. Like things are in a better place. Maybe it's resignation, not peace. All I know is something has eased in me. Like I've come back to myself after a long time away.

Washington seems changed when I make it back. Thousands of enslaved people have been coming to the city, fleeing the South. A woman called Elizabeth Keckley—a former slave herself and dressmaker to none other than Mary Todd Lincoln—has founded a Contraband Relief Association, gathering necessities to help these refugees. It's hardly enough. Every alleyway has become a warren of canvas and tin, sometimes just cotton bedding, dividing the lanes into makeshift shelters for fugitive arrivals. I look into the eyes of people as I drive the wagon by, wondering how one city can be packed with such misery. Then I remember how much worse the miseries must have been back home that they fled.

I arrive at the agency's offices to find Pinkerton gone for a few days. George Bangs tells me he's been working more and more in the field alongside General McClellan. While I wait for a new assignment, Bangs sets me up with a desk in the back room.

I read letters, send telegrams, file receipts and other paperwork. I receive field reports through couriers from agents in Baltimore and other Southern cities. I scour newspapers for anything about Hattie, Lewis, or Tully. In short, I do *Thorough and Complete*.

I think on Scobell constantly. Looking over his field reports and receipts from the past months, I try to imagine what he's doing now. A receipt for the cost of hand tools, and I picture Scobell getting work as a hired handyman in a rebel household. A report on troop numbers, and I see him in the dark on the outskirts of an army encampment, risking life and limb to count supper fires.

It's strange. Knowing he's out there, but not being with him—it's not as torturous as I imagined. Knowing he loves me is a comfort. No, comfort doesn't equal the feeling it confers. It shores me up. Gives me the strength to keep doing the work. I'm doing it for him. Him and me, both.

It's a week after I return that Pinkerton finally appears in the offices. Bangs is on some errand, so I'm alone. Pinkerton comes in full chisel but stops when he sees me. His face reddens with feeling. "A terrible business." Webster's death, the loss of four agents, the certain betrayal by Tully or Lewis, it's all in his voice. "A terrible, terrible business," he says once over.

The door to the offices opens again softly. Bangs steps inside, clutching an envelope. "Transfer order for one Rose O'Neal Greenhow."

It's the first I've heard of the widow since her damning letter was printed in the *Richmond Whig*.

Pinkerton looks at me with a smug satisfaction. "She's going to prison at long last."

I can't believe she remained in her own home for so long. The fortune of being a reputable lady appreciated by powerful men.

"Well, get up," Pinkerton interrupts my thoughts. "You're coming with me to transfer her."

My guts get cold. I don't want to go back to her house.

As always, Pinkerton sniffs out my feelings without me saying a word. "Don't balk! I need a female to oversee her packing so it won't offend the lady's 'propriety.'"

It's a lie; Pinkerton doesn't give a damn about her propriety. "You want to punish her by bringing me back," I guess.

He holds my gaze. "She sees you, she won't be trying any foolishness."

I'm quiet in the carriage. I keep seeing Little Rose in my head. Her in her mother's garden kicking flowers, her sleeping across my leg in the widow's bed, her standing in the doorway of her sister's desecrated room. "Did the widow finally confess?" I ask, to clear my mind. "That why she's finally going to prison?"

Pinkerton seethes quietly a moment. "She was caught waving different-colored handkerchiefs from her windows in some kind of code. She's a bloody devil. Incorrigible! Unrepentant!"

As the carriage approaches "Fort Greenhow," I'm surprised to see about a dozen people gathered outside the house. "What's this?" I ask Pinkerton, but he doesn't know either.

We find out from the officer in charge. "Word spread that Greenhow's going to prison. People want to see the 'fiery rebel' make her exit."

"It's not a goddamn play!" Pinkerton bellows as we step into the house.

It's altogether changed, the house. Boards have been nailed over the windows, blocking out much of the light. The floors are scuffed and tracked with dirt. There's four guards visible just from the foyer: one guarding the front door, two taking women prisoners into the dining room, another walking a woman upstairs. It doesn't feel like a private residence anymore. A house of female detention, indeed.

The officer sends a guard to fetch the widow. Pinkerton and I wait alone in the front parlor. My heart pumps unevenly in my chest. The room feels full of ghosts. I remember me and Tully and Scobell searching the place. Scobell and me loving each other on the couch.

There's footsteps on the stairs and a moment later, the widow appears in the front parlor door, a guard at her side. She hasn't seen me yet. Her face reads of fatigue and worry, but she stands as proud as Marie Antoinette. A queen to the end.

Behind her, Little Rose bobs into view. She looks thinner, rangier. Her eyes cast about the parlor warily. She's the first to see me. Her eyes get wide. She pulls on her mother's skirt.

The widow looks over and finally notices me. Her breath catches. She smooths it out and addresses Pinkerton, "I heard a spy was hanged in Richmond. It seems the good Lord didn't answer my prayers that it was *that one*."

Pinkerton doesn't blink. He holds up the envelope with the transfer order. "You've got two hours to pack!"

The widow isn't thrown; maybe she expected something like this with Pinkerton's reappearance after so many months. "Pack for where?" she asks evenly.

Pinkerton gives her a dark look. He places the envelope on a table by the couch and folds his hands comfortably at his waist. "The Old Capitol building. It's been repurposed." He waits to see her response. It's the very boarding house the widow's aunt once ran. The same building where the widow lived as a young woman with her sister.

The widow's face remains closed, but she's quiet.

Pinkerton goes on, "Incarcerated where you were nurtured into the bigot you became."

The widow gathers herself. "Two hours is hardly sufficient for Little Rose and me to pack."

"Who said anything about Little Rose?" Pinkerton asks with feigned innocence.

The widow gets stock-still. "Surely my daughter will be permitted to come with me."

"It's prison, not a holiday!" Pinkerton half laughs.

"She is eight years old!" the widow cries. "I am her only living parent!"

"Should have thought of that before committing treason," Pinkerton whips back.

"This is revolting, inhumane . . . " She starts to shake.

Pinkerton gets right up in her face. "Do you know how many mothers and daughters have been taken from one another in the South? Ever asked your own cook what happened to her mother?" Pinkerton remembers the interview I did of Minnie Ann. "Your outrages are nothing to me."

It's true. Everything he's saying is true. I feel it deep down: this woman deserves nothing. And yet, something in me falters at what he's doing—what we're doing. She doesn't deserve better, but her girl does.

I'm moving before I know what I'm doing, walking over to the table where the transfer order lays. I pick it up. Pinkerton shoots me a questioning look.

The guard is still in the front parlor doorway, blocking any egress by the widow. I nod Pinkerton through the red gauze curtain separating the front parlor from the back. His puzzled look is shifting to a dubious anger, but he follows me.

"Couldn't the girl go with her mother?" I whisper. We're standing in the back parlor by the floral couch right where Pinkerton and Lewis first interrogated the widow.

"To prison?!" Pinkerton snarls.

The words come out before I know I'm saying them: "I was born in a one-room cottage with dirt walls. Hunger, cold, and everything besides, I would've stayed there beside my mam if I could've."

Pinkerton is hardly moved. "I'm not giving that woman a thing!"

In my mind, I see the widow as I did after I destroyed her daughter Gertie's room. A broken heap on the floor. "It's hard to be on the side of right," I say his own words back to him.

Pinkerton motions to the transfer order in my hand. "Per government order, I'm delivering *one* prisoner." He reaches for the envelope.

I pull it away from him, fury growing in my guts. "Let the girl stay with her mother!"

Pinkerton tenses, readying for a fight. "Don't do this, Kate." He grabs for the envelope again.

I'm too quick for him. I whip around the far side of the couch.

Pinkerton rounds on me, eyeing the distance between us. "This will not end well for you!"

I know it. Just squaring off with him has surely cost me my job. I see the choices laid out: give in and maybe remain a Pinkerton. Keep going down this road and give it all up. Give it all up for a bigot. But I'm not doing it because she deserves it. I'm doing it because her girl does.

And because I do. I'm not the widow. I'm not Hattie. Or Pinkerton. And taking a girl from her mother is not who I am.

Behind the couch, I slip the order from its envelope. I hold it up between my fingers. "I'll tear it up!"

Pinkerton moves almost at the same time, diving across the couch, knocking the whole thing to its back with a crash. But I'm already dashing around behind the other couch. Pinkerton scrambles off the ground and charges over, roaring in fury.

I give the paper a small rip, and he stops short. His breath heaves with effort. "Kate, you tear that paper, you're destroying an official government document. I'll be hauling you to prison too!"

"The girl goes with her mother!" I hiss.

Pinkerton's face is taut with blood as he calculates his next move. I give the paper another small tear.

Pinkerton gives a wild groan. Then, all at once, he reaches down and tears off a shoe. He hurls it at me. I duck. The shoe hits a vase, shattering it in a spray of glass. "Fine, then!" he pants. "I will offer the widow the choice to bring her daughter to prison!"

"Swear it?" I say, my fingers still on the order.

"I swear"—he glares witheringly at me—"on my own mother's soul."

I look in his eyes, just to be sure I believe him.

I do.

I slide the order back in the envelope and offer it to him.

Pinkerton snatches it. I let go a breath, my whole body softening in relief.

His eyes narrow. "Don't be getting comfortable, girl." He stabs the air in front of me with a sausage finger. "When this is done, we talk."

I look toward the front parlor. Little Rose's face glows pale behind the red gauze. She darts back to her mother's side as Pinkerton stalks into their room.

"The girl may accompany you," Pinkerton tells the widow, as if she could have missed our altercation.

She doesn't give a word of thanks, just nods in acknowledgment, as if it's the least she deserves. Then she extends her hand for Little Rose. "Time to pack, dear."

Three hours later, we're escorting the widow, Little Rose, and a mountain of luggage out the front door of 398 Sixteenth Street.

When we step outside, I can't believe my eyes. The dozen people waiting to get an eyeful of Rose O'Neal Greenhow, Southern lady spy, has grown. Hundreds now pack the street. It looks like a veritable parade route.

The widow surveys her audience, pats her hair, and lifts her chin. She takes Little Rose's hand and walks proudly to the carriage. Little Rose waves to the onlookers.

Pinkerton offers his hand to the widow as she steps into the covered carriage, but she declines. Imitating her mother, Little Rose, too, scrambles up on her own.

There's so much luggage, Pinkerton directs me to stay behind and arrange its transport. Then he climbs into the carriage with the widow and girl and shuts the door. He raps for the carriage to go.

Just as they pull away, Little Rose's tiny face peeks out the canvas carriage cover. Her eyes find me, and she calls out, "Thank you, Mary Kate!"

Mary Kate. I'm stunned to hear it. Then I remember I told it to her once in her mama's garden when she asked me my name. My true name.

The face vanishes abruptly as she's yanked back inside the carriage. By Pinkerton's hands or her mother's, I don't know.

I return to the offices to await Pinkerton. I sit at my desk in the back room, knowing my days at the agency are over. Loneliness grips at me, a heavy sort of feeling. This work took me from being a mill girl and turned me into a storybook hero.

Bangs comes into the back room to refile a ledger. He reads my dismal mood and offers a sympathetic look.

I manage to work through a field report from Sam Bridgeman, who's at work in Baltimore, noting a request for supplies. I expect my feelings of dread to worsen as Pinkerton's return draws nearer, but strangely they don't. Instead, there's almost a relief. I find myself wondering on what else I might find for work. Maybe something alongside Consider Pritchett. Or for the Contraband Relief Association.

The door's slam in the late afternoon tells me Pinkerton's come back. I step warily into the front room, where he stands with his hat still on. "The mother and daughter are incarcerated at the Old Capitol," he announces. "That woman called me a tyrant and a brute, and a third thing I won't mention in present company."

Bangs, sitting at his desk, gives Pinkerton a small nod of appreciation.

Pinkerton turns to me. He's so puckered, he looks like he's about to be sick all over the floor. I wait for the words that will end it. "I went to the War Department after depositing the widow," he starts. "My mercy toward Greenhow was evidently noted by the public circus in the streets." His words are full of scorn. "While *some* felt it too lenient"—Pinkerton plainly counts himself in this number—"certain *others* felt it was a step toward rebuilding the War Department's reputation after the widow's infamous letter in the papers. They approved of my choice." His face contorts into a grimace. "I don't like being wrong, Kate. But I can admit, in this case, your instincts were sound."

There's a long silence. Finally, Pinkerton takes a breath. "So, what is it you want?"

I don't understand the question.

"What assignment do you want?" he hisses impatiently. "You want to go undercover in Richmond? Join Bridgeman in Baltimore? Tell me."

What do I want? Every time I try to predict this man's next move, he does the contrary. I half laugh, then cover it swiftly with a cough. Because suddenly I know exactly what I want. "A safehouse," I say.

It's not what he expected. I quickly try to make a case for it. "This whole calamity with Webster might have been prevented if he had had a private place to recuperate from his illness instead of the hotel where Lewis was recognized."

Pinkerton looks at me sharply.

"We need a safehouse in Richmond. A proper safehouse all to ourselves. Somewhere an agent can hide out if need be. I'd run the place."

Pinkerton's eyes narrow. "You're only ever pushing me for harder assignments. What's this now?"

"Guess I've changed," I tell him, knowing I haven't changed; I've just finally figured out who I already was. "I'd pose as a widow who takes on boarders now and again to support herself. I'd be a drop for couriers. I'd still make use of my eyes and ears."

Pinkerton looks at me hard. "You've thought on this."

In truth, I haven't. But I've dreamed on it. A castle in the sky.

"Do it." Pinkerton grunts. "Soon as possible."

— Twenty-four —

The same day I purchase the property in Richmond, Scobell comes up the road carrying a bag of tools. "Heard you might be hiring a man to help with the house," he calls.

"You heard right. You have references?" I playact for the neighbors.

"I can direct you to my last employer. Cook at Walker's Tavern."

"Come back late tomorrow," I say. "I'll have an answer for you."

The next afternoon, when he steps in the back door, the playacting ends. The sun's just starting to set, light streaming through the curtain's edge into the kitchen where we stand, drinking each other in.

"I know this isn't forever," Scobell says. "But it's something, isn't it?"

"It's something," I say back. I extend my hand for his.

He hesitates. "I got to tell you. There's things I carry. What I lived. It's in me and isn't going nowhere. If you're with me, for however long we got—months, weeks, days—you'll be in that with me." He holds my eyes. "That scare you?"

Knowing what all he's lived, I feel a tug to run, even as my hand opens toward him. "Yeah, it scares me," I whisper.

Scobell gives a bitter laugh. "Well, you're honest. Probably best." I can feel his subtle tensing. His thickening skin.

I remember the riot and clamor of the cotton mill—the clamor that shook my bones. I took that fear and brought it in deep. Let my very heart take it up so it became part of my being and had no thrall over me. I try it now. Not hardening against my fear, but softening into it.

Our softest parts are our bravest parts.

"I'll be in it with you," I tell him. "Scared or no."

Something eases across his face. And deeper. An ease and exhalation through his whole self. He takes my hand and pulls me into his arms. I'm wrapped in the scent of home.

"Look at that. I got my Eurydice out of hell," Scobell whispers.

The old myth of Demeter and Persephone comes into my head—the other couple who was stuck in hell. The gods divided Demeter and Persephone, but Demeter went down, down, down into that dark well and moved those very gods. She remade the world so it became a circle: winter—summer—winter—summer. I never saw it before, but all at once, I do: the world didn't become whole again in the way it was; it was a broken world, divided in two and never reconciled. But it moved on. It found a way. Persephone and her mother lived side by side half the year and were whole again. The ending's still the old ending, but I'm seeing something new in it.

Scobell and I can't erase what we've lived, but we can help each other live with those stories, and maybe find new things within them. And maybe we'll get our half-is-whole love story. Not side by side for always in the sun, but a love story all the same.

A last shimmer of light comes from the window, flickering across his face. I kiss John Scobell for the first time in daylight. I kiss him, look into his eyes, and say, "I'll be beside you. But I need you to do one thing for me."

"What's that?" he asks softly.

"Will you call me Mary Kate?"

AFTERWORD

History has its account of how Kate and the Pinkertons' story went on.

Allan Pinkerton tried for prisoner exchanges for the agents still incarcerated in Richmond. Hattie Lawton was finally released in June 1862. Through her whole imprisonment, she was known in the newspapers only as Mrs. Webster.

John Scully (renamed John Tully, because the name was so similar to John Scobell) and Pryce Lewis were released in September the following year. Publicly, Pinkerton never apologized for them or judged them. When pushed, he said, "Who, in our day, can claim their possession in the very face of death and dishonor?"

The demise of Rose O'Neal Greenhow unfolded a year later in 1864. After months in the Old Capitol prison, the Union set her free without trial on the condition she would remain on Confederate land and provide no aid to the rebels. She was celebrated in Richmond as a war hero.

Soon after, Jefferson Davis sent her to England as his emissary to convince the English to acknowledge and support the Confederate government. In England, she dined with Queen Victoria. She captivated the Second Earl of Granville, and they became engaged. She published a memoir, its sales intended to refill her dwindling coffers, alongside the Confederacy's.

Greenhow boarded a ship back to America, bringing the proceeds of that book—gold and silver amounting to thousands of dollars—home. Considering the dangers of the journey, she left her young daughter, Little Rose, in the care of a convent.

On October 1, 1864, Greenhow was aboard the *Condor*, a blockade runner headed for South Carolina, when the ship ran aground. Seeing what they believed to be a Union gunboat, she and a few others took to a lifeboat to avoid capture. But the waters were rough. The boat capsized.

The funds she had recently raised were in a pouch attached to her person. The others from the lifeboat were able to swim ashore, but Greenhow—weighed down by such a purse—drowned. The justice is almost too poetic to be believed.

After the Civil War, Pinkerton's agency returned to detective work. Kate Warne continued as an agent, running his "female detective bureau" and, at times, posing undercover to catch murderers and thieves. She died of pneumonia in 1868. Pinkerton buried her in his family plot.

That same year, Pinkerton suffered a major stroke. His sons, William and Robert, had just begun working for the agency. They took over its direction.

The agency's work shifted more and more toward big business interests. The Pinkertons were hired by the railroads to catch outlaws like the Reno gang and Jesse James. Gradually, the Pinkertons became the fist of the moneyed, infamously and violently working against labor activism.

Pinkerton died in 1884. Less than ten years later, the government issued the Anti-Pinkerton Act to curb the use of mercenaries and private military forces—which indicates what the agency had, by then, become. Was Pinkerton innocent of the transformation? He couldn't have been entirely ignorant of it. The agency never recovered its name, its abolitionist work effaced by its ignominious end.

———

Allan Pinkerton recounted the exploits of his agency during the Civil War in a book published in 1883, complete with heart-stopping turns and subtitled illustrations:

> The Spy of the Rebellion; Being a True History of the Spy System of the United States Army During the Late Rebellion.

Rose O'Neal Greenhow had already published her memoir, including an account of her arrest at the hands of the Pinkertons in 1863:

> My Imprisonment and the First Year of Abolition Rule at Washington.

Pinkerton's book was prefaced with the promise:

> The events narrated have all occurred. The record is a truthful one.

But events breed memories, as we all know—recollections as distinct from each other as siblings, maybe all with the same weak chin, but possessing different souls entirely. And these two "historical" records stand in contradiction to one another.

Did the Pinkertons arrest Rose Greenhow before or after she signaled her conspirators? Did they manage to obtain her cipher key before she destroyed it? There are different answers in different accounts.

Other elements are simply unknown. Allan Pinkerton wrote of an agent, John Scobell, who was a former enslaved person. No mention of him has been found in Pinkerton's employment records or elsewhere, leading some to believe he was Pinkerton's literary invention.

And what was the identity of the female Pinkerton agent present during Greenhow's house arrest? Pinkerton never mentioned her by name. Kate Warne is a definite possibility; she was Pinkerton's first female detective and an active agent during the Civil War.

Pinkerton was meticulous in describing his female agents as both daring *and* possessed of womanly virtue. He never alluded to any romantic relations between any of his agents. He knew his audience and wrote accordingly.

———

Pinkerton and Greenhow both claimed their books to be true accounts of history. This novel, by contrast, is fiction. It takes history as a starting point, a tether from which it might range like a kite on currents of imagination.

Several story points differ from the known history. Kate Warne's background is largely unknown; the version I present before 1856 is invented. The Tremont Cotton Mill is based on the Lowell mills of Massachusetts. Rose Greenhow was transferred to the Old Capitol prison in winter 1862, not spring. There was purportedly a Black woman spy named Mary working in the Davis house in Richmond during the war, but she worked for the Union through Elizabeth Van Lew's spy ring, not Pinkerton's. Some claim her name was Mary Elizabeth Bowser. Others believe she was called Mary Richards Denman. There are other, smaller alterations in the book as well. In particular, crafting the point of view of a historical character is always a challenge. Ways of thinking have changed dramatically since the nineteenth century. Historical fiction is a balancing act between past and present, fact and fiction. What I can say is, like Pinkerton and Greenhow, I wrote with my audience in mind. Thank you for reading.

SHORT SELECTED LIST OF REFERENCES AND SOURCES:

Greenhow, Rose O'Neal. "Letter from a Southern Lady In Prison to Seward," *Richmond Whig*, November 17, 1861. https://library.duke.edu/rubenstein/scriptorium/greenhow/1861-11-17/1861-11-17.html

Greenhow, Rose O'Neal. *My Imprisonment and the First Year of Abolition Rule at Washington*. Richard Bentley, 1863.

Pinkerton, Allan. *General Principles of Pinkerton's National Police Agency*. George H. Fergus Printer, 1867.

Pinkerton, Allan. *The Spy of the Rebellion; Being a True History of the Spy System of the United States Army During the Late Rebellion*. M. A. Winter & Hatch, 1883.

Wilson, Henry. "Love Letters from Henry Wilson to Mrs. Rose O'Neal Greenhow," National Archives online, 1861. https://catalog.archives.gov/id/1633526

I drew from several Richmond newspapers for the articles regarding Pryce Lewis and John Scully's arrests, including:

"Yankee Spies." *Richmond Enquirer*, March 4, 1862.

"Condemned Spies." *Richmond Dispatch*, April 5, 1862.

Minnie Ann's story was drawn in part from:

Browne, Margaret Griffith, *Autobiography of a Female Slave*. (E.O. Jenkins, 1857), "Documenting the South," University of North Carolina https://docsouth.unc.edu/neh/browne/browne.html

"The Relentless Seas" was adapted in part from:

Arthur, T.S. "Taking Boarders," *Godey's Lady's Book* Vol. 42 (January, 1851).

The idea of a person as a "blank page" or *tabula rasa* is a very old idea, but I've drawn specifically on the pedagogy of Jacques Lecoq, as taught at L'Ecole Internationale de Théâtre Jacques Lecoq, in which the body is described as "a blank page on which drama can be inscribed."

ACKNOWLEDGMENTS

Merci mille fois to my fabulous agent, Stephanie Cabot, and to Neyla Downs, Helena Sandlyng-Jacobsen, Mark Kessler, Lauren Wendelken, and the entire team at Susanna Lea.

Thank you so very much to my amazing editor, Loan Le, and the excellent people at Atria Books including Elizabeth Hitti, Crystal Watanabe, and Liz Byer. Special thanks to the inimitable Trish Todd for her guidance and insight along this journey.

To Sarah Heller—your belief in this story carried me through. I've been truly grateful to have you as a reader and friend.

To Boomie Aglietti, Emily Epstein, Blake Habermann, and Amy Reisch—many, many thanks for reading drafts. Your notes were invaluable.

To my Civil War fact-checkers, Jake Valter, Paul Quigley, and Thomas Rudolph Seabrook—I was so lucky to have you. Any errors that remain are mine.

To Ann Blackman, author of *Wild Rose: The True Story of a Civil War Spy*—you were so kind to speak with me many years ago about Rose Greenhow. I am grateful for your excellent research.

To the good people at the Lowell National Historical Park—thank you for keeping so many women's stories alive.

To the original Pinks, with whom I first explored this story in play form, Max Dana, Jay Dunn, Tara Giordano, Blake Habermann, Kevin

Lapin, Adam Paolozza, and Siobhan Towey—thank you for your *jeu* and *complicité*. R.I.P. Crout, Sukey and Betty Duvall, who didn't make it into the book.

To the Salyers & Hurand family—my heartfelt thanks for your loving support.

Cate, thank you for talking through character and psychology with me.

Mom, thank you for always cheering me on.

Dad, you are my first and most thorough reader. Thank you for your thoughts and insight, for traveling to Lowell to see the mills, and for telling me stories of Mary Alice Heaney.

And thank you to G, A, and K. Together we make MAGK.

ABOUT THE AUTHOR

MEGAN CAMPISI is a playwright, novelist, and teacher. She has been a forest ranger, a sous-chef in Paris, and a physical theater specialist around the world. She attended Yale University and the École Internationale de Théâtre Jacques Lecoq. In 2019, she received a Fulbright Specialist award to travel to Turkey and give master classes at Tatbikat Theatre. Her first novel, *Sin Eater*, received the Debut Crown award from the Historical Writers' Association in 2021. Originally from the San Francisco Bay Area, Megan lives in Brooklyn, New York, with her family.